More Golden Than Day

Book Three
The Last Werewolf Hunter

by

William Woodall

Jeremiah Press   ·   Antoine, Arkansas

Jeremiah Press
PO Box 3
Antoine, AR 71922

First published by Jeremiah Press on 02/14/2011.

Printed in the United States of America.

This book is printed on acid-free paper.

ISBN 978-0-9819641-8-8

Library of Congress Control Number: 2011904378

More Golden
Than Day

For Cody,

For greatness of heart.

The Curse-Breaker Books
By William Woodall:

The Last Werewolf Hunter Series

Cry for the Moon
Behind Blue Eyes
More Golden Than Day
Truesilver

The Stones of Song Series

Unclouded Day
Many Waters
Bran the Blessed

The Tyke McGrath Series

Nightfall
Tycho
Avenger
Freedom
Elysium

Unrelated Novels

The Prophet of Rain
Beneath a Star-Blue Sky
(short story collection)

Guard your heart above all things,
For it is the wellspring of your life.
                    -Proverbs 4:23

Thoughts of a Werewolf Hunter
By Zach Trewick

"God is love, even to the lost, and to know Him at all is to know this."

"As long as I live, when I think about Louisiana, I'll remember glistening mist on a Cajun girl's hair, and walking together under those live oak trees, and being happy."

"There are only three questions a man ever needs to ask: What is the nature of God, what things are worth living for, and what things are worth dying for. And the answer to all of them is the same: only love."

"The only reason we ever love anybody or anything in the world is because they remind us of God in some way, like the reflection of the sun in a dew drop. I believe that with my whole heart, and when Jolie told me about the Hope of the werewolf hunters, how could I keep from loving her for that?"

"Sometimes you have to just be, to take time to praise God in silence like the rocks and the trees and the clouds in the sky do, so that you get closer to Him and see with His eyes. If you spend your whole life running hard, then you never have time to grow."

"There are a thousand ways to say I love you."

"You should never be too busy to stop and enjoy things, cause you only live once and you better make it count."

"Sometimes you find yourself in a position where the only thing you can do is to spend your life as dearly as you can."

"I once thought it was foolish to cry for the moon, to long for the impossible, to wish for things that can't be so. But God often has a different idea of what's possible than I do, and He never plants dreams to no purpose."

"I hope that because of everything I've gone through, I've learned to be a little more like Him, to see with His eyes, to feel with His heart, and to carry inside me just a bit more of that Light more golden than day."

"If you want to deal with a wicked person, search their heart and try to find whatever that original seed of goodness was before it went sour, and then teach them a better and truer way to fulfill the deepest desires of their heart, if you can."

Contents

Chapter One

The first time I ever saw Jolie was at the Four States Fair, the year I turned sixteen.

It didn't seem like one of those days when your whole life changes, and if you'd told me I was about to get dragged into the most dangerous and amazing experience of my entire life, I never would have believed it.

Or maybe I would have, come to think of it. I've been through a few tight spots in my life, and if I've learned anything, it's that you should always expect the unexpected.

I remember it was about nine o'clock or so, and me and Cameron were just getting ready to grab a bite to eat before we headed home for the night.

That's when I saw her, standing by the ticket booth and sipping on a can of Cherry Coke. I wouldn't usually have paid much attention, but she was so pretty I couldn't help giving her a second glance. She had long red hair with blonde streaks that glinted in the carnival lights, and she reminded me of a basketball player or maybe Lara Croft in *Tomb Raider*. Very athletic.

She must have noticed me looking, because she turned in my direction and smiled at me with a little wave. I smiled back and then walked over to say hi to her, since she caught me looking. Cam was too busy playing a game to notice.

"Hey, I'm Zach. Have we ever met before? You look so familiar for some reason," I told her when I got close enough. That was sort of a half-truth; she didn't really look familiar, but then again she kinda did. I couldn't decide for sure.

"No, I'm new around here, I'm afraid. I don't know much of anybody," she said.

"Really? Where are you from?" I asked.

"Natchitoches, Louisiana. Nowhere you ever heard of, I'm sure," she laughed.

"No, I guess not," I admitted.

"I didn't think so. Nobody ever has. My name's Jolie, by the way," she said. There was a pause, and I tried to think of something else to say.

"So what brings you up this way?" I finally asked.

"Oh, I just came to stay with my aunt for a few days. She lives up here all by herself, and she needs some help now and then," she said.

"Well, hey, me and my brother are fixing to go get somethin' to eat. You want to come with us?" I offered.

"Sure, why not?" she said.

She grabbed my arm as we left the ticket booth and I was kinda surprised at that. Most girls are not that flirty with somebody they just met, you know. I also noticed she was wearing what looked like a guy's high school ring on her left middle finger, and that made me wonder if she might have a boyfriend somewhere. If she did, then it was even stranger that she was being so touchy-feely.

I can't help noticing things like that, you know. Eileen always tells me I'll make a great scientist or a detective someday because I pay attention to little details that everybody else overlooks. Maybe so.

Cameron was done with his game by then, and when he saw us walking together he smiled.

"Hey, who's your friend?" he asked.

"Uh, this is Jolie. I asked her if she wanted to come eat with us," I said, and he turned to look at her.

"Hey, I'm Cameron. Don't believe anything Zach tells you about me," he told her.

"Oh, I'll try not to," she laughed.

She hooked one arm around mine and the other one around his, and the three of us walked together that way until we came to the food stands.

Me and Cam ordered some chili cheese fries, and Jolie got a basket of tater logs with nothing but salt on them, not even any ketchup. Maybe she didn't want to get anything drippy on her clothes; they looked kind of expensive, even though it was only jeans and a sweater.

The picnic tables were crowded that night and we had to squeeze close together to find a place for all three of us, but nobody minded that. We all laughed and joked and talked like we were old friends, and I remember thinking what a cool person she was.

Cam must have thought so too, because he snapped a picture of the three of us with his phone, like he always does when he's having a good time.

After a while Jolie put her arm around me and leaned over close like she was about to lay her head on my shoulder. I'm not sure what I would have done if she had, but as it turned out that's not what she had in mind.

"They're watching us," she whispered in my ear instead. She was so close I could feel her breath tickle the hair on my neck.

I have to confess I wasn't at my sharpest right then, and for a second I drew a total blank.

"Huh?" I said stupidly.

"Hush and don't look surprised. It's dangerous if they think this is anything but me having a good time at the fair. I don't know for sure if they can see us right this second, but I know they've been following me all day. Werewolves. Now kiss me and make it look good, like that's all we're thinking about," she said.

And that's exactly what she did.

I have to say, that was probably the last thing on God's green earth I was expecting. It felt more like a scene from *Mission: Impossible* than anything else. Go ahead and laugh if you want to, but I swear that's exactly what popped into my head, and I had to bite my tongue to keep from laughing.

Nevertheless, I managed to keep a cool head and kiss her back. Sort of.

She quickly slipped a piece of paper into my hand, and then she got up and looked at her watch like she just realized what time it was.

"Sorry, boys. Got somewhere I have to be in a little bit. See y'all later," she said, and then turned and walked away.

I watched till she was out of sight, still too astonished to comment, and then I looked down at the slip of paper she gave me. It said *Call me tomorrow!* and below that was a phone number. Cameron saw it too, and he just sat there looking at me with an annoying grin on his face.

"Oh, you got it bad, Zach," he finally said with a laugh.

"No I don't," I said. It was definitely one of the weirdest experiences of my life, and I didn't have a clue what to make of it yet, but I definitely didn't want Cameron thinking I was all swoony and calf-eyed over a girl I barely met. That was just too cheesy by half.

"Yeah, whatever. She's pretty awesome, though," he said.

"You think so?" I asked.

"Yeah, I do. You should give her a call tomorrow," he said.

"I don't know; maybe I will," I said.

"You'd be dumb if you didn't," he told me.

"Well, anyway, let's get out of here," I said, changing the subject.

It took forever to get out of the fairgrounds because of all the traffic, and I let Cameron drive. My mind was much too full to pay attention to the road right then. I've been told before that sometimes I think too much, but this was one time when I had a good reason for it.

Being kissed by beautiful and mysterious strangers who pop up out of nowhere isn't something that normally happens in my life, believe it or not. That by itself was enough to knock me back for a week, whether I admitted it to Cam or not.

But it was kinda scary, too, the more I got to thinking about it. Who *was* this girl, and how did she know about the wolves? And why did she think they were watching us on the midway tonight?

There was something else, too. She must have already had that slip of paper written out before I ever went up to talk to her at the ticket booth, because I would have noticed if she'd done it while we were sitting together at the picnic table. That meant she must have planned the whole thing ahead of time, before we even met.

Justin likes to say that things are not always what they seem to be, and in this case I was definitely willing to go along with *that*. On the surface, it looked like a boy and a girl ran into each other by chance at the fair, and then shared some food and a quick kiss before they went home. Nothing very unusual about that, especially if she made it look like we already knew each other. I wondered now if that's what all the arm-holding and sitting close together and all that jazz was supposed to be for. . . so the kiss wouldn't seem out of place, if anybody was watching us.

But why would anybody go to that much trouble? It didn't seem worth it, if all she wanted was to warn me about the wolves and slip that phone number in my hand. It seemed like it would have been a lot easier just to call me or send me a letter, instead of going for all that cloak and dagger stuff.

I looked at the crumpled slip of paper in my hand and thought about how utterly insane it all was, but one thing was for certain.

I had to see her again.

* * * * * * *

We got home maybe an hour later, and slipped indoors without a peep. Justin and Eileen were already in bed by then and we didn't want to wake them up. They were having a baby in December, and Eileen always seemed tired nowadays and couldn't sleep very well.

Cameron knew all that as well as I did, but I guess he couldn't resist teasing me, even if it did make some noise.

"So when are you bringing your girlfriend home to meet Justin and Eileen?" he asked in a hushed voice, like it was something I might not want them to overhear.

"She's not my girlfriend," I said tiredly.

"Really? It sure looked that way when y'all were smooching all over each other tonight," he laughed.

"Oh, shut up, Cam. You don't know anything about it," I said, half embarrassed and half irritated. I love Cameron to death and we're as close as two brothers could ever be, but I have to admit he can also be the most aggravating person you ever imagined.

"Sure thing, bubba. I'll shut up and let you daydream about her in peace," he said.

I groaned and rolled my eyes. He was impossible sometimes.

"Look, there's more to it than you think," I said carefully, when we got to our room and shut the door.

"I knew it! So when are you getting married, then?" he joked.

"Cameron, I'm serious. Stop it with the stupid jokes and listen to me," I said. That sobered him up a little bit.

"Okay, then. What's up, Zach?" he asked, without even a smile.

"She only kissed me so she could get close enough to whisper in my ear," I said.

That was the wrong thing to say, because Cam started to smile again and I knew he was getting ready to hit me with another zinger about my so-called girlfriend. Then he saw the look on my face, and the smile faded.

"I'm guessing she said something besides how much she loves her sweet little Zach, huh?" he said.

"Yeah, you could say that," I said dryly.

"So what was it?" he asked.

"I don't understand what she said. She told me there was somebody watching us at the fair tonight and she thought it was a werewolf," I told him.

"Huh?" he said, and the look of surprise on his face was almost enough to make me laugh, if things hadn't been so serious.

"Yeah, that's what I said, too," I agreed.

"But why would they be watching *her?* Or even us for that matter? Who is she?" he demanded.

"I don't know, Cam. I only know what she told me, and now you know as much about it as I do," I reminded him.

"That's all she said?" he asked.

"Yeah, pretty much. She said it was dangerous and to make it look good when I kissed her, so nobody would think it was a serious discussion if they saw us talking," I said.

"Dangerous how? And for who, you or her?" he asked.

"She didn't say. But if she went to that much trouble to make it look like I was just a boy she was flirting with at the fair, then it's probably nothin' to laugh at," I pointed out.

"That's crazy," he said.

"May be. I'm clueless," I told him, and he furrowed his brows and thought for a minute.

"Well, I can't think of any good reason why the wolves would care about you and me anymore. We're done with all that. So even if they *are* watching us for some unknown reason, they'll surely get tired of it after a while when they find out there's nothing to see. It'll never amount to anything, Zach," he finally said, hopefully.

I tried to tell myself he was right and there was nothing to worry about, but deep down I wasn't so sure. People don't do things for no reason, and I didn't think it was very wise to just blow it off that way.

But Cameron very clearly didn't want to hear that, and I can't say I blamed him; not after everything that happened last time we tangled with the wolves. He was happy with his life, for probably the first time he could ever remember, and he didn't want anything to mess that up. I understood him better than he thought I did, sometimes.

I wasn't real anxious to open up a whole new can of worms either, for that matter, but I had an uneasy feeling in the pit of my stomach that there might be trouble coming, and I knew it wouldn't go away just because I wished it would. I don't think I worry for nothing, but I don't shut my eyes to things I don't like, either.

I decided it wasn't the time to argue about it, though. It was late, and both of us were too sleepy to care about much of anything except going to bed at that point. I could wait and see what Jolie had to say when I called her tomorrow, and then if it seemed important enough I could sit down and try to make Cameron listen.

"I don't know. Maybe you're right," I finally said.

"Sure I am. Don't worry about it," he agreed, and that was all we said about it that night.

I was antsy all day long at school the next day. I kept playing with that slip of paper with Jolie's phone number on it and thinking about what to say when I called her. I couldn't focus on my work or pay attention to anything else; I thought three o'clock would never come.

Me and Cameron both had baseball practice after school that day, but I decided it probably wouldn't hurt me to miss it for once, much as I hated to.

The city was offering a fall baseball league that year, like they sometimes do, and that's why we were having off-season practice like that. Me and Cam always used to sit around at school with our best friends James and Levi to talk about playing for the Texas Rangers someday, believe it or not, and all four of us signed up for Fall Ball because we knew we needed all the practice we could get. Maybe it sounds like a wild and crazy dream that'll never happen, but hey, you never know. I won an All-Star trophy last summer during the regular season, and I don't think I've ever been prouder of anything in my life. So. . . we'll see.

But in spite of all that, what I really wanted more than anything right then was to call Jolie and get some answers. Practice could wait. I had Cameron drop me off at home before he drove to the ball field, and as soon as he was out of sight, I pulled out my phone.

She answered on the first ring.

"Hello?" she said.

"Hey, it's. . ." I started, but she cut me off before I could get another word in.

"Meet me at the soccer field at Spring Lake Park in half an hour," she said quickly, and hung up on me.

I looked at the phone for a second. How did she think I was supposed to get to the soccer field? Flap my wings and fly? That was all the way across town, and Cam had the truck.

I muttered something under my breath about rude girls who expected too much, and then I called a taxi to take me down there. It was the only thing I could think of on such short notice, even though it cost me twenty bucks that I couldn't really spare. I might have been more annoyed, if I hadn't still been dying of curiosity.

Anyway, it took longer than thirty minutes for me to get to the soccer field; more like forty-five, to tell the truth. Some little kids were playing a game on the field itself when I got there, and Jolie was nowhere to be seen.

I finally found her sitting on a bench under an oak tree, watching the kids play. I almost didn't recognize her at first because she was wearing a green scarf that covered her hair and some big black sunglasses that made it hard to see her face very well. But when I got close enough, I knew it was her.

I sat down on the bench beside her without saying anything, and she took off the sunglasses and turned to look at me.

"You're kinda late, boy," she said mildly. That aggravated the tar out of me, but I bit my tongue and didn't say so.

"I got here as soon as I could," I told her.

"Well, I don't guess it matters. We're both here now," she agreed.

"Don't you think you should tell me what's going on now?" I told her.

"Yeah, but not here. I don't think anybody's trailing me today, but you can never be totally sure. Come on," she said, standing up.

I got up too, and she headed for the parking lot at a brisk walk. I had to trot to keep up with her.

She led me to a brand new banana yellow Volkswagen Beetle and unlocked the doors. The windows were tinted so dark they looked like black mirrors, and she had a Louisiana license plate that said "SMOKIN".

That made me want to laugh, and when I thought about it for little while, I decided maybe that was the whole idea behind it. She was poking fun at herself in a subtle kind of way, like she knew she was pretty but didn't take herself too seriously because of it. I kinda liked her for that.

I got in the passenger seat without saying anything, though, and she drove out of the park.

"Where are we going?" I asked.

"Nowhere, really. We're just driving so we can talk without anybody hearing what I have to tell you," she said.

"You couldn't tell me on the phone?" I pointed out.

"Nope. Anybody can pick up cell phone calls. Not secure enough," she said.

I wondered why anybody would care enough to try, but I shook my head and let it go.

"Okay, so tell me. I'm all ears," I said.

"All right, Zach, I'll get right to the point. I know what you and Cameron did with the Trewick pod two years ago, and there are some things I'd like to ask you about that," she began.

"Pod?" I asked.

"Yeah. You know, a flock of birds, a herd of cows. A pod of werewolves," she said, and I wanted to laugh again.

"That's silly," I told her.

"Maybe so, but that's the word. Better not think they're silly, though," she said. That reminded me of what happened in Tennessee at my mom and dad's place, and I didn't feel like laughing anymore after that.

"Yeah, you're right about that," I admitted.

"Anyway, it was good work. I'm impressed," she told me.

"Uh, thanks, I guess," I said, wondering all over again who she was and how she knew so much.

"You're welcome. But like I said, there are some things I'd like to ask you," she repeated.

"Yeah, there are some things I'd like to know, too," I told her.

"All right, then. I tell you what; you tell me something I want to know, and then I'll tell you something you want to know. We'll take turns. Deal?" she asked.

"Fair enough," I agreed.

"Okay, then. First question: How did you destroy those wolf stones?" she asked.

"We had some help. There used to be a spring of holy water not far from here, and if you sprinkled some of it on one of the stones and prayed over it, then it broke the curse," I explained.

"There *used* to be?" she asked.

"Yeah, the wolves found it not long after we did, and they blew it up with dynamite. We barely had enough to finish," I told her.

"I see," she said, half to herself.

"Okay, my turn to ask a question. Who are you, really, and what have you got to do with all this?" I asked.

"Well, you already know my name. That's who I really am. And as for what I've got to do with all this. . . I'm a professional werewolf hunter," she said, without a trace of a smile.

"Does that pay pretty well?" I asked her dryly.

"A lot better than flipping burgers after school," she said, equally dryly.

I had to laugh.

"How do you get involved with something like that?" I asked. I couldn't help wondering, you know. It's not like they could put an ad in the paper.

"Oh, it's the family business, you might say. We've been doing it for centuries. We fight the wolves wherever we find them, however we can, but there are always more pods popping up out there," she explained.

"*More* pods?" I asked, not liking what I was hearing.

"Surely you didn't think there was just one pod in the whole world, did you?" she asked. I remembered wondering about that very thing a few times, now that she mentioned it, but it never seemed very important before. Not till now.

"How many pods are there?" I asked grimly.

"I'm not sure, total. I know of at least ten right this minute. There's one in New Mexico, and another one in Wisconsin, and a third one in Ohio. I know of others in England and France and Australia and-"

"Okay, I get it," I interrupted, a little bit sourly this time. She was making me feel like I hadn't accomplished anything at all by stamping out just one pod.

"No need to be tetchy," she scolded.

"Sorry," I said.

"In any case, my turn now. I know you grew up in a pod, so how come you decided not to join them?" she said. That was a harder question than the first one, and I had to think about it for a minute to give her a good answer.

"Well. . . I was only twelve when I ran away, you know. At the time I wasn't even totally sure why, except I knew I didn't want to be a monster. I think I could always tell they didn't really want me, you know, and maybe that's why I started to look somewhere else," I said.

"What made you think they didn't want you?" she asked.

"Because there was an old tradition they had, about how the seventh-generation boy with blue eyes was supposed to be the Curse Breaker and destroy all the *loup-garous*. I fit the description, so I guess they didn't like that very much. Cam did too, and they never could make up their minds which one of us it was," I explained.

"Interesting. So where did that tradition come from? Any idea?" she asked.

"Yeah, Cam knows more about it than I do because he was with them longer, but he told me it was something Daniel Trewick said; the one who started our pod," I told her.

"That makes sense. Pod leaders tend to know things like that. Most of them are way too curious for their own good; that's usually what gets them in trouble in the first place," she agreed, nodding.

"All right, my turn now. Where do those wolf-stones come from in the first place? Why is it only certain ones that work?" I asked. That was one of the things Daniel Trewick never mentioned in his journal, and the five stones for that pod had been scattered out in such weird and far-flung places, I couldn't help being curious.

"Oh, that's no big secret. Whenever somebody wants to form a new pod, they take some dust from Mont Mouchet in France, and they sprinkle it on a piece of sandstone somewhere in the right sort of place, curse it with certain ceremonies, and then they're in business. It's not very hard, actually, if you know how." she told me.

"Okay, but why choose places so far apart? My pod had five stones, scattered out everywhere from Tennessee to Texas. Why just those and no others?" I asked, and Jolie shrugged.

"There's no telling about that part. Your pod leader picked them for some reason. Maybe he traveled a lot and decided to curse every stone he came across that looked like the right kind, or maybe he just found several old ones that other pods didn't use anymore. That happens sometimes, too," she said.

"So what's the right kind of stone?" I asked.

"I don't remember *all* the rules; I know it has to do with the rock formations in the area, and it can't be cracked, and there are a couple of other things, I think," she said.

"But if somebody does find the right kind, all they have to do is sprinkle it with that dust from Mount Moosejaw or wherever it is, and that's it?" I asked.

"Mont Mouchet," she corrected, "and yes, that's pretty much it. That and speak the curse. That's how most new pods are formed, although like I said, now and then you get one where somebody finds an old stone from another pod and figures out how to use it. That's kinda rare, though," she said.

"So what if somebody destroyed that mountain?" I asked.

"Nice idea, but it's a *mountain,* Zach. You can't destroy a whole mountain," she said.

"Well. . . no, maybe not," I admitted.

"All right. My turn, and last question," she said solemnly.

"Go for it," I said.

"How would you like to be a werewolf hunter?" she asked. I have to admit, that one caught me totally flat-footed.

"Huh?" I asked, not sure I heard her right.

"You heard me. We always need some good recruits," she said.

"I thought you said it was just a family business," I reminded her.

"Yeah, it is, but we do make exceptions now and then, for the right person," she told me.

I felt a thrill of excitement at the thought; I won't deny that, and I wanted to say yes like I'd never wanted anything else in my life before. There are certain things that touch your heart instantly and make you thirst after them like water on a hot day, you know. That's what it felt like.

But then on the other hand, I remembered how Cam almost died, last time we got involved with something like that. The danger to people I loved was very real, and this time there wouldn't be any sweet water to save them if anything went wrong.

"I'd have to think about that for a while," I finally said, reluctantly.

"Yeah, I thought you probably would. Here's my card, whenever you make up your mind," she said.

And believe it or not, she handed me a hot pink business card with shiny red letters that said *Jolie Doucet, Werewolf Hunter,* with her cell phone number down at the bottom. It was surreal. I guessed she was a Cajun, with a French last name like that, although you wouldn't have guessed it by looking at her. Most Cajuns have dark hair.

I stuck the card in my pocket without thinking too much about it.

"I'll have to let you off somewhere downtown, if that's okay. Like I said, I don't think anybody was trailing me today, but you can never be totally sure. It might not be safe for you if one of the wolves saw us together, especially not close to your house; some of them are mean customers," she said.

"Why are they following you all the time, anyway?" I asked.

"There's such a thing as revenge, Zach," she said cryptically, with a sad sort of smile.

That shut me up from asking any more questions for a while; I wasn't sure I wanted to know the answers.

She pulled in at the south end of the mall and parked the car, then turned to look at me.

"Think about it for a while before you make up your mind, Zach. We could do a lot together, you and me," she said.

There was a long pause, and then she did something I wasn't expecting. She lifted her hand to my cheek, and trailed her fingers across the bit of golden stubble I was just starting to grow. It tickled, and the way she did it was almost shy, like she wasn't sure what I might think.

"Call me sometime anyway, Blue-Eyes, if you want to," she said, and all I could do was nod. I'm not usually that tongue-tied, but for once I seemed to have forgotten how to speak.

I stood there in the parking lot and watched her drive away until she disappeared amongst the traffic on Richmond Road, and then I slowly raised one hand to my face. I swear my skin still tingled where her fingers had touched.

My thoughts were too confused at that moment to even begin to write them all down, so I won't try. But one thing was certain: she'd given me an *awful* lot to chew on.

I glanced at my watch and saw that it was only four-thirty, so that meant I was stuck downtown for at least an hour before anybody could come get me. Cam would still be at baseball practice for another thirty minutes, and Justin and Eileen wouldn't be off work till then, either. There was nobody else I could call for a ride, and I didn't have enough money for another taxi.

I didn't mind so much, though. I walked over to Books-A-Million and browsed the shelves for a while, just to see if there was anything new and interesting. I love that place. There's always something I haven't seen before, and they don't mind if you pull up a chair and read for a while. It's like a huge library with books about anything you could imagine, and if you like something especially well you can always buy it. What could be better?

I went to the section that has books about werewolves and such things, and found one that was called *Hunters of the Night: Real-Life Tales of Monster Slayers.* It sounded cheesy, but Jolie had me interested in the subject and I had nothing better to do at the moment.

I didn't really study it all that close, just flipped through the pages and read whatever caught my eye for a second. But there was nothing about Mont Mouchet, or *loup-garous,* or even Cajun werewolf hunters with flaming red hair.

I still wasn't sure what to think about what she said; *either* part of it. The idea of becoming a werewolf hunter myself was a huge thing to think about, but even that was *nothing* compared to the thought that she might really like me.

Yeah, yeah, I know; roll your eyes and laugh at me if you want to, but what can I say? She was beautiful and interesting and even funny sometimes, and it's not every day that you meet somebody like that, you know. I'm no more immune to a pretty face than anybody else is.

I couldn't help wondering *why* she liked me so much, though. Jolie was beautiful enough to take her pick of almost any boy she wanted. I've been told a few times that I'm cute, it's true, but I don't measure up to *that* level and I knew it as well as anybody. We hadn't talked long enough for her to be all that impressed with my warm and loving heart, either. So if it wasn't my insides and it wasn't my outsides, then what could it be?

It always makes me uneasy when things don't add up, you know. It means there's something missing from the way I'm trying to understand the world. It crossed my mind that Jolie was smart enough to *pretend* she liked me for her own purposes without meaning it; that's what she did at the fair that night, after all.

But nevertheless, I won't lie about it; I kinda hoped she really meant it this time and that we could talk and get to know each other better, regardless of what happened with the werewolf hunting thing.

It was after five o'clock by then, so I called Justin to pick me up on his way home from work. He did, and by the time I got home Cam was there too.

"I thought you stayed home today," he said when I saw him.

"Yeah, I decided to go to the bookstore for a while, that's all," I said.

I was kinda shy about telling him what happened with Jolie that afternoon. I knew he wouldn't like the werewolf part, and I could just imagine what he'd say if I told him about her touching my cheek; I'd never hear the end of it if he ever sunk his teeth into *that* juicy little tidbit.

But he didn't ask about her, surprisingly enough.

"So how was practice today?" I asked, mostly to turn the conversation to something else.

"Oh, it was okay. Jake hit a ball all the way over the back fence and we lost it in the ravine," he told me.

"Seriously? Jake never hits anything," I said, mildly curious. Jake was what you might call the team mascot, more than anything else. He was the kind of kid who'd trip over his own feet if they weren't attached to his legs. Sometimes even then, actually.

"Yeah, he really did. I saw him do it," Cameron said.

"I almost wish I'd been there, now. That's the kind of thing you don't see every day," I said.

"For sure," Cam agreed.

I didn't think any more about it right then. At the time, Jake's home run just seemed like a passing curiosity, here today and forgotten tomorrow. Before long I'd have good reason to think a lot about it and what it meant. But for the time being I was still blissfully unaware.

Chapter Two

I thought a lot about everything for the next few days; in fact, I think it's safe to say I hardly thought about anything else. I was so distracted at baseball practice on Thursday afternoon that I got bonked on the head with a flyball, and I'm *never* like that. I remember even James asked me what was on my mind, and he's not exactly the sharpest knife in the drawer when it comes to noticing that kind of thing.

It was several things. I kept remembering that kiss at the fair, and the way Jolie touched my face and asked me to call her, and even that silly SMOKIN license plate that made me laugh; I chewed endlessly over what it all meant and whether she really liked me or whether she had some other plan up her sleeve. It was driving me crazy.

But it wasn't only that. I was starting to worry about the whole werewolf hunting thing, too. Yeah, at first it thrilled me like nothing I ever felt before, but after a while I figured out why that was. Jolie had just finished telling me about all these pods that still existed, which meant the Curse was still very much alive, and then right in the middle of my disappointment she handed me what seemed like a second chance to break the thing. That was a powerful lure, you know. Especially for me, the one who was supposed to be the Curse-Breaker. *That's* why it touched such a deep place in my heart and set me on fire the way it did. When God gives you work to do, it's not something you can forget about so easily.

But the more I thought about it, the less certain I was that Jolie was offering me anything even remotely like that. She wanted help fighting wolves, and that wasn't quite the same thing. In fact, I couldn't help but wonder what it was that a werewolf hunter *did,* exactly.

Did it mean she carried a box of silver bullets in her pocket and a pistol in her purse, and that she hunted werewolves the same way some people hunt deer? That's kinda what it *sounded* like it meant, and that was an awfully dark and gruesome thought, you know. There was no way I wanted to get involved with something like *that.* I wasn't even sure I wanted to talk to somebody who was, no matter how beautiful and interesting she might be.

Maybe I was tying myself up in knots over nothing, and I guess the smartest thing to do would have been to call her up and just ask her about all that stuff, of course. But that's where the whole does-she-like-me thing came back into play again; I was afraid to say the wrong thing and make her mad at me, or even worse, laugh at me. Girls who are that pretty can be hard to talk to even at the best of times, believe it or not, and this was light years from the best and easiest of times.

So I dithered and dawdled and put off calling her while I tried to sort it all out inside.

Saturday morning I went out to Red Lick like I usually do, to mow Miss Edith's grass and do whatever else she might need done around the house. She was almost a hundred years old and she wasn't up to that kind of thing anymore.

I liked my visits out there. She always made me tea and cookies, or "sweet biscuits" as she sometimes called them, and usually we sat and talked for a while on the verandah after I was done with everything.

That particular Saturday started out pretty much like usual. I got to her house about nine o'clock and weeded the front flower beds, then repainted the trim on the garage with dark green paint.

I got done with all that about three o'clock, and then I sat down on the verandah to cool off a bit before I headed home. Miss Edith brought out the tea in a glass pitcher full of ice, and some sugar cookies on a lace platter cover.

You shouldn't think that was anything unusual, though. She always used to tell me it was the little things that mattered most, and you should always make your guests feel like royalty, no matter who they might be. She was one of those gracious old Southern ladies, and that's just the way she did things. I loved her to death, but there was always a certain level of good manners you had to maintain at her house, too.

So I sat there in my white wicker chair and I was careful to eat politely and not just wolf down my food like I might do at home.

"Zachary, you seem a little bit distracted today. Is there something on your mind?" she asked me that afternoon. She always used my full name like that for some reason, but I was used to it by then.

"No, Miss Edith, but I met this girl at the fair a few days ago and I guess I've been thinking about her a lot," I admitted. She smiled.

"Oh, I see. Well tell me all about her!" she said.

"Her name is Jolie, and she's got red hair and she's from somewhere down in Louisiana. Nackadish or something like that," I said.

"Do you mean Natchitoches?" she asked.

"Yes, that's it," I agreed.

"I take it you like her, then?" she asked.

I couldn't help thinking again about the whole werewolf hunting thing, and maybe I hesitated just a bit too long before I answered.

"Yes, ma'am, I really do. She's a lot of fun to be around," I finally said.

"Hmm. . . You don't seem too sure of yourself when you say that, Zachary. Is there something about her that bothers you?" she asked. Miss Edith is a wonderful person to talk to about most anything, and I decided it couldn't hurt to see what she thought.

"It's not exactly that. It's just that she does some things I'm not sure I like, that's all," I said.

"Care to tell me about it?" she asked.

"Well. . . she says the world is full of other werewolves besides just that one group me and Cameron had to deal with, and she says she's a werewolf hunter," I said.

"Which means?" she asked.

"I'm not sure. I guess it means she kills them. I didn't think to ask her about that part," I admitted.

"It seems strange that such a person would meet you by accident at the fair, don't you think?" she pointed out.

"Oh, no, it wasn't an accident. She came looking for me because she wanted to ask me some questions and offer me a job as a werewolf hunter, too," I explained.

"And what did you tell her?" she asked.

"I told her I'd have to think about it for a while," I said.

"But you wanted to say yes?" she prodded.

"Maybe if I knew for sure it wasn't anything bad. But even then I'm not sure. I want to break the Curse, not fight wolves forever. Besides that, I know Cam wouldn't be happy about getting wrapped up in something like that again. I'm not even sure Justin and Eileen would be very pleased right now, not with the baby coming so soon. I know it puts them all in danger, at least a little bit. It's just that I feel like we didn't finish the job we were supposed to do, if there are still all these pods out there. So if I had a chance to finish it now, then don't you think I ought to try?" I asked her.

Miss Edith didn't answer at first, just took off her gold-rimmed spectacles and polished them on the hem of her dress.

"You're a good boy, Zachary. You already know the answer to that question without me needing to tell you, don't you?" she asked.

"Yes, ma'am, I guess I probably do, and maybe working with Jolie is a good way to get started. It just bothers me the way her family is going about it, if they're really killing folks. What the wolves are doing is evil, but that doesn't mean it's right to go after them with silver bullets, either. They're still people, aren't they?" I asked, hesitantly. It was hard to put into words exactly what I felt.

Miss Edith smiled again.

"Oh, indeed they are. I'm glad to see you can still remember that, and think of them that way," she said.

"Love the sinner, hate the sin," I said weakly. I meant it as a joke, but Miss Edith took me seriously.

"Exactly!" she cried, "Always remember that, and you'll never become a hard and cruel man."

"I try," I said, half to myself. Miss Edith looked at me long and searchingly for a minute, and then she seemed to reach some kind of decision.

"Come with me, Zachary. There's something I want to show you," she went on.

I got up from my seat and followed her inside. She walked slowly, so it wasn't hard to keep up with her. She crossed the dining room and took a key from under a white ceramic cat on a shelf, then used it to unlock the cellar door. I'd never been down there before, so I was a little bit curious about what it was she wanted to show me.

She took her time going down the stairs, holding on to the railing carefully to keep from falling. When we got to the bottom she pulled a string to switch on a single dusty light bulb that didn't do much at all to light up the place.

It turned out to be a wine cellar. There were three of those wooden shelves that hold wine bottles, all of them stacked full, and that was about it.

I was disappointed, to tell the truth. I'd been expecting something a little more interesting than that. Miss Edith went slowly to the closest shelf, pulled out a dusty green bottle, and then handed it to me.

I dusted cobwebs off the label, which was something French and dated for 1965. I don't know much about wine, but I did remember that older is supposed to be better. 1965 was pretty old, so I guessed it was a fairly valuable bottle, if it came to that.

"Taste of it," Miss Edith said.

"Huh?" I said, totally forgetting my manners for a second in shock. Miss Edith was not at all the kind of person I would have expected to offer me alcohol.

"Don't grunt, Zachary; you're not a pig," she scolded me, "Now do as I say, and taste of it."

I glanced at Miss Edith out of the corner of my eye, just to see if she was really serious. She certainly looked that way, and I figured one sip of wine wouldn't kill me, after all. I popped the cork out and lifted the bottle to my lips, and then I took a small drink.

It wasn't wine.

It was water, with a faint taste of honeysuckle blossoms.

My eyes widened, and I looked at Miss Edith again. She was watching me, with a smile on her face.

"Always plan ahead, Zachary. I filled up these bottles for years, whenever I went out to the spring. Now it's gone, but these are still here. There are about two hundred bottles full, more or less. I've never told anyone else on earth about this place, except you," she said.

"So why are you telling *me*?" I asked, too stunned to think of anything else to say.

"I have good reason, Zachary. I've been wanting to tell you for a long time, but I needed to see what kind of boy you'd turn out to be, first. But I've known you for two years now, and we've talked about all kinds of things, and I believe you're the one I should leave it to," she said.

"Leave it to?" I repeated.

"I'm ninety-nine years old, Zachary. I won't be here much longer. But I couldn't trust all this to a stranger. It matters too much. I hoped and prayed that God would send me someone who could take it up, before I had to lay it down. I believe that's you. So I'm giving it to you, child, to do with as you see fit. All I can tell you is to use it wisely, and never tell anyone you have it. Not even your best friends," she said.

"Miss Edith. . . " I began, but she laid a finger on my lips to shush me.

"Hush, Zachary. My grandfather told me the secret and left me this place when he died in 1932, and I've kept it faithfully all these years. Now I'm asking you to do the same thing. There's no spring to guard anymore, but that only makes this place all the more precious. Use it wisely and use it well," she repeated.

I went home that afternoon lost in thought, and for a while I even managed to forget about Jolie, believe it or not. I was thrilled to find out there was a secret stash of sweet water somewhere when I'd thought it was all used or destroyed, and that cast a whole new light on the question of what I should do about the wolves.

I took it as a sign, for one thing. I don't believe in accidents, you know; not when it comes to things like that. I knew the water was a miracle, meant to be used to break the Curse. So if the Curse was still around, then it didn't surprise me that God made sure there was enough water left to finish the job He meant it for. No werewolf could frustrate that plan, not even with dynamite, and maybe at the same time He was encouraging me to remember that I was still the Curse-Breaker and my work wasn't done yet.

That was all fine and well, as far as it went. But at the same time, there had to be some other purpose for the water than just breaking wolf-stones like I did before. I could never finish all of them that way, not even with two hundred bottles full; not as long as people could keep going to Mont Mouchet and forming new ones. There had to be something else it was meant for than just that. If I could only figure out what it was.

It changed the way I looked at the werewolf hunting issue, too. In fact I was tempted to call Jolie right then and tell her I'd decided to take her up on the offer, as long as I didn't have to kill anybody. It seemed to have come along at exactly the right time, and I didn't think that was an accident, either. *She* might not think of the job as a stepping stone to breaking the Curse, but that didn't mean I couldn't use it that way.

I still had to wonder about the personal stuff, of course; whether she really liked me or not, and what I thought about it even if she did. That mattered, too, but I figured if we were working together we could sort out all that when there was time.

"How was Miss Edith today?" Eileen asked me when I walked in the door.

"Oh, she was fine," I said, still lost in thought.

"Something came in the mail for you this morning, Zach," she said.

"Really? What is it?" I asked her, mildly curious. I don't often get any mail, so whenever I did it was always interesting.

"Here it is," she said, handing me a pale pink envelope. It was addressed to me, sure enough, but there was no return address on it at all. The postmark was from Natchitoches, Louisiana, three days ago. When I saw that, I knew it had to be from Jolie; she was the only person I knew from down there.

I moseyed out to the barn and sat down on the bench beside Buster's stall to read it, just to have some privacy. I like to go out there sometimes when I want to be alone, or if I want to talk to somebody without worrying what they might think. Horses are good listeners, you know. They just turn their ears around in your direction and take in whatever you're saying, and they hardly ever talk back.

Nobody else was out there, so I opened my letter and started to read. The paper was pink, too, and it smelled like wild cherries.

Hey Blue-Eyes,

I hope everything is okay with you. I forgot to tell you I'll be back at my Aunt Angie's house this weekend, and I thought we might get together and have lunch sometime or maybe go see a movie if you want to. Here's her number, just in case. See you soon!

Jolie Doucet

She ended the letter with a bunch of x's and o's, and I smiled a little when I saw that. Eileen told me once that those are supposed to mean "hugs and kisses", which I never would have guessed if she hadn't told me. I always used to think they were just some meaningless doodly thing that girls like to put on letters for some reason, the same way they draw hearts and butterflies and flowers on everything they can get their hands on.

I still didn't think it meant *that* much, honestly, but nevertheless it made me feel warm right down to my toenails, cheesy as that sounds. It's amazing how a little slip of cherry-scented paper can do that, isn't it?

Anyway, I decided it was an excellent time to go ahead and call her. She ought to be at her aunt's house already, if the letter was right, and I had more than half a mind to ask her if she wanted to go have some ice cream and see a movie. It was still plenty early enough. We could talk, and she could explain exactly what it meant to be a werewolf hunter, and then if all went well I was ready to tell her I'd take the job. Everything else could wait till later.

I saved her aunt's number in my phone so I wouldn't lose it, and then I pushed the call button.

It didn't go through. Instead, all I got was a recorded message telling me the number was out of order. I tried it again just to make sure I hadn't made a mistake, and when it still didn't work I tried the number on the business card she gave me. That one went straight to her voicemail.

I furrowed my brow in disappointment and kinda wondered if maybe something was wrong. Surely she wouldn't ask me twice to call her and then not answer the phone, would she? She had to know it was me; she'd have caller ID on her cell phone even if her aunt didn't have it at home.

Maybe any other time I would have just shrugged it off and tried again in a day or two, and that's what I almost did even now. But I couldn't help remembering all that stuff she said about the wolves following her around and wanting revenge, you know. That put a little bit different twist on things, so I sat there and chewed my bottom lip for a while, trying to make up my mind what to do.

I finally decided it was worthwhile to drive over to her aunt's house for a minute, just to make sure everything was all right. So I called information and got the address that went with the number: 933 Ash Street. I knew vaguely where that was; somewhere downtown near the post office, if I remembered right.

Justin gave me and Cam his old Dodge Ram 4x4 when he bought a new one last year, and most of the time we don't fight much about who gets to drive it and when and where. It's our pet project, and it spends about as much time parked under the hickory tree behind the house as it does anywhere else. We bought some chrome wheels and bed rails for it, and a glass pack muffler that makes it just loud enough to sound mean when you step on the gas.

We had plans to get a cold-air intake and some other stuff like that, when we had the money. Justin says neither one of us can have a job except on Saturdays or during the summer, so it's hard to rake up the cash for those kinds of things. Especially for me, since I was always at Red Lick on Saturdays, doing stuff for Miss Edith.

Anyway, the keys were hanging on the wall next to the front door, so I went in there intending to take them and go.

"Going somewhere?" Cam asked. He was sitting on the couch watching a movie and looked up when I opened the door.

"Yeah, just downtown for a minute. I'll be right back," I said.

"Mind if I come along?" he asked.

That put me in an awkward position, because of course I really didn't want *anybody* to come with me, but it was hard for me to say so.

"Sure, I guess," I said grudgingly. If I had to, I could come up with some excuse for stopping at the house on Ash Street. Cam probably wouldn't quiz me too much.

So we hopped in the truck and drove down there, and I went to the post office first, since I had to come up with another reason for going downtown than just to check on Jolie.

"Eileen already checked the mail this morning," Cameron said when we got there.

"Did she?" I asked.

"You know she did, Zach. You got that pink letter today," he reminded me.

I hadn't known he knew about that, but then of course you can't keep secrets very well when you live with somebody. He must have seen it on the kitchen table earlier.

"Yeah, I guess I forgot about that," I lied, and Cam laughed at me.

"No you didn't, Zach. I saw you go out to the barn with that letter in your hand and then as soon as you came back in, you wanted to come down here. That's why I wanted to come, so I could see what was up. So whatever it is, you might as well spill it," he said.

I sighed.

"All right. But if I tell you then no laughing about it, Cam," I told him.

"Okay, that's fine," he agreed.

"I wanted to stop by Jolie's aunt's house and check on her, just to make sure she's all right," I said.

"Really? Why wouldn't she be, and why do you care, and what do you think you could do about it anyway?" he asked.

All tough questions.

"Well. . . that pink letter was from her. She said she'd be in town this weekend and she asked me to call her so we could maybe go do something together; that's all." I said.

"And?" he asked.

"So I called her and I keep getting a message that says the number is out of order. It's probably nothing, but I just want to go check it out since it's not that far anyway," I explained.

"So you *do* like her. I knew it all along," he smiled.

"Cam, you promised. No laughing," I reminded him.

"Oh, all right; I won't. I just think it's sweet, that's all," he said. I wasn't exactly sure what *that* was supposed to mean, but I knew better than to ask him about it. If I did, that would just keep the whole topic alive for that much longer. So I didn't take the bait.

"Okay, let's go down to the old lady's house and see what's up," he said after a while.

Ash Street was only a couple of blocks from the post office, just like I thought, and as soon as we found it we drove slowly north, counting house numbers.

Before long we came to a black mailbox with 933 on it, and that's when we got a nasty surprise. The house was a burned-out wreck. All the windows were busted out and the front door was gone, and there was black soot and smoke stains everywhere. There was nothing left but a gutted ruin.

No doubt that was why the phone number didn't work. It looked awfully recent, too; the place was even still smoking a little bit, here and there. Besides that, Jolie wouldn't have been talking about staying here for the weekend, if she knew it was burned down. That meant it couldn't have happened more than three days ago at the most.

"Are you sure this is the place, Zach?" Cam asked me.

"Yeah, it has to be. This is the right address, and there are no other houses close to this one. Let's take a closer look and make sure, though," I said.

We got out of the truck and slowly picked our way up the concrete walkway and onto the steps.

"Look, here's the 933," I said when we got closer, pointing to the metal numbers that were still attached next to the missing front door. I wondered what had happened.

Oh, I know it was a house fire, of course; I'm not stupid. What I meant was, I wondered if maybe it was more than just an accident. Maybe one of the wolves had spotted Jolie while she was there and then torched the place on purpose.

There was a string of that yellow plastic *"Do Not Cross"* tape wrapped around the house to keep people from going inside, but I ignored that and ducked underneath it.

"What are you doing, Zach? You want to get arrested?" Cameron hissed at me.

"I just want to look, that's all. Go wait for me in the truck if you want to, or else come in here yourself and then nobody can see us," I told him.

He must have decided he couldn't change my mind, because he followed me inside without saying anything else about it.

There wasn't much to be seen in there, at first glance. Just burned and scorched furniture, covered in black soot and still soaking wet from the fire hoses. It stank like you wouldn't believe.

But there *was* a half-melted computer sitting on a desk against the wall, and I decided that was worth looking at first. I couldn't possibly do any more damage to it than there already was, so I tore the cover off the tower part and rooted around inside until I found the hard drive. It didn't seem to be damaged, but after going through that much heat you could never tell for sure. I disconnected it from what was left of the CPU and slipped it in my pocket.

"What's that for?" Cam asked.

"Just curious. Might find out something, if it still works," I said.

We took a quick look around the rest of the house and didn't find anything else worth mentioning. Fire is really good at destroying things, you know.

I was uneasy about spending too much time in the house because, like Cameron pointed out, they put up that yellow tape for a reason, and you can get in trouble for crossing it when you're not supposed to. And besides that, burnt-out houses are dangerous places to be. You never know when the floor might cave in or the ceiling might collapse on your head, and there's broken glass and rusty nails everywhere.

As soon as we glanced at everything, we got out of there. We were both smudged with greasy black soot and stank to high heaven just from the short time we'd been inside.

"Do you really want to get in the truck like this? It'll stink for a week," Cam pointed out.

"No, but I think it'll be okay if we throw somethin' over the seat," I said. I looked in the bed to see if there was a tarp or a blanket or anything like that. There usually would have been, but apparently not today.

"Never mind. We'll just have to clean it out real good," I said.

As soon as we got back home, that's exactly what we did while we still had some daylight left. We wiped down the seats and sprayed them with Febreeze and put a can of Eileen's French

Vanilla air freshener in there. Neither one of us especially likes that flavor; it smells like stale birthday cake to me. But it was all we could find, and it was way better than smoke and water smell.

"I guess that will have to do," I said.

"Yeah, it will. So what are you doing with that hard drive?" Cam asked.

"Watch and see," I told him.

As soon as we got back inside, I took the cover off my computer and then plugged the hard drive from the burnt computer into one of the empty slots reserved for extra internal hard drives.

You might have noticed that I really like computers. Most people don't know much about them except how to use whatever software they like, but they're amazing things and they can do wonderful stuff if you know how to play with them the right way.

Anyway, I put the cover back in place without screwing it down, and then turned everything back on. It started up as usual, and as soon as it was ready I clicked my way through to the screen where all the drives were listed. Sure enough, there was a new one there.

"Bingo," I said to myself.

I clicked on the new drive to look at the files, and of course there were tons of them. I expected that. But I didn't care about the operating system files or solitaire or any of that crud. I wanted documents or spreadsheets or databases; anything that might have useful information in it.

I soon discovered that the hard drive had been damaged pretty badly by the fire. Heat does funny things to magnetic memory, which is why they always tell you not to let your computer get too hot. That drive was chock full of corrupt files that couldn't be opened anymore, or if they could then they didn't show anything but gibberish. I'd be willing to bet that way more than half the memory was either erased or ruined.

But not all of it.

I found one file that contained what seemed to be locations of *loup-garou* pods and basic information about them. There were a lot more of them than I expected, and I was discouraged all over again about how little me and Cameron had actually done. One pod was just a drop in the bucket, it seemed.

There was also an entire folder full of in-depth case files on each pod from the list, but most of those were unreadable and the rest of them were badly damaged.

There was another file that looked like an amateur family tree and history of the Doucet family since 1767, which was apparently when they first got into werewolf hunting. That one was mostly just a list of names and dates and who was related to whom and some of the notable things they did, but in places Angie had expanded it to read like a storybook. The tail end of that one was corrupted, too, so I could only read the first few pages of it.

I guess I was so absorbed in looking at files that I forgot Cameron didn't already know about all the werewolf hunting stuff. But he's not stupid. He was looking over my shoulder when I opened that file with all the pod locations, and he knew what it meant as soon as he saw the word *loup-garou.*

"What do these people have to do with the wolves, Zach?" he asked me quietly.

There was no way to keep it a secret anymore after that, so I told him.

"Jolie and her family are werewolf hunters. She came to find us because she heard about how we destroyed all those wolf-stones, and she hoped I could help them fight some other pods," I said.

"Pods?" he asked.

"Yeah, she said that's what you call a group of werewolves. I never knew that before," I admitted.

"And what did you tell her?" he asked.

"I told her I'd have to think about it for a while; that's all," I admitted, not wanting to look him in the eye.

"I see. Well, it sure looks to me like you're doing a whole lot more than just *thinking* about it," he said, crossing his arms over his chest and starting to scowl.

"I just want to make sure she's all right, Cam. You saw that house today," I reminded him.

"Yeah, all I saw was a burnt-out house, and that could happen to anybody. She doesn't even live there," he pointed out.

"No, but it seems awfully fishy, anyway. She stays there a lot, and she kept talking about the wolves following her around and wanting to get revenge, remember?" I asked him.

Cameron thought about that for a few seconds, but if it softened his mood at all he sure didn't let it show on his face.

"I guess she didn't bother to tell you which *pod* it might be that hated her so much, did she?" he asked sarcastically.

"No, she didn't. But I'm sure a lot of them probably have grudges and scores to settle against her family. They *are* werewolf hunters, after all," I said, and Cameron shook his head sadly.

"You're getting dragged into another fight, Zach, and this one's not even yours," he said.

"I'm trying not to, Cam, but I can't let anything happen to her," I said.

"Bubba, this is not just about her and you know that as well as I do," he told me.

That was the heart of it all, right there, and we both knew it. Cameron knew I could never turn my back on breaking the Curse till it was finished. I might say I was just thinking about it, or just helping a pretty girl, but he knew me better than that. He knew my heart's desire was to crush the Curse forever, and I was a fool if I pretended not to know it myself. I was trying to help Jolie, true, but that wasn't the whole story by a long shot.

I sighed. It never feels good when somebody yanks the warm rug of make-believe out from under your feet, but it's usually better when they do. I wasn't being completely honest with Cameron about my plans and purposes, and he was right to call me down for that. People will risk their lives for the truth sometimes, but never for anything less.

"Cam, do you remember, a long time ago, when you told me about the prophecy of the Curse-Breaker and then we all fought the wolves together?" I asked him.

"Yeah, I remember. What about it?" he said.

"Well. . . I saw the way you acted, back then. You used to think it mattered to break the Curse; I know you did, even though you never talked about it much. That day when you went down to the deer camp all by yourself, I thought that was the bravest thing I ever saw anybody do in my whole life. So, if there are still all these pods out there, and especially if they're hurting people, then don't you think we ought to finish what we started, or at least try?" I asked him. That was stark truth, straight as an arrow, and all I could do was pray that he'd listen.

He didn't answer me right away, though. He just looked out the window where the sun was setting across Coca Cola Lake, and played with the bullet on a string that he still wore around his neck sometimes. When he spoke again, he sounded moody.

"I never wanted to fight wolves all my life, Zach. I want to go skating, and play ball after school, and cruise State Line and whistle at pretty girls, and hang out at the mall, and all that stuff normal people do. I want. . . oh, I don't know. I want to get a good job someday and fall in love and have three or four kids and go to church every Sunday and live happily ever after. That's *all* I want, Zach. I'm not like you. I don't want to be a crusader or a dragon-slayer or whatever you want to call it. That's not who I am," he said after a while.

It's not like Cameron to be that serious, or even to talk about stuff like that at all, and I knew I must have hit a deep nerve.

"I know that, Cam, and I don't want to do it for always, either. I want to end it this time for good and all, if we can find a way. But I need your help, bubba; I can't do it by myself," I said.

He looked at me for a long time with that same scowl on his face, and I could almost watch him struggling inside between how much he loved me and how much he hated crusading.

"You know I'll help if I can," he finally said, although he still didn't sound very happy about it.

"Yeah, I know," I told him heavily. Maybe he knew he was making me feel bad, because he wiped the scowl off his face with an effort and gave me a crooked smile.

"All right, then, where do we start?" he asked.

Chapter Three

We started by transferring all the usable files from the scorched hard drive over to mine while we still could. You never could tell when some or all of the others might go bad. Then as soon as that was done, we started digging. The first thing I wanted to do was to make sure Jolie and her aunt were safe, and when that was done then we could start trying to figure out what to do about breaking the Curse.

Angie Doucet must have been a werewolf hunter for a long time, because she had files on dozens of pods and probably hundreds of individual people. Like I said before, almost all of them were damaged in spots, some worse than others, and it makes for tiresome reading when you can't finish anything you start on. The case files were the worst, and I didn't even *try* to read those yet. They could wait for later when we had more time.

I found other things, of course. There was a map of southern France with Mont Mouchet marked on it, and some photos of people I didn't know, and a list of books Angie had swiped from every library within a thousand miles. That one mystified me since it never explained the purpose behind it. People don't normally drive that far just to steal a book.

"I thought you wanted to find out what happened to Jolie," Cameron asked after a while.

"I do," I agreed.

"Well. . . I really don't think she was kidnapped by a mad librarian in Oskaloosa, Kansas," he pointed out dryly, and he was right, as usual.

"No, I guess not," I sighed, and closed the screen. I was tired of reading, anyway. The files were interesting, but not very helpful at the moment.

"Any other ideas, then?" he asked.

"The only thing I can think of is to drive down to Natchitoches and see if she's at home. I already tried calling her phone," I said.

"You really think that's necessary?" he asked, with a raised eyebrow.

"Yeah, I'd feel a lot better if we did, just to make sure. If we've got the gas for it, anyway," I said. The tank was about half full, and I still had maybe fifteen dollars or so. I wasn't sure how far it was to Natchitoches, but I was pretty sure that was cutting it awfully close.

"Well. . . I still have a hundred bucks left over from that hay baling job I did last week while you were out in Red Lick, if we need it," Cam offered.

"Aw, I couldn't take your money, Cam. You need that for other stuff," I said, embarrassed. In fact I already knew what he wanted it for; he was saving up for an almost-new four-wheeler he wanted to buy from Levi's uncle. He already had most of what he needed, and if I took that hundred bucks I knew it would set him back at least a couple weeks.

He held up a hand and shook his head.

"Look, I said I'd help if I could. I don't mind paying for gas, but if I give you the money then I need you not to make me feel weird about it, okay?" he said.

"Well. . . I guess you have a point. Thanks, though," I said.

"No problem. When do you think we should go?" he asked.

"It's probably too late to make it down there today and still have time to do anything. We'll have to go tomorrow afternoon," I said.

"Sounds good to me, but what about Justin and Eileen?" he asked.

"We'll tell them tonight, before we go to bed," I said.

So that's what we did.

They were pretty calm about the whole thing, I have to say, but then of course they usually are.

"I think y'all are biting off a pretty big piece of trouble," Justin said soberly, after we explained everything.

"What do you think we should do?" I asked him.

"It sounds to me like you should do exactly what you just said. Go down to Natchitoches and see what you can find out, and then try to help this girl if it turns out she needs it. I'm proud of you for wanting to, and I wish I could come with you," he said. I was pretty sure that's what he'd say, but it still felt good to hear it.

"I know you can't go this time. We'll be okay though," I promised him.

"Just be careful and don't do anything stupid, boys. You know what I mean. Don't start thinkin' you're in a monster movie and you can just throw popcorn and switch the channel if somebody gets hurt," he said.

"We know," I said.

"Well, then, all I can say is be as careful as you can, and trust God, and be brave boys. I love you both," he said. Then he pulled out his billfold and handed me a hundred dollars.

"Here, you might need that, just in case somethin' happens," he added. I took it with murmured thanks and stuck it in my pocket.

Cameron grabbed the .22 and a box of silver bullets from the gun case, also just in case, and stuck it down behind the truck seat where nobody could see. You never knew when you might need it.

Before we left the next day I drove out to Red Lick to see Miss Edith one more time, too. I wanted to take a bottle of sweet water with us, *also* just in case.

She wasn't home when I got there, and I figured she was probably still at church. But that was okay, because I knew where the extra key was. She always kept it under a pot of red geraniums next to the front door. She wouldn't mind if I went inside without her there, but I meant to leave her a note anyway, just so she'd know it was me.

The cats swarmed me when I stepped inside, just like they always did, but they scattered again when they found out I didn't have anything to feed them. I went downstairs to grab a bottle off the wine rack, then came back up and left my note on the dining room table beside the silver serving tray. I made sure to lock both doors before I left, and that was that.

The wine bottle was glass, of course, so I carefully wrapped it in one of my old t-shirts before I stuck it down behind the seat next to the gun, wedging it in so it wouldn't roll around and break.

"What's that for?" Cameron asked me.

"Just something we might need," I said lightly. As far as he knew it was only a bottle wrapped in an old t-shirt, and I wanted to keep it that way. It's not that I cared for him knowing, but Miss Edith had told me to keep the water a secret and I was trying to do what she asked.

He didn't comment, and we left Red Lick without saying anything else about it. If he wondered about the bottle at all, he kept his guesses to himself.

As it turned out, the trip wasn't nearly as bad as I thought it would be. There wasn't much to look at except pine trees and cotton fields, and if I'd been by myself it probably would have been pretty dull. But since I had Cam with me it wasn't so bad. We always had stuff to talk about.

So we talked about the Fall Ball Classic that was coming up in a few weeks, and old man Webbers' hay baler that was always breaking down, and the new mud tires we wanted to get for the truck, and things like that. We never mentioned wolves at all, even though I'm sure we were both thinking about them. I know I was, deep down. But sometimes when you're worried about something, it helps to put it out of your mind and talk about other stuff, you know. We both knew we might be walking into a pretty nasty situation before long, but neither one of us wanted to think about that until we had to.

We got to Natchitoches around three o'clock, more or less. That didn't leave a whole lot of time for nosing around before it got dark, but I hoped it would be enough.

We found a phone book and soon discovered there was no shortage of Doucets in town. That complicated things, since we didn't have any way of knowing which was the right one. Jolie had never given me her address or even her parents' names.

I pulled out her business card again to make double sure there was no address on it, but it only had her cell phone number. Probably sensible, if you don't want uninvited guests, but it didn't make it any easier for us to find her.

"There's no way we'll have time to go visit all these people in the phone book," I said disappointedly.

"Well, we could always go to the mall and show her picture around. I've still got that picture on my phone that I took at the fair last week," Cam suggested.

"Yeah, that might work. Let's give it a try," I agreed.

So we went to a UPS store first and got them to print a couple of those pictures from Cameron's phone so we'd both have one, and then we went to the mall and started roaming around showing the pictures to anybody who looked like they might be in high school.

We talked to several people who thought they'd seen Jolie before, but nobody seemed to know where she lived or who her parents were. After a couple of hours we were just about ready to give up the ghost.

"This ain't workin' too well, bubba," I said, pointing out the obvious.

"No, it's not," Cameron agreed, "but I can't think of anything better to do, unless you want to go visit every Doucet in town."

"No. . . let's just keep trying for a little while, I guess," I said.

We tried asking some of the shop owners in the mall, and that's when we got our first good lead.

"Oh, yeah, I've seen her. That's Jolie something-or-other. I can't remember her last name. She comes in here all the time with her mom, though," the clerk at the Upscale Retail Boutique told me.

"Really? Do you remember her mom's name?" I asked.

"Umm. . . Sonya, or Sheila, or something like that," she said, like she wasn't too sure. It sounded like a pretty slim clue, but I thanked the girl and left.

There was a pay phone next to the restrooms, and I looked in the phone book again to see if there were any Doucets with a name like that. There were two possibilities, in fact. John and Sarah Doucet lived on Hickory Street, and Robert and Celine Doucet lived on La Salle Circle.

We adjourned to the truck and drove to John and Sarah's house first, mostly because that was the closest one. We still had enough daylight to check both places, and if they both turned out to be wrong then we'd just have to sit down and think of something else.

That house on Hickory Street was pretty impressive, I've got to admit. It was a three-story red brick thing, with a wrought iron fence and a tall hedge and two huge magnolia trees on each side of the front walkway.

That whole street was a no-parking zone, so we had to drive a few blocks down to find a place to leave the truck. There was a parking lot at an old Piggly Wiggly grocery store that wasn't open any more, and that's where I pulled in. It was no more than a ten minute walk back to the house.

"Go on," Cameron told me, when I didn't get out.

"What do you mean, go on? You're not coming with me?" I asked.

"No, I'll sit here and guard the truck," he said with a grin.

"But-" I started.

"Seriously, Zach, it's probably better if only one of us goes up to the door, don't you think? They're more likely to talk," he pointed out.

"Well. . . yeah, I guess that's true," I admitted, even though I didn't like it much.

I got out and walked back down the street to that big wrought-iron gate, then took a deep breath before I went inside. I pushed the door bell, and heard chimes ringing faintly somewhere deep inside the house.

After a long time, a tall lady in a gingham dress opened the door. She looked about forty, maybe, but she was in really good shape for her age. I also noticed she was wearing a silver ring almost exactly like the one Jolie had been wearing at the fair, and on the same finger, too.

"Yes?" she asked.

"Excuse me, ma'am, are you Sarah Doucet?" I asked her.

"Yes. Can I help you?" she asked.

"I hope so. Do you know a Jolie Doucet?" I asked her.

"I have a niece by that name," she said, frowning a bit.

"Can you tell me where she lives or how I can get in touch with her? It's very important," I said, trying to act like it wasn't. If you get upset then people are less likely to do anything for you.

"I'm afraid I can't do that without asking Jolie first, young man. If she wants to see you then she can give you that information herself," she said, disapprovingly, and started to shut the door.

"Listen, I hate to bother you, but I'm afraid she might be in trouble and I don't know who else to tell. Will you at least check on her?" I asked. She stopped shutting the door and looked at me for a long time before she answered.

"All right, child. I'll tell you this much, since you seem to be a friend of hers. Jolie's been missing since Thursday night. But there's nothing you can do about that except pray she comes home safe, which I'm sure she will. Now, good night," she finally said.

"Just one other thing, please," I asked. The woman looked impatient.

"Yes?" she asked.

"I know about the *loup-garous*. I need to know which pod took Jolie," I said. That was kind of a gamble, since I didn't really know for sure if that's what happened or not, but I figured I had nothing to lose by asking.

"I have no idea what you're talking about," the lady said, in a tone that meant the discussion was over.

Somehow I knew she was lying; sometimes you can see it in people's eyes, you know. But I could tell she wasn't going to help me, so I didn't waste any more time on her.

"I'm sorry I bothered you, ma'am. Good night," I said, and walked away. She watched me until I shut the iron gate and went out of sight behind the hedge.

"That's Jolie's aunt, but she wouldn't tell me anything except that Jolie's been missing since Thursday," I told Cam as soon as I got back to the truck.

"So we go to the other house, then?" he asked.

"Sure, why not?" I said sourly. Talking to Sarah Doucet had put me in a bad mood.

It was almost dark by the time we made it to the other place. That one was at the end of a little cul-de-sac, way back from any other houses. It was a nice neighborhood, just like the other one, but this time instead of a brick mansion we found nothing but another gutted ruin, even worse than the house in Texarkana had been.

"Uh-oh. That doesn't look good, bubba," Cameron said, and I had to agree. When I saw that, I *knew* there was trouble. One house fire might be an accident, but not two of them.

"Let's go check it out," I said.

So we got out and dug through the debris for a while, till it got too dark to see. I don't know what I expected to find. Maybe another computer drive I could look at or something else that might give us a clue what happened or another place to go look. But there was nothing like that.

I did find what had to be Jolie's room, though. It was painted a dark pink color that would have looked funky most places, but it seemed to suit her. That part of the house had survived the worst of the fire, so there wasn't as much damage as there was elsewhere.

She had a dresser by her bed with a big mirror above it, and almost the entire mirror was covered in photos she'd taped to the glass. There were pictures of her standing with other people I didn't recognize, and showing off a trophy from a beauty pageant, and holding up a rainbow trout she'd caught, and some other things like that.

I noticed there was an empty spot on the glass where she'd pulled off a picture and not replaced it, and when I poked around the room a bit more, I found the missing snapshot lying on her pillow. It had to be the same one, because one of the corners was torn off, like somebody had ripped it loose in a hurry from where it was taped to something.

It didn't seem to be anything special, when I picked it up; just a picture of her standing in front of a tree, and I was curious why she pulled that particular one off the mirror and then left it there like that. I flipped it over to look at the back, and as soon as I did, I saw something written there in purple ink.

Love you, Blue-Eyes.

That was all it said, but I knew as soon as I saw it I knew that she meant for *me* to find that picture. I was the only one who'd know what "Blue-Eyes" meant. Maybe she had to be cryptic so nobody else would guess what she was trying to say or who she was trying to say it to. The only problem was, *I* wasn't even sure what she was trying to tell me.

I turned the picture back over and studied it again, more closely this time. Like I said before, it didn't look too unusual. It was just a snapshot of Jolie in a red t-shirt and blue jeans, standing in front of a big pine tree. There wasn't anything in the background except more trees, and she wasn't holding anything or standing next to anybody.

There was something written on her t-shirt, but she was standing too far away from the camera for me to be able to tell what it said. I might possibly scan it into my computer and blow up the picture and be able to read it that way, but it didn't seem likely to mean much.

On the other hand, she had to mean *something* by wanting me to see that picture, if I could only figure out what it was.

I took it with me, just in case.

There was nothing else in the bedroom that seemed worth messing with, and it was almost dark by then, so we gave it up after that.

"Come on, Cam, let's go home," I said, discouraged.

We didn't talk as much on the way back home as we did going down there. I guess both of us were too wrapped up in our own thoughts, or maybe it's just that the mood was darker than it was going down there.

We pulled into the driveway a little past eleven, and since it was a school night we both went straight to bed. I could deal with the picture tomorrow.

School seemed to drag by slower than cold pancake syrup the next day. I was already looking at the clock by nine thirty, and it only got worse from then on. I was seriously tempted to go home at lunchtime, and I almost never do that. I played football with James and Levi instead, and that was intense enough to distract me for a while, at least until lunch was over and I had to sit through history class for an hour.

Anyway, three o'clock finally got there, and since there was no baseball practice on Mondays I was able to go directly home after that.

When I got to my room, I took out Jolie's picture and scanned it into my computer. Then I blew it up four times as big as it used to be, to see if I could read what was on her t-shirt.

It was a picture of a hairy Bigfoot-looking thing, with a caption that read "The Boggy Creek Monster." Which, needless to say, didn't seem to shed much light on the subject of where she might be or who took her. At least not at first.

The Boggy Creek Monster was vaguely familiar for some reason; I could have sworn I'd heard that name before, but I couldn't remember when or where. So I did the obvious thing and looked it up. As soon as I saw the first entry, I remembered where I'd seen it.

There's a little town called Fouke, maybe ten or fifteen miles from Texarkana, and there's a Boggy Creek not far from there. I guess they call it that because it's swampy down there. But anyway, it's sort of a local legend that there's a hairy monster that lives in the woods around Boggy Creek, and they sell trinkets and t-shirts and things like that about it.

I'd never paid much attention to it, honestly, but you can't live around here without at least hearing about it. So the next question was, what did it mean?

It might not mean anything at all, of course. Jolie could have bought the t-shirt while she was visiting Angie and it might not even have anything to do with what she was trying to tell me. It's easy to think you've got it all figured out sometimes, when you're really just seeing the reflection of your own silly face.

On the other hand, maybe there was a werewolf pod down in Fouke, and they were the ones who had the grudge against the Doucets at the moment. It would have been easy for them to come burn down Angie's house, and even Natchitoches wasn't that far, if they wanted to sneak down there and attack the others too. It seemed like a wire-drawn train of thought to wring all that out of the picture on one old t-shirt, but right then it was all I had to go on.

I combed through Angie's list of werewolf pods and I did indeed find one in Fouke, but it was marked as destroyed ten years ago.

I went to the case file for that pod, and it turned out to be one of the more intact ones, thankfully. It still had a lot of damage in places, but not so much that I couldn't read it.

It was pretty grim stuff, I have to say. Angie never actually said she killed anybody; but she kept saying she "collected" thus and such a person, whatever *that* was supposed to mean. I couldn't help wondering if it was some obscure code word for whacking people and she just didn't want to come right out and say so.

Anyway, after she "collected" them she apparently robbed the house, because she listed a bunch of stuff she took from the place: two thousand dollars in cash, a 1994 Ford Taurus, a diamond wedding set, a Mossberg hunting rifle, and a few other odds and ends. As soon as that was done, she set the place on fire.

There was a lot more, but that's all I could read. The text trailed off into a bunch of undecipherable gibberish that went on for five or six pages.

I wondered if that was how the Doucets got so rich, by looting whatever they could from the werewolves they hunted. I was willing to lay pretty good odds that was at least part of it.

In fact, after reading all that I started to think maybe being a werewolf hunter might be almost as bad as being a werewolf, when it came right down to it. No wonder the wolves hated them so much and wanted revenge, if that's the way they acted.

Justin told me once that it's very easy to start out doing something good and then gradually let it get twisted into something even worse than the problem you were fighting to begin with. It's the most dangerous and deadly of all snares, and you take the first step down a very dark road when you start thinking that the ends justify the means. I've always believed that you never did wrong by doing right, but the opposite saying is true, too. You never do right by doing wrong.

Justin never let us make that mistake, when we were fighting the Trewick pod. We took away their ability to lead more people into evil, but we didn't hurt them or steal from them or anything like that. I don't doubt they hated us for that, but there are all different levels of hate, you know. The Trewicks hated us enough to want nothing to do with us and maybe even enough to shoot us if we came around them anymore, but not quite enough to come after us later on.

The Doucets were a lot more radical, though. They "collected" people and robbed them and burned their houses down if they could, and surely that was the kind of thing that might make any survivors hate them enough to want to do the same thing if they ever got the chance.

If somebody came to our house one day and killed my family and stole everything they wanted before they set the place on fire and destroyed everything else, I'm not sure I could keep from hating them for that. Oh, I'd know I wasn't supposed to, and I'd try, but I'm honestly not sure if I could do it or not. The wolves wouldn't even have the benefit of knowing better.

I was getting dangerously close to thinking maybe the Doucets deserved whatever they got, and that was a really bad attitude for me to have. Start thinking that way and you'll soon forget how much grace you've been given in your own life, and then you'll turn into a harsh and prideful person. I didn't dare be judgmental, not even to the werewolf hunters.

Nevertheless, I started to seriously rethink my impulse to become a werewolf hunter myself. There are certain things which are so bad you just have to turn your back on them, you know. . . no matter how useful they might be as stepping stones. There's such a thing as honor.

I guess what bothered me even worse than that about the whole thing was how Jolie felt about it all. She hadn't *seemed* like a cruel and hateful person, but after reading all that, what else could I think? If she had any heart at all, then how could she be involved in something like that? I wasn't sure I wanted to risk my neck for a thief and a killer, you know, if it turned out that's what she was.

I was full of thoughts like that when Cameron walked in.

"What's up, bubba? Why the long face?" he asked.

"Nothin'; just thinking about some stuff," I said.

"Oh, okay. Did you look at that t-shirt like you said you would?" he asked.

"Yeah, it's got a picture of the Boggy Creek Monster on it; you know, that thing they have down in Fouke," I told him.

"Really? So she might be in Fouke, then?" he asked, hopefully.

"I don't know. Maybe. They wiped out a pod down there ten years ago, so maybe they missed one or somethin'. There's no telling; it might not even have anything to do with it," I said.

"But it might, though," he said.

"Yeah, I guess it might," I shrugged.

"You don't seem too enthusiastic about it," he said.

"I don't know. I was just looking at those files again. Angie Doucet seems like an awfully cruel person, that's all," I said.

"So now you're wondering if Jolie is the same way," he said. It wasn't quite a question, but I treated it like one.

"Yeah, maybe," I admitted.

"I knew that was it," he said.

"She didn't *seem* like that kind of person," I said, half to myself.

"So maybe she's not. You don't really know her well enough to say," he pointed out.

"That's true," I agreed, and I couldn't help feeling a little better after that.

"So do you still want to try to help her?" he asked.

"Yeah, I do," I finally said. As long as I didn't know for sure, I could still believe she was different; stupid as that might be. Sometimes things look worse on paper than they truly are, and it's always possible there's a good explanation for things. You never know unless you ask. I was willing to give her the benefit of the doubt, at least for now.

I don't know why I cared so much anyway, about somebody I barely knew and had every reason to think was a thief or even worse, but for some reason I did. Maybe it was the way she touched my cheek that day in the car, or the way she said she loved me on the back of the picture. Or maybe it was something else completely. Nobody understands himself all the time.

"Okay then, where do we start? Go down to Fouke and show her picture around, like we did in Natchitoches?" he asked.

I have to give Cameron credit; I knew he didn't want to be involved in all this, but he promised me he'd help if he could, and he really was trying to. He's nothing if not loyal.

"No, if we do that and she *is* there, then they might just move her somewhere else. They'd hear about us showing her picture around, probably a long time before *we* heard anything," I said.

"What should we do, then?" he asked.

"I don't know. It's like looking for a needle in a haystack," I said.

"We could ask Jake; he's from down there, I think," he suggested.

"And what would *he* know about it?" I asked.

"Well. . . probably nothing, but you never know; it's not that big of a town. If nothing else, he could keep his ears open and let us know if he hears anything. He's the only person I can think of that we know from down there, and we'll see him at baseball practice tomorrow anyway. I could ask him then," he offered.

"I guess it couldn't hurt," I said. I thought it was a waste of time, to tell the truth, but Cam was trying to be helpful and I didn't want to discourage him.

"I wish there was a way to find out more about that old pod in Fouke. These files are so damaged and corrupted, it's hard to tell much," I complained.

"Well, what *do* you know about them?" Cam asked.

"Um. . . not much, actually. They lived in Fouke, there were three of them, and they got collected and their house burned down on November 28, exactly ten years ago. That's about all I can tell from this," I said.

"No names, no address, nothing like that?" he asked.

"No, everybody has a number. 243-A, B, and C, whatever that means. That's how I knew there were three of them," I said.

"I bet you could go to the library and look through the old newspapers and find something. They usually report house fires and things like that, don't they?" he suggested.

"Well, yeah, sometimes I guess they do," I agreed. I was thinking to myself how tedious and dull that would be, leafing through microfilmed newspapers from all those years ago. They don't always index those articles, you know, so the only way you can find what you want is to read the whole dadgummed paper.

Not to mention the library closed at five o'clock and that meant I'd have to skip baseball practice again. I could just imagine what coach would have to say about *that* next time I saw him, but I didn't see any other choice.

I sighed.

"I'll go do it tomorrow," I finally said.

Chapter Four

I drove to the library after school the next day, and sure enough, the *Texarkana Gazette* wasn't indexed for that long ago. I ended up having to look at microfilms until I was ready to pull my hair out; ten year old news is about the most utterly boring thing you can possibly imagine. Justin and Eileen taught me a lot about how to do research, but that doesn't mean I'm patient enough to enjoy it. Maybe when I'm older I might, but not yet.

Anyway, I did eventually find a teensy weensy little blurb about a house fire in Fouke in the December 2nd edition of the *Gazette,* way back on page 18 wedged in between an article about the Union Pacific Railroad laying off some people and another one about what to do if your cat starts scratching the furniture. Fascinating stuff.

The blurb only said that apparently nobody was home at the time of the fire and that the residence was a total loss and that it belonged to some people named Jason and Charla Golden. It also gave an address on County Road 211 and said that foul play wasn't suspected. That made me want to laugh, in a sad kind of way. I couldn't help wondering how Angie managed to get away with something like that so slick. Lots of practice, no doubt.

There was nothing else in the article worth mentioning, but at least now I had names for the people and an address for where they used to live.

That was the only helpful thing I found after almost two hours of searching. About 4:45 one of the librarians came by and told me I had to shut off the microfilm machine because the library would be closing in a few minutes, so I gave up on finding anything else that day.

There were still maybe two hours of daylight left when I got done at the library, and I decided it was worthwhile to go ahead down to Fouke to see if I could find the place itself, or whatever was left of it after all this time. There might be more clues.

Fouke is not a very big place. But even so, I still had to stop at a gas station to pick up a Miller County road map before I could tell where to start looking. I had no idea where County Road 211 might be.

It turned out to be close to Boggy Creek, believe it or not, and that made me think maybe I was on the right track, after all.

That monster t-shirt had been an awfully subtle and oblique hint, and I couldn't help thinking Jolie was putting an awful lot of faith in my ability to notice things and figure out what they meant. I was sorta flattered, in spite of the fact that I didn't know for sure yet if that's what she even meant by it.

Anyway, I found the road without too much trouble, and finding the house itself wasn't too difficult either, once I knew where to look. I just cruised down the road and counted mailbox numbers until I came to the right place.

At first I was afraid the mailbox would be gone after all this time, but as it turned out I was worrying for nothing. It was still there, kinda rusty and faded, but you could still read the numbers if you squinted a little.

It looked like the Goldens had lived in a mobile home, because even though the whole place was incredibly grown up with sumac bushes and Johnson grass and little pine and sweet gum saplings, you could still make out where the driveway used to be and you could still see the remains of the trailer itself. It was totally burned up at one end and the roof had caved in on about half of it, but the other end was still more or less intact.

I parked the truck in the old driveway and glanced around to make sure there was nobody in sight. There didn't seem to be, and I decided to risk a little exploring before it got too dark.

I picked my way through saw briers and Johnson grass higher than my head to reach the front steps, and I was covered in cockleburs and beggar lice by the time I got there. I looked down at my jeans ruefully; Eileen was going to kill me if I carried all that into the house when I got home.

The front door was partly melted when I got close enough to see, and it looked like somebody had kicked it in at some point. I had to duck down and crawl under it to get inside.

As soon as I got through I found myself in the remains of the living room, and I nosed around in there for a while just to see what I could find. The fire had been pretty bad in that section of the trailer, but I still found an old gas bill addressed to Jason and Charla Golden. That proved I had the right house.

You wouldn't think something like that would survive a house fire, but paper is a lot tougher than you might imagine. I found the bill in a corner where the heat must not have been bad enough to burn it up. I read somewhere once that it has to get to 451 degrees before paper will burn, and that's pretty hot, you know.

There was also an ancient issue of *Bassmaster* magazine lying crumpled up next to the gas bill, partly scorched but still readable in places. The little address sticker was gone, but I found one of those auto-renewal notices inside the back cover with Jason Golden's name already pre-printed on it. There was an interesting article in there about using grubs for summer smallmouths, and I decided to take it with me to read later.

The kitchen and everything on that end of the trailer was totally destroyed, so I headed down the hall toward the master bedroom instead. It was on the other end of the house and that area wasn't burned too bad.

The first thing I found back there was a ten year old calendar, open to November and stained brown with smoke. I flipped through it just out of curiosity, and among the notes about when the water bill got paid and such things, I found a note on June 24th with a lot of little hearts and stars and the name "Jacob" in a girl's handwriting. I guessed it was somebody's birthday, although I couldn't be totally sure of course. I took the calendar with me, and it left a clean spot on the wall behind it when I took it down.

The closet was still full of stuff, and while I was rummaging around in there I came across an old shoebox full of snapshots. They'd gotten wet at least once and most of them were stuck together in a big sticky wad, but I was able to pull a few of them apart. There were several pictures of a young couple that I guessed were Jason and Charla, and in one of them they were holding a little kid between them. There was a caption on the back that said *Jason, Charla, and Jacob, September 22.*

I guessed that was probably the same Jacob whose name was on the calendar; he looked like he was maybe five or six years old in that picture. They all looked happy, and even though I knew they were werewolves and therefore who could guess what kind of evil they'd done, I couldn't help feeling sorry for them.

I took the box of pictures too, just in case I needed them later. I didn't find anything else worth mentioning, just some moldy clothes and rotted furniture and stuff like that, most of it badly burned or smoke-damaged, and I wondered again what really happened to these people. They obviously never came home again after that day, that's for sure.

That's another thing you wouldn't think I'd care about very much, would you? After all, whatever it was that happened, it was a long time ago and there was nothing I could do about it now. But I did care, for some reason.

It's easy to talk about wiping out pods when they're just numbers in a list, but it's a lot harder to do that when you can see a little kid's smiling face in a picture, or read a girl's loopy handwriting on a calendar for her baby's birthday like Charla did, or when you know that a young man likes to read *Bassmaster* or wear camouflage jackets like Jason did. It makes them a lot more real.

And yet I learned all those things about them just from a quick walk through their house over ten years after they disappeared. Angie had to have seen those kinds of things too, when she came there to take what she wanted and do whatever she did to them.

Maybe I still didn't want to believe that anybody could be so heartless and cruel as to wipe out a whole family like that. It was hard to swallow, you know. I struggled with it and couldn't decide how I felt.

Justin always taught me that there's no such thing as evil; there's only spoiled goodness. He says no matter how wicked and rotten something seems, there had to be something good there first before it could get twisted and spoiled. And if that's so, then the real key to undoing evil and pouring light into the darkness lies in finding out what that original good thing was, and trying to restore it. He says I shouldn't treat bad people with hate or fear; I should remember what Jesus said about the people who crucified him. . . that they didn't know what they were doing.

And so he would say, if you want to deal with a wicked person, search their heart and try to find whatever that original seed of goodness was before it went sour, and then teach them a better and truer way to fulfill the deepest desires of their heart, if you can.

Maybe that's true. I guess Justin would know. But I have to wonder sometimes if there might be people who are too far gone into evil to save like that, who have learned to love the darkness too well and don't care about finding any other way, better or not. In fact I'm sure there are such people, rebels to the bitter end, or else there'd be no one in hell.

But then again, you never can tell who might listen and who might not, so I guess Justin is right after all. . . treat them all the same. I don't know. It's hard, and I'm not wise enough to figure it out yet. Sometimes I wonder if I ever will be.

I say all that because I started to wonder if maybe the real purpose God led me to get involved with the werewolf hunters was because I was supposed to try to search *their* hearts and teach them a truer and better way to do things. It was a staggering thought, and a terrifying one, too. They seemed wickeder than anybody I'd ever seen or imagined, even though I was pretty sure they were at least *trying* to do something good. One thing was certain; I could never be one of them myself, unless they somehow found that better way. It might not matter to them right now whether or not they lifted everything up to God, but it made an awful big difference to me. So I was taught, and so I've always believed, ever since I was old enough to understand what it meant to be the light of the world.

I walked out to the truck thinking hard, and slipped the calendar and the pictures and the magazine behind the seat where nobody would see them. I was just about to leave when an old man came walking out of the trees on the far side of the road. He didn't look pleased to see me.

"Can I help you, son?" he asked, in a tone of voice that didn't sound like he wanted to help me much at all. He had on one of those blue shirts they use as uniforms at tire shops and places like that, and the name on his pocket said "Bobby".

"No sir, I, ah, I just had to use the bathroom, that's all. I was just leaving," I explained quickly. It sounded stupid even to me, but it was all I could think of on the spot like that. Bobby-the-old-guy looked disgusted, but I guess he had no reason not to at least halfway believe me.

"Well this is private property and nobody's allowed out here. There's broken glass and sharp metal and all kinds of things that could get a kid hurt. Get gone, and next time I catch you out here I'm callin' the law," he said.

"Yes, *sir*," I said, and I didn't waste any more time taking his advice. Going to jail was *not* my idea of a fun evening, and he seemed like the kind of guy who might really do it. He stood there in the front yard and watched until I disappeared around a curve in the road, and I breathed a sigh of relief when I saw the last of him. I wondered who he was and why he thought he had the right to come out there and yell at me for poking around in that dumpy old trailer, because he sure acted like he had a right to.

I stopped at the gas station in Fouke for a few minutes, to get me a cold Dr. Pepper and put some gas in the truck. I'd been doing a lot of running around lately and the tank was almost empty again. I also took the time to pick the cockleburs and beggar lice off my clothes and off the truck seats, so I wouldn't get in trouble with Eileen.

Nobody was home when I walked in the front door, so I went to my room and sat down at the desk. Justin and Eileen had to work late now and then at the oil company, so that was nothing very unusual, but I might have thought it was strange that Cameron wasn't home yet, if I'd stopped to think about it. It was after six o'clock and baseball practice had been over for almost an hour already.

But I was still wrapped up in thinking about the Goldens, and it didn't cross my mind at the time to wonder where everybody else might be.

I was curious about Bobby whats-his-name, so I fired up my computer and did a search for anybody with that name on that particular road in Fouke. I soon discovered there was a Bobby and Sandra Lee just down the road from the burnt-out trailer. It had to be the same dude, because I hadn't seen the one at the trailer drive up in anything. He had to have come from somewhere close enough to walk.

After that, I went to the county website to look up the property records for that area, and I soon found out that Bobby Lee also owned the trailer itself, and that he'd had it for almost twenty-five years.

I put two and two together and decided he must have owned the place when Jason and Charla lived there, and therefore he must have known them, some way or other.

I guess I could have done the obvious thing and gone to see the man to figure out what he knew and how much he was willing to tell me, but I decided that probably wasn't such a great idea. He hadn't seemed very friendly, for one thing, and we hadn't exactly gotten off to a good start, either.

But the fact that he owned that place while the Goldens lived there and the fact that he was an old dude made me wonder if maybe he might be some relative of theirs, maybe even Charla's dad.

That was something else which was possibly checkable, so I started out by searching the county marriage licenses for that time period. Sure enough, I found a record of where Charla Lee got married to Jason Golden seventeen years ago, when she was 19 and he was 22. I still couldn't tell if Bobby was Charla's dad or her uncle or what exactly he might be to her, but something he surely was. I couldn't prove it yet, but I was willing to lay pretty good odds he was her dad.

I did a quick name search for Charla Lee on Google and came up with nothing useful, but that didn't really surprise me. Just for kicks I tried all the others' names, too. I finally got a hit on Jacob Golden's name, but it was just a birth announcement that somebody had posted on an old message board.

I was amazed it was still there after all this time, but sometimes you get lucky that way. I could have found the same thing in the newspaper, most likely, but I would have had to wait till tomorrow to do that, because I would have had to go back to the library to use the microfilm machines again.

It was definitely the right Jacob because it mentioned his parents' names, and then a little later on it said that he was the grandson of Robert and Sandra Lee of Fouke. Good enough. That meant Bobby had to be Charla's father.

"Dang straight," I murmured to myself.

I felt pretty smug about figuring all that out, but on the other hand, I wasn't sure it was really all that useful. It still didn't get me any closer to figuring out where Jolie was, or how I could help her. The only person who might know something was Bobby Lee, and I was willing to bet a dime to a doughnut that *he* wasn't talking. If he even knew anything to tell.

It's frustrating to get all these tantalizing tidbits of information and then not be able to figure out how they fit together, or if they even mean anything in the first place. The whole thing might be a wild goose chase, for all I knew. Jolie might not even be in Fouke at all. I had nothing but a bunch of guesswork to go on, and that's a pretty flimsy foundation.

I put my face down in my hands and rubbed my eyes. I was tired of thinking for a while.

I wanted to talk to Cameron about it, or Justin, or Eileen, or *somebody*. Sometimes when your brain is worn out, it helps to bounce ideas off another person and see what they think.

Cameron still wasn't home by then, and I finally started to wonder where he'd gotten off to. I tried calling him and got no answer, but that by itself wasn't so unusual. Cell phones are not the most reliable things in the world.

I knew it was unlikely he'd still be at the park, but I decided to drive down there just in case. He might have had to stay late today for some reason.

I didn't see him anywhere along the main route, and when I got to the park there was nobody out on the ball field and no lights on. Everything was dark and empty.

I started to worry just a little bit, to be honest. Cameron isn't the type of kid who goes off somewhere on a whim and never tells anybody where he's at or when he thinks he'll be home. I'm worse about that than he is.

Of course, his phone might be dead or something minor like that, or he might have called Justin or Eileen to let them know where he was instead of talking to me. I would have thought he'd call me today to ask if I found out anything at the library, but then again maybe not.

I decided to call Justin.

"Hey, Justin, do you know where Cam is?" I asked him when he answered.

"No, I woulda thought he'd be home by now," he said.

"Yeah, me too. That's why I wondered if he called you or not. But there's nobody at the practice field and I didn't see him on the road between here and there," I said.

"That's kinda strange. I know he didn't call Eileen because we're both in the lab today. If he'd called her then she woulda told me," he said.

"What should I do?" I asked.

"Well, don't get your knickers in a knot. It's not even seven o'clock yet, so he might still show up any time now. Maybe he went out to eat with some of the other guys after practice today or somethin' like that," he said.

"But wouldn't he call somebody, if that's what it was?" I asked, and Justin didn't quite answer me.

"If he's not home by the time me and Eileen get there, then we'll go look for him. We won't be here much longer. In the meantime, go home and stay there in case he shows up," he told me instead. That's how I knew he was worried; Justin almost always gives a straight answer to a straight question, and if he doesn't then something's wrong.

I told myself it was a good plan, though, and I drove home hoping I was worried for nothing. When I got there, I sat down on the couch and tried to watch a rerun of *Star Trek* on TV for a while. Justin and Eileen would probably get off work in less than an hour, and all I had to do was wait till then.

That's harder than you might think, though. I'm an action kind of guy and I don't like just sitting and twiddling my thumbs when something's going on.

Cam never did show up, and by the time Justin and Eileen got home I was *seriously* worried. It wasn't like him at all to just disappear like that.

"I called Mrs. Robinson at the school and she said Cameron left from there with James Bray as soon as class was out. She didn't know where they went," Eileen said as soon as she walked in the door.

"James is on the baseball team. He probably just gave him a ride down to the park, since I had the truck today," I said.

"Yeah, that's what I thought. I called the coach and he said Cam was there for practice this afternoon and that he left when everybody else did, but he didn't know where he went after that or who he was with," she said.

"He's still not answering his phone, either," I told them.

"Yeah, we know. I tried calling him twice," Justin agreed.

"I think it's safe to say something's wrong. Cam wouldn't stay out this late without telling somebody," Eileen said.

"What do you think could have happened to him?" I asked.

"I don't know, Zach. Did he say anything yesterday or this morning that might give us some idea where to look for him? Was there anything he might have done today that was unusual?" she asked.

"I can't think of anything. He was supposed to talk to Jake about helping us look for Jolie down in Fouke, but that's the only thing I know of," I said.

"Who's Jake?" Justin asked.

"He's a big, clumsy kid from Fouke. I don't know him that well but he plays on the baseball team with us," I said.

"Do you know his number, who his parents are, his last name, anything like that?" Justin asked.

"No. Like I said, I barely know the boy," I admitted.

"We need to find out; he might have been the last person who talked to Cam today, so he might know something. We need to call the other boys too, because he might have gotten a ride with one of them after practice. He wouldn't have tried to walk this far. If we call everybody then one of them has got to know something. Babe, do you know where we put that contact sheet they gave us last month when the boys signed up for Fall Ball? It ought to still be here somewhere," he said, turning to look at Eileen.

"Sure, it's in the kitchen in the mail holder," she said. I wasn't surprised she knew where it was without having to hunt for it; Eileen never loses anything. The contact sheet had the name, address, phone number, and parents' names of everybody on the baseball team, so we could get in touch with them if we needed to. I was glad Justin thought of it.

He got up and went to fetch the contact sheet, and after leafing through papers for a while he found it and came back into the living room.

"Okay, here it is. It looks like there's only one Jake on the list. Jacob Golden, County Road 211, Fouke, parents Bobby and Sandra Lee. Let's call them and see if they know anything," he said.

I'm not dumb. As soon as I heard those names, my mind leaped ahead and I knew instantly what happened to Cameron. Like I said, I don't believe in coincidences like that. Bobby and Sandra weren't Jake's parents, they were his grandparents, and he had to be the same Jacob from the Golden pod. Never mind what he was doing living with his grandparents or how he survived being "collected" by Angie Doucet or any of that stuff. He had to be the same one.

And if he was, then he of all people had reason to have a grudge against the Doucets in general and against Angie Doucet in particular, and if somebody was so full of hate that he'd set two houses on fire, then who knew what else he might do. Especially if somebody came up to him and started asking inconvenient questions.

I remembered something else, too. Jake had always been a clumsy, goofy kind of kid, and Cameron had said something about him hitting a home run a few days ago. The old Jake could never have done anything like that, but if he'd found his parents' old wolf-stone and if he knew anything about how to use it, then he could have become a *loup-garou* and then he'd be strong and swift enough to hit all the home runs he wanted. It was the right time of year for it, too; the Hunter's Moon had been a little over a month ago.

It explained so many things I hadn't understood till then; even that silly Boggy Creek Monster t-shirt that Jolie had been wearing. She must have known who Jake was and hoped I'd figure out it was him, if she gave me the right hint. It was a pitiful poor clue, to be sure, but in the end it had turned out to be enough.

It only took an instant for all that to run through my mind, and I'm willing to admit there were still some pretty big holes in it. But when it came down to the basic outline, I knew I was right just as sure as taxes.

"Stop. Don't call them," I said out loud.

"Why not?" Justin asked, looking at me curiously.

"Because that's where Cameron is, and Jolie too. I think Jake is a *loup-garou* and I think he's got them both," I said.

"That requires a little bit of explanation, Zach, don't you think?" Eileen said.

So I laid it all out for them, and they listened, and when it was all said and done they agreed with me.

"We need to go down there right now," Justin said.

"You don't think it might be better to wait till in the morning when everybody will be gone? I know Jake will be in school, and the old guy Bobby still works somewhere. I know that from the shirt he was wearing when I saw him. I don't know about the lady, but it's a good bet she'll leave at some point during the day," I suggested.

"No, that's not a good idea. If we knew Cam was safe, then I'd say yes. But we don't know what might happen to him or Jolie between now and then. We don't dare wait that long," Justin said, and then he turned to Eileen.

"Babe, you stay here, and me and Zach will go see what we can do. Keep your phone turned on and be ready to do whatever you need to do if we call," he told her.

Eileen doesn't rattle very easily, but this was one time when I could tell she was scared, whether she admitted it or not. She was never like that during the whole time we fought the Trewick pod, not even when they were shooting at us in the rock quarry. But we were all together then, and she wasn't having to watch us go off into danger and leave her behind. That's hard to do. But there was the baby to think about, and she knew what she had to do.

"Be safe, both of you," was all she said, but the way she kissed Justin before we left said more than any words ever could.

Justin was quieter than usual on the way down there. He's never much of a talker while he drives, but he does sing to himself or listen to the radio sometimes. Not tonight, though, and his mood rubbed off on me too. I told him which way to go when we got to Fouke, and the rest of the time I kept my mouth shut. He slowed down a bit when we came to the burnt-out trailer.

"I don't think we should just go up and knock on their front door; not yet. If they've got Cam and Jolie then they wouldn't tell us anyway, and it would just tip them off. Might even get us nabbed," he said.

"So what do you think we should do, then?" I asked.

"I think we should park a little bit down the road and scout the place to see what's up first. I wish we knew if they had dogs or not," he fretted.

I knew what he meant without asking; dogs bark, and that would attract attention and maybe even cause somebody to come outside and see what was up. We had to avoid that at all costs.

"All we can do is hope," I said.

Justin parked in that same driveway where I had my run-in with Bobby Lee, and then killed the lights and the engine.

We got out and shut the doors as quiet as we could, and then stealthily started walking down the gravel road. It would have been shorter to cut straight through the woods, but Justin said it was too easy to get lost out there in the dark. Besides that, people might possibly believe it if you said you had car trouble or some such thing if you were walking along the road at night. It's a lot harder to convince them you're not up to no good if they catch you sneaking through the woods behind their house.

So we stuck to the road for the time being, our shoes crunching softly on the gravel. It was so quiet we could hear every footstep.

Maybe my imagination was running away with me, but it felt just like the calm before a terrible storm hits. Sometimes my mind is entirely too good at feeding me images like that, especially when I least want to think about them. I hadn't had to fight a *loup-garou* since that last time in Caddo Gap two years ago, and I wasn't anxious to do it again.

Chapter Five

It wasn't long before we saw a light up ahead that had to be the place, and we stopped walking before we got too close. We didn't dare be seen.

The Lees lived in a one-story house made of brown brick, with a couple of sheds and a well house out back. It was nothing special as far as houses go.

Unfortunately, the whole front yard was lit up by a porch light right next to the front door, so there wasn't a snowball's chance in a blast furnace of getting close to the place without being spotted.

"Look," I whispered, pointing to one corner of the porch. There was a gray and black striped cat eating from a dish by the top of the steps, and Justin let out a sigh of relief when he saw it.

"Okay, good. Hopefully that means no dogs. Let's duck into the edge of the woods and slip back behind the house where it's still dark. Then maybe we can find out somethin'," he said.

We crossed the ditch and climbed over a barbed wire fence to get in amongst the trees, which were so thick you could barely stretch an arm out in any direction without touching a trunk or a branch. We had to move slowly and carefully to keep from crunching on fallen limbs or shaking the bushes too much. There was no way to get through without making at least a little noise, but it must not have been enough for anybody inside to hear us.

After about twenty minutes we made it around to the back of the house, and it was dark as the inside of a velvet purse back there, because of the shadows of the trees. We crept up behind one of the outbuildings and regrouped.

"What should we do now?" I whispered.

"Let's check these buildings first, and then if we don't find anything we'll try the house," he whispered back.

The first building turned out not to have anything inside it except some lawn and garden tools and things like that. There was no place you could have hidden a mouse in there, much less a person. Justin risked using the penlight on his keychain for a second, just to make sure we didn't miss anything. We pulled the door shut behind us to hide the light, but even so he clicked it off as soon as possible.

The next shed had a padlock on the door, and that was a problem.

"Let's skip this one for now and see what's in the last one," Justin said.

We soon found out that the last building had nothing inside it but a deep freeze with some wrapped-up deer meat inside.

"Come on, let's go back to that first one. I think I saw a pair of bolt cutters in there," Justin whispered. We went back to make sure, and there was indeed a pair of bolt cutters. They were small ones, like the kind you can buy at Wal-Mart for ten bucks, but with a little luck they should do the trick. We quickly fetched them out and went back to the second shed.

"Are you sure we can do this without making a lot of noise?" I asked anxiously.

"All we can do is try. If we do it slow then maybe," he said.

Justin fitted the bolt cutters to the padlock, and then he slowly started squeezing the handles. He didn't dare put his weight into it, and I could hear him gritting his teeth from the effort. The blades bit into the steel slowly but surely, though, and it really wasn't long before the lock broke in half.

Justin let out a deep breath and wiped sweat off his face.

"Dad *gum* it," he whispered under his breath.

I pulled the lock off the hasp, and then slowly started to open the door. It let out a loud rusty creak and I froze instantly.

"Hold on a minute; I know how to fix that," Justin said, and then he spit on his hand and rubbed it into the hinges real good until they were dark with wetness. The rust left a dark brown stain on his hand that I could see even in the dim light.

"Try it now," he said, and this time the door opened with only a faint creak. Justin slipped inside and I stayed by the door to watch and make sure nobody was coming.

He wasn't in there long, but when he came back out he had a puzzled look on his face.

"What is it?" I whispered.

"I'm not sure. Somethin' with Cam's name on it. I'll show you when we get back to the truck," he said.

We closed the door and put the broken lock back on the hasp so it wouldn't swing open and give us away.

"All right then, nothin' left but to check the house," Justin said glumly.

We crept up close to the back wall, making sure not to trip over anything in the yard. When we got there, we soon discovered that it was much too dark to see inside the windows. The kitchen light was on, to be sure, and we could see into that room just fine. In fact, I could see all the way across the kitchen and into the front living room, where three people were sitting around watching TV. I recognized Jake and Bobby, and the other one was an older woman who I guessed must be Sandra.

Well. That accounted for everybody we had to watch for, so the next step was to check inside all those dark rooms.

We ended up having more of them to look at than we thought, because it turned out the house wasn't really one story. It looked like it from a distance, but when we got closer we realized there was a finished basement level too, with some narrow windows down low to the ground.

Justin used his pen light just long enough to shine it in each window for a second and see what there was inside, and before long we knew there was nothing interesting on the main floor. Then we got down on our hands and knees and checked the basement rooms. We came up empty handed there, too, but there were still three or four more windows across the front of the house that we hadn't checked yet.

The problem was, that whole area was lit up like Christmas, and all it would take would be for somebody to glance out the big picture window at the wrong time. If that happened then our goose was cooked, because there was nowhere to hide.

But maybe, just maybe, if I stayed slicked up against the wall and crawled on my hands and knees, I'd still be out of sight. Unless one of them came to the door or something really unlucky like that, of course.

They say fortune favors the bold, so I decided it was time to be bold as brass. I *knew* Cam and Jolie had to be here, somewhere.

"We still have to check those basement rooms across the front, Justin," I whispered.

"Yeah, I know," he whispered back, and he didn't look too happy about it.

"I'm smaller and faster, so let me go do it. If you stay here then maybe you can distract them or help me if I need it," I said. Justin knows good sense when he hears it, so he nodded and squeezed my shoulder.

I got down on all fours and slipped around the corner quicker than a flea on a dog's back, before I had time to talk myself out of it. It was scary, being right out in the open like that with the light pouring down, but I held my breath and didn't let myself think about it.

The first window I looked in on another spare bedroom, just like I thought it probably would. The next one was harder to reach because it was underneath the porch. The porch by itself wasn't the problem; it was about two feet up off the ground, and there was plenty of room for a person to crawl up under it with no trouble if he needed to. The problem was, I couldn't get under there without removing the wooden crosshatch trellis that went all around the edge.

I crept up close to see if there was any way to pull it loose, and it didn't take me long to figure out that it was only held in place with wood staples. *That shouldn't be too hard to get off,* I thought to myself, so I gripped it in both hands and gave a swift yank.

In fact it turned out to be a little bit *too* easy. I pulled harder than I needed to, and when the staples came loose I lost my balance and tumbled backwards into an azalea bush, with the trellis lying on top of my legs. It made so much noise that I was sure somebody must have heard it, and to my horror I saw a shadow get up and move across the window by the door.

I had only seconds before they saw me, so I quickly scrambled under the porch and pulled the trellis back in place against it, trying to keep from breathing too hard.

A split second later I heard the front door open, and somebody walked out onto the porch above me. I could see the bottoms of his bare feet through the cracks in the decking when I looked up.

Whoever it was went to the edge of the porch and put his hands on the railing for a minute, but when he didn't see or hear anything unusual I guess he didn't think any more about it.

"Stupid cat," I heard him mutter to himself, and I recognized Jake's voice.

Jake went back inside before long and shut the door behind him, leaving me alone again under the porch while I recovered from my heart attack. I was shaking from the close call, but I took a deep breath and decided now was no time to get rattled.

There was a light on in the room under the porch, and when I eeled my way close enough to peek inside, I was rewarded with one of the two things I most wanted to see right then. There was Jolie, sitting on a twin sized bed in the corner with her knees pulled up to her chest. She'd been crying, I think, but it was hard to tell from that far away.

I tapped on the window, real soft so nobody would hear it upstairs. Jolie looked up instantly, and I tapped on the glass again.

She jumped up off the bed and rushed to open the window. I guess they didn't bother to lock it since it was way too small for anybody to slip out of anyway.

"You sure know how to make an entrance, Blue-Eyes," she whispered.

"Yeah, I guess. I like to have never found you," I whispered back.

"Yeah but you did, and that's all that matters. Look, Jake is a *loup-garou* and he- " she started.

"I already know all that. But where's Cam, and how can we get y'all out of here?" I asked.

"I don't know where Cam is. I haven't seen him. But I can get us both out if you'll do just one thing for me," she said.

"What is it?" I asked.

"Bring me my ring. It's silver, with a star sapphire on it. I wore it that day at the fair, if you remember," she said.

I've heard stranger things before, and unless Jolie had suddenly gone totally off her rocker I wasn't inclined to doubt her.

"Where is it?" I asked.

"It's in Natchitoches, in my bedroom. If you pull up the corner of the carpet beside my closet, there's a loose piece of wood in the floor. Under that you'll find a locked steel box, and here's the key," she said, taking off her necklace and handing it to me. There was an ornate little key on it, which looked more like jewelry than it did a real key. If I'd seen it anywhere else, I would have thought that's all it was.

"It's in *Natchitoches?*" I asked, hardly believing it.

"Yes, I'm afraid so. Jake caught me off guard in the middle of the night and I didn't have a chance to grab it. He managed to get inside the house without setting off the alarm system, somehow. All I had time for was to leave that picture where you'd find it," she said.

"That was awfully risky, don't you think? What if I'd never found it?" I asked.

"Oh, I knew you would, Blue-Eyes. I know you better than you think I do; you never give up. But you go get that ring for me and bring it here and then everything will be just fine," she promised.

"That might take a while, you know. They won't hurt anybody between now and then, will they?" I asked anxiously.

"I don't think they'll do anything right away, Zach, since they haven't yet. But of course I don't *know,* so I'd hurry if I were you," she said.

"I'll be back as soon as I can," I promised.

"I know you will, Blue-Eyes. But hurry and go now, while you still can. And whatever you do, *don't lose that ring!*" she said.

She kissed the first two fingers of her left hand and laid them against my dirty cheek, and I felt all warm and brave inside, like I could slay forty dragons to get her out of that place, if I had to. I smiled at her, and then she closed the window and went back to her bed.

I didn't waste any more time after that. I pushed the trellis loose again and replaced it behind me after I scrambled out from under the porch. I was covered in dirt and grime and crushed azalea leaves, but I couldn't have cared less.

I crab-walked my way along the front wall and slipped around the corner as fast as I could, and Justin breathed a sigh of relief when he saw me.

"Anything?" he asked.

"Yeah, I found Jolie. But come on and let's get out of here fast. I'll tell you why in a minute," I whispered.

Justin, as usual, took me at my word. We hotfooted our way back through the woods and got out of there faster than a rattlesnake on roller skates.

"Did you ask her about Cameron?" Justin asked me, as soon as we were back in the truck.

"Yeah, she said she hadn't seen him," I said.

"Well, maybe not, but those people have *somethin'* to do with him, anyway," he told me.

"How do you know for sure?" I asked.

"Because I found this in the shed," he said, and pulled something out of his pocket. I couldn't tell what it was at first, but when I turned on the dome light I saw that it was a little plastic bottle, like the kind people put on a spice rack in the kitchen to keep nutmeg or cinnamon in. It was about half full of reddish-brown powder that looked a lot like cinnamon, in fact. There was a handwritten label taped on one side, and I turned the bottle around to read it better. It said *Cameron Parker,* with today's date written below it.

"What's that supposed to mean?" I asked, perplexed.

"I have no idea. I just picked it up because I saw Cam's name on it and I wondered why," he said.

"Is it poison?" I asked, unsure what to make of it.

"I don't know, Zach. But I wouldn't open it if I were you, just in case," he said.

He didn't have to worry about that. I had no intention of opening that little bottle until I knew for sure what was in there.

But in the meantime, I stuck it in the glove box of the truck and forgot about it. There were more important things to think about than that. We were just coming to the interstate, and I had to tell Justin which way to go.

"Turn south," I said. Home was the other direction, and he'd just been getting ready to turn that way.

"What for?" he asked, slowing down.

"We've got to go to Natchitoches tonight, and hopefully be back by morning," I said.

"And why is that?" he asked.

"Jolie said she could bust them both out of there with no problem if I'd bring her a ring from her bedroom in Natchitoches. She told me where to find it and gave me the key," I explained, holding up the necklace she gave me.

"I see. Do you remember how far that is, Zach? We'd be driving all night long," he reminded me.

"Yeah, I know that. But I believe her," I said, stubbornly.

Justin didn't say anything, exactly; he just got on the southbound ramp and then called Eileen to let her know we were okay and what was up, and told her we'd be home some time in the morning. Then he drifted back off into his normal silent-driver mood.

There wasn't much traffic on the road that night, and once again I had nothing much to do except look out at the cotton fields. Sometimes I wish Justin didn't have that one particular habit. I don't get to talk to him as much as I used to, and sometimes I really miss that. I learn a lot from him, whether he knows it or not.

He stopped at a gas station in Shreveport and got a large coffee for him and a large Monster energy drink for me. Anything with enough pizzazz in it to keep us both awake till morning.

I really hate staying up all night, I have to say. I know some people are night owls and truly seem to enjoy it, but I'm not one of those people. I'm neither a bat nor an armadillo, thank you very much. If I'm not in bed by at least one o'clock in the morning, I feel cruddy all day long the next day.

We made it to Natchitoches about midnight, and when we got to Jolie's house we got straight to business. I took the penlight on Justin's key ring, went directly to her bedroom, scooped up the ring, and then got the heck out of there. I didn't want to spend the night in the parish jail just because one of the neighbors saw us snooping around in the middle of the night.

But that didn't happen, and after we slipped out of town, I took the time to take a closer look at Jolie's ring while I still could.

Like I said before, it sorta resembled a high school ring, but not exactly. It didn't have a school name on it, for one thing, just some flowery stuff carved on the outside of the band. Her name was engraved on the inside, but that was the only writing I could see.

But the most interesting thing about it was the gem. It was a star sapphire, midnight blue like the sky, and the little star glittered bright and white down in the depths of the jewel, even in the weak light from the dome lamp. It reminded me of the way Venus looks sometimes when it's the brightest thing in the sky right after the sun goes down, and you can't see any of the other stars just yet; just that one bright spark in the middle of all that midnight blue. It was a beautiful piece of work.

But pretty or not, I couldn't help wondering what it was for and why Jolie wanted it so badly and how exactly she thought it could help her escape. I guessed I'd find out soon enough.

We had to pull over on the side of the road about two o'clock and sleep for at least a couple of hours. You can only stay buzzed on coffee and Monster for so long before you crash, you know, and it's not safe to drive like that.

We got back to Fouke not long before sunrise, and Justin wearily drove us back out to that dirt road where the Lees lived. He didn't go to the burnt-out trailer this time; he just pulled over on the side of the road a bit closer to the house. Somehow we found the strength to stumble our way to the edge of the front yard, and there we stopped.

The whole place looked quieter than a graveyard, and I almost dared to hope that nobody was awake yet. But it was getting lighter outside every minute, and if they weren't up yet then they soon would be.

There was no time left to think about it, so I patted my pocket to make sure the ring was still there, and then crouched down and trotted across the yard to the front corner of the porch. I was pretty sure nobody had seen me, but I didn't stop to catch my breath. I yanked loose the trellis and slipped behind it quicker than a hen could snatch a tick from the grass. Jolie had left the window open a crack, and I put my mouth down close to it.

"Jolie! Are you there?" I called, as loud as I dared. I heard somebody's feet hit the carpet, and she was there before I could take another breath.

"Did you get it?" she asked urgently.

"Yeah, here it is," I said, fumbling in my pocket for the ring. As soon as I got hold of it, I pulled it out and passed it through the window to her.

"Thank God!" she whispered, her eyes shining. Then she turned all business.

"Okay, Zach. Get away from here as fast as you can so I know you're safe, and I'll meet you at your house sometime this afternoon. If Cam is here I'll bring him too, and if not then I'll see if I can find out anything. Don't worry; I've got it all under control now, I promise," she said.

"Are you sure?" was all I could think to say.

"I'm absolutely and totally sure. These guys are mincemeat, the minute they open that door. Don't worry about it a bit," she said.

She seemed so utterly firm and sure of herself that once again I had to believe her. And besides that, I was so exhausted I think I could have gone to sleep right there under the porch. Two or three hours of sleep kicked back in a truck seat on the side of the highway just isn't enough.

So I left, and trusted her to know what she was talking about. Me and Justin drove home without saying a word, and as soon as we walked in the door we hit the beds. School be danged for the day.

I slept hard, and it was almost noon before I finally woke up. My head hurt and I felt heavy and tired just like I knew I would. Justin was still asleep, so I drank a glass of orange juice and popped a vitamin and some ibuprofen tablets, then laid down on the couch to rest some more. I half watched an old sci-fi movie on TV just to keep myself occupied. *Alien,* I think it was, but I wasn't really paying much attention to it. I was mostly just waiting to see if Jolie showed up like she said she would.

She took her own sweet time about it, I have to say, because it was nearly two o'clock when I finally heard somebody knock on the door. I rushed over there to open it, and sure enough, there she was. She'd apparently taken the time to go shopping, because she was wearing another one of those expensive-looking shirts and some new shoes, and I noticed she'd had her hair and nails done too.

I was tempted to be mad at her for wasting time to do all that when she knew I was sitting at home worried and waiting, but I was too glad to see her to stay mad for long.

"Hey, Blue-Eyes. Did you miss me?" she asked with a smile.

"You have no idea how much," I said, and then threw my arms around her. I didn't really plan on that ahead of time; it just sorta happened. But she only laughed and hugged me back.

"Yeah, I missed you too, Zach, but seriously, sit down and let's talk," she said.

I stepped aside to let her in, and that's when I noticed for the first time that she didn't have Cameron with her. When I saw that, most of my good feelings dried up.

"You didn't find Cam?" I asked.

"No, Zach. He wasn't there, or if he ever was then I don't know where they put him. They wouldn't tell me anything when I asked them. We'll find him, though; it's just a matter of time," she said confidently. I wanted to believe her about that, too, so I held my peace and asked her the one other question I was dying to know the answer to.

"So how'd you get away?" I asked.

"I told you I'm a werewolf hunter, Zach. I put them to sleep," she said, smiling.

"Put them to sleep? What does that mean?" I asked.

"Never you mind about that. It's enough for you to know that they'll never bother you or anybody else ever again," she promised.

"What about when they wake up?" I asked.

"Yeah, well. . . that will never happen," she said.

"You mean you killed them?" I asked, horrified, and every doubt and fear I'd ever had about what she did as a werewolf hunter came flooding back. But Jolie only laughed like that was the funniest thing she ever heard.

"Of course not! We never *kill* anybody, Zach. I put them to sleep, and sleep is what they'll do, unless somebody wakes them up someday," she said.

She had me totally confused, and it must have shown on my face, because she gave another little laugh.

"Poor Zach. I know you don't understand, but they'll be all right, honest," she promised. Then she furrowed her brow and gave me a long cool look, like she was trying to decide whether to tell me something more.

"If I tell you something, can you keep a secret?" she finally asked.

"Yeah, sure. What is it?" I asked.

"Look here," she said, and pulled a little plastic bottle out of her purse. It looked just like the one Justin found in the outbuilding that had Cameron's name on it. Except the name on this one was Jacob Lee Golden. Jolie handed me two others, labeled Sandra Jane Lee and Robert Edward Lee. I recognized Jolie's handwriting, and all of them had the same date scribbled below them. Today.

I looked up at her, still not sure what she meant by it all.

"That's Jake and Bobby and Sandra, right there in your hands," she said.

"Huh?" I asked.

"That's them. That dust inside the bottles. That's what my ring is for. It turns people to dust if I touch them with it. That's how we hunt the werewolves and don't get caught," she explained.

Maybe it was fitting that it was Halloween; you sort of expect to hear spooky things like that, and they don't seem quite so unbelievable as they would other times.

Any other time I would have asked her a thousand questions about the whole thing, but not then. All I could think of at that moment was the bottle of dust sitting out there in Justin's glove box; the one with Cameron's name on it.

"But there's a way to wake them up again, right?" I asked, sick at heart.

"Papa always said there was, but he never told me how," she said.

"Would he tell you if you asked him?" I asked, with a little more hope. Somehow I didn't want to tell her about Cameron. Maybe deep down I thought as long as I didn't say it out loud then it couldn't really be true. Stupid, foolish wishful thinking, that was, but sometimes there are things so awful you just can't bear them right away.

A cloud passed over Jolie's face, and she sounded sad when she spoke again.

"I'm sure he would, but I can't ask him, Zach," she said.

"Why not?" I asked.

"This is why," she said, and one by one she pulled out six more bottles of dust from her purse. I read the names as she set them down on the table, and some I recognized and some I didn't. All of them shared the same last name as Jolie, and I could only assume one of them was her father.

"Jake broke into Angie's house a few days ago, and somehow he got hold of her ring and used it against her before he burned her house down. Nobody knew he had the ring until it was too late, though. He caught my parents, and my aunt Sarah and uncle John, and my cousin Matthieu too. He put them all to sleep and took their rings. I'm the only one left, and God only knows why he didn't do the same thing to me, too," she said softly.

"I'm sorry," I said. I didn't know what else to say, to somebody who lost that much. No words seemed good enough.

"Oh, it's not as bad as you think, Zach. They're only sleeping, not dead. All I have to do is find out how to wake them up again. I'm just thankful he saved their dust instead of letting it blow away," she said.

"But how did he know how to do all that?" I asked, puzzled.

"I'm not totally sure. He was five when Angie put his parents to sleep, and I know he saw her do that. So maybe he remembered enough to make some good guesses," she said.

"You think he'd remember that much?" I asked, doubtfully.

"Well, yeah. . . I know he remembers what happened, because he talked about it several times while I was locked up in that house. That's why he hates us so much," she explained. I still had my doubts, but there was something else I wanted to know.

"Okay, so why did Angie not put Jake to sleep at the same time?" I asked.

"She was supposed to, but Angie is a soft-hearted old thing, and she couldn't bring herself to do it to a little kid. So she carried him next door to his grandparents instead, and made them understand that if they wanted to keep breathing they'd never say a word about it to anybody. It was Angie's case, so nobody else could tell her not to handle it that way if that's what she decided to do," she said.

"Was it Jake that was watching us that night at the fair?" I asked.

"I think so. It was only a day or two later when he broke into Angie's place. He was probably trailing me so he could make sure I wasn't at the house with her when he hit the place. Easier to deal with just one of us at a time, you know," she said.

"All right, that makes sense, but if Angie was the one who handled that pod, then how come *you* know so much about them?" I asked.

"Well, yeah, it's Angie's case. But she's getting kinda old for field work now and I told you sometimes I come up here to help her with things. She thought it was a good idea to keep an eye on Jake now and then, just to make sure he didn't decide to follow along in his parents' footsteps someday and become a *loup-garou*. So we checked up on him maybe once or twice a year. That's how I knew who he was when he caught me and that's why I had that Boggy Creek t-shirt in the first place. I bought it one time when I was up here with Angie," she explained.

"Yeah, well. . . it looks like y'all really missed the boat on that one," I said dryly, and she shrugged.

"Maybe so, but things can blow up really fast sometimes, Zach. That's the way things are in this business. It's not all fun and games," she said, tapping the bottle that held Jake's dust.

"No, I guess not," I agreed. In fact it seemed like the Doucets had danged near met their match after all this time. In *Jake Golden,* of all people. I never would have believed it, if I hadn't seen it with my own eyes.

"Zach. . . I still want you to become a werewolf hunter, if you want to. We need you, now more than ever. Somebody needs to take Angie's place, so she can go ahead and retire. Have you thought about it at all, since I asked you?" she asked.

"Yeah, I've thought about it a lot, actually," I admitted.

"And?" she asked.

"I think I need to know a few more things first, before I can say yes," I told her. It was a huge relief to know that hunting wolves didn't mean killing anybody, but I was still determined to know *everything* before I agreed.

"Absolutely. What do you want to know?" she asked.

"Well, first of all, what do you do with all these people after you collect them in the bottles?" I asked her.

"We have to go put them in the storeroom so they'll be safe. In fact that's what I need to go do with these ones today. Would you like to come with me? I'll show you some things," she offered.

"Sure, why not?" I agreed, and she got up to leave. I followed her, and when we got outside I saw her banana-yellow bug parked out front.

"Where'd that come from?" I asked.

"Oh, I left it at the airport that day when I dropped you off at the mall. I had to go take care of some loose ends out in New Mexico and there wasn't time to drive that far. Then I rode home with Daddy and Matthieu after we got done out there. Turned out to be a good thing, huh?" she said.

"Just another day in the life of an international werewolf hunter," I muttered under my breath.

Chapter Six

That's how I ended up driving back down to Natchitoches for the third time in three days. I was getting to be a real expert on that route, it seemed.

Jolie was in a good mood and we talked about a lot of things that day. A lot of it had to do with Jake, and *loup-garous,* and all that stuff, but not all of it. A lot of the time we just talked about life and what we thought about this and that, things we liked and didn't like, places we'd been or might like to go someday, stuff like that. She reminded me of a little kid, the way she had so much enthusiasm for everything.

We stopped to have a late lunch at some Cajun place in Bossier City that she knew about. I remember she ordered *boudain* sausage with red beans and rice, and I decided to go the safe route with fried catfish and hushpuppies; that was one of the few things on the menu that I recognized. She laughed at me, but I didn't mind.

It was almost sundown when we got to Natchitoches, and she drove directly to that big brick house where Sarah Doucet had been so unfriendly to me last time. The driveway was full of cars, so she ended up leaving the bug in that same parking lot where I left the truck last time.

When we got to the big front door she flipped open a metal panel and punched in an access code on a keypad. A little light changed from red to green, and I heard a small *click.* Then she shut the panel and turned the doorknob.

It was dark inside the house, but she didn't turn on any lights. She just led me down a hall and into the kitchen, and then outdoors into a formal flower garden behind the house. It was surrounded by a high brick wall on all sides, and there were still quite a few plants with late blossoms, here and there.

Jolie paid no attention to the scenery, though. She went directly to a spot where a purple hydrangea plant grew right up next to the wall, then reached behind it and pulled out a brass key on a chain.

She didn't explain what it was for; just led me to the south wall. It was cut deeply into the slope of a hill on that side, and that whole section of the wall was draped with some kind of evergreen vine so thick and matted you couldn't even see the bricks anymore.

I didn't understand why we were there until she slipped her hand behind a tangled mass of vines and pulled them aside to reveal a low passage into the hill behind. I would never have guessed it was there in a million years, if she hadn't showed me.

"Come on," she said quietly.

We walked maybe fifteen feet down a narrow tunnel, and then we came to a locked steel door. Jolie turned the key in the lock, and then gestured for me to go inside.

I opened the door, and at first it didn't look like much in there. Just a dimly lit room with stone walls, and some wooden shelves running all along both sides. Most of the shelves were full of little bottles like the ones we found at Jake's house, all of them neatly labeled and standing in rows. There must have been hundreds or even thousands of them in there; way more than I could count, anyway.

Besides that, there was a wooden table and some chairs in the center of the room and an old fashioned chandelier right above it which was giving off what little light there was, and then down at the far end there was a set of steel filing cabinets. It felt chilly and damp in there, and it reminded me of a root cellar.

"This is it?" I asked, disappointed.

"Yeah. Come look," she said.

I followed her to one of the shelves nearby, where she carefully put Jake and Bobby and Sandra's bottles in an empty spot. She'd brought in the bottles that held her own family, too, but she put those on the table instead of finding a place for them on the shelves.

"I've got to write down where I put Jake and the others, so we can find them again if we need to. It'll just take a second," she said, and then quietly went to the filing cabinet to pull out a manila folder with some papers in it. She grabbed a pen from the table and started making notes, and before long she was absorbed in what she was doing.

While she was busy writing, I went to the nearest shelf and ran my finger along the top. It definitely wouldn't pass the white glove test, because my finger came away black. The shelf was divided into sections that were labeled with letters and numbers, probably to help keep things organized.

I picked up one of the bottles at random, just out of curiosity. It was dusty and old, and it looked like nobody had handled it for a long time. I noticed that it was glass, too, instead of the plastic ones I'd seen so far.

"On all that you love, don't drop that," Jolie told me, when she saw what I was doing. I hadn't planned on dropping it, but she was being so solemn and serious about it that I decided it was best to be super careful. I held it with both hands, and turned the bottle around to read the label.

John Dreyfus,
March 31, 1947

That was all it said, and I wondered who he was. I'd certainly never heard of him.

"Who's John Dreyfus?" I asked out loud.

Jolie must have been done writing down whatever she had to write, because she closed the file and came to see what I was looking at.

"He was a *loup-garou*. That's all I know about him. I'm sure he'd be in the files somewhere, if we wanted to look him up. We always put their name and the date they came into the storeroom on the bottles. The files are organized by year, so that's all we really need to know," she said.

"You mean he's been here since 1947?" I asked, amazed.

"Yeah. Some of them have been here a lot longer than that. We bring them here and keep them safe so nothing will happen to them, and Papa always told me they'll all wake up at the end of the world, on the last day," she said, in a hushed voice.

That was kind of a spooky idea, you know, and *again* I started having second thoughts about werewolf hunting. Or maybe it was forty-second thoughts by then; who can tell? Because it seemed to me like there wasn't much difference between killing somebody and putting them to sleep until the end of time, when push came right down to shove. They were both pretty dadgummed permanent, if you asked me.

"It doesn't sound much different than dying, to me," I said out loud. Jolie looked uncomfortable and wouldn't meet my eyes.

"It may not sound like it, but there *is* a difference, Zach. All these people are still alive, and we could wake them up at any time if we wanted to," she reminded me.

"I thought you didn't know how to do that," I reminded her.

"No, *I* don't, but it's *possible,* though," she insisted.

"How do you even know it's possible, if nobody's ever done it?" I asked.

"All I know is what Papa told me. He always said there was a way," she said stubbornly.

I probably shouldn't have been so hard on her about the whole thing. I think it's just that seeing all those people locked up in that place for so long gave me a horrible fear that we'd never find a way to wake up Cameron, and that made me feel guilty and angry and all twisted up inside.

In fact there were a lot of harsh and bitter things I wanted to say right then because of the pain in my heart, but I knew it wouldn't help anything if I took it out on Jolie. It wasn't her fault. So I bit my tongue, hard, and forced myself to calm down before I ruined everything.

"So your father knows how to wake up the sleepers, then?" I asked.

"Yes. That's what he always said," she agreed.

"But we can't ask him because he's asleep, too. Does anybody else know?" I asked.

"Some of the older ones might, but none of them are left, either," she said sadly.

"It seems to me like that's something *you* would have wanted to know before now," I said, a bit reproachfully. She winced a little, and I bit my tongue again, even harder this time, to remind myself to shut up before I said something I couldn't take back.

"Yeah, I probably should have, Zach, looking back. But I never thought it mattered that much, till now. There was never any reason to need to know it before," she said.

"You never thought you might want to wake up any of these people someday?" I asked, sweeping my hand at the bottles. I was very careful to control my voice and not say it in a mean way this time, but that question cut right to the bone of every doubt and fear I'd ever had about her because of the werewolf hunting. She was sweet and beautiful and awesome in a thousand ways, but as much as I liked her, I had to know what her heart was like deep down before I let it go any farther.

"Of course not. Why would I want to wake any of *them* up?" she said.

"What do you mean, why? Because it's not right to do something like this to people, that's why. I can understand putting them to sleep for a while, maybe, but not forever," I said, almost letting my temper get the best of me again. Jolie noticed my bad mood, I'm sure, and she sighed.

"That sounds really good, Zach, but you better think about it a little more before you judge us too harshly. If you woke these people up, they'd still be just the way they were when we put them down here. They'd still be cursed, they'd still be dangerous, and there'd be nothing you could do about that except turn them loose on the world again," she said.

I thought about Mama and Daddy and Laura and the other wolves I knew. They might be high-handed and they might be ungodly and a hundred other things I could think of, but dangerous wasn't something that came to mind right away. I remembered Cameron telling me his mom liked to kill horses and cows, but even that was fairly small potatoes, you know.

Of course, there was that one incident in Lebanon. Cameron got a bullet in the chest for that one, and it still makes me shiver when I think about it sometimes. But then again, they probably wouldn't have done that if we hadn't been there trying to break their wolf-stone like we were.

I guess I wasn't really disagreeing with Jolie that being a *loup-garou* was a bad thing. But still, I could think of worse things people do, and nobody turns them to dust and puts them in a spice bottle to wait for the end of the world because of it.

"It just seems like too much, that's all," I finally said.

"Too much?" she asked.

"Yeah, kinda. I mean, do they really do that much harm, that you need to do all *this?*" I asked, waving again at the rows and rows of bottles on the shelves. There had to be whole families locked up in there, sleeping the years away.

Jolie gave me another sad look.

"Zach, you have a soft heart, but you don't know as much as you think you do. You don't understand," she said.

"What's that supposed to mean?" I asked.

"Well, pods are different, you know. Some of them are pretty mild and just chase animals and such now and then. It's like a game or a hobby for them. But others are vicious and cruel, and some of them are even worse. Think for a minute about all the werewolf stories you ever heard and what kinds of things the wolves in those stories did. Don't think for a minute that things like that never happen, because I'm here to tell you they do. I've seen things you don't even want to think about, Blue-Eyes, and if you'd been with me and seen them too, then you wouldn't be asking me why we do this and why we leave them down here. That pod in New Mexico, now that was a bad one," she said, and I could have sworn I saw her shiver.

I thought about some of the horror flicks I'd seen now and then, and I quickly decided she had a point. I didn't want to think about those things happening in real life, and if there were other pods that were involved in those kinds of things, then maybe it *was* better for them to sleep until Judgement Day instead of being left out there to terrorize the world. The Trewick pod must have been one of the milder ones, and for that I was thankful in my heart of hearts. If they hadn't been, I might never have gotten away from them in the first place.

My heart softened a little bit, when I thought about all that. But there was one other thing I had to understand before I could let it go.

"Okay, so I see your point about locking up the really bad guys this way. But you just said yourself that not all the pods are like that, and some of them don't do much harm. Why go after them?" I asked.

"Because there's always the chance they could turn vicious at the drop of a pin, Zach, and we can't risk it. Pods are hard enough to locate anyway, and when we find one we wipe it out immediately. Not just for that reason, either. As long as there are active pods out there, then it means the knowledge of how to form one is out there, too, and that's why even the milder pods are a threat and a danger. They corrupt people and they spread the curse. We can't just leave them alone to do their own thing, much as we might like to sometimes. And if you're tempted to feel sorry for them, you need to remember that every single person in this room made a choice. Every one of them deliberately chose to be cursed and to become what they are, and this is the consequence for that choice," she said.

I was silent at that. I chewed my lip for a few minutes and did some hard thinking, and after a while I decided I wasn't mad at her anymore for doing what she did, even though I still didn't see how it was much different than killing people. If you had the power to wake somebody up but you never chose to do it, then how was that any different than not being able to do it at all?

Maybe it makes some difference, on some level, somehow. It seemed like splitting an awfully fine hair to me. But on the other hand, she had a point about trying to eliminate the curse and having to go after even the mild pods because they corrupted people. She was trying to do the same thing I wanted to do, more or less; wipe out the Curse, or at least minimize it as much as she could. I understood the wish, and even the reasoning, but I still didn't have to like it.

"I still feel sorry for them," I said softly.

"Yeah, so do I sometimes. But it has to be this way, Zach. There's no other way, unless you want us to go after them with silver bullets," she said.

"I don't believe that. There has to be some other way to break the Curse than killing the wolves or putting them to sleep forever. You have to give them a chance to see what they did wrong and turn away from it," I said, and Jolie shook her head.

"If you can find another way, Zach, then tell me how. I wish there was. But my family has been in the werewolf hunting business for two hundred years or more, and we never found any other way," she said.

I didn't say it, but I thought to myself that maybe that was part of the reason why they *hadn't* found any other way. People don't like change very much, you know, and two hundred years is a long time to be doing things one way.

In fact, maybe the Doucets didn't really *want* to get rid of the werewolf curse. It gave them a secret purpose and something exciting and noble to do in the world, and besides that it also made them filthy rich from looting all the wolves they turned to dust. Those are pretty powerful reasons not to want to change things.

Oh, I don't doubt they meant well; I don't mean that. I just mean they had a strong reason not to look for ways to put a permanent end to the problem. If they ever found one, it would put them out of business, so to speak.

But I couldn't tell Jolie all that. She'd be insulted at the very least, and I didn't want to start a fight over things I didn't even know for sure were true. I might be totally wrong about them.

"What about stealing all their stuff and burning down their houses; why do you do that?" I asked her.

"Well. . . Papa always said it was kind of like a fine you have to pay if you get a speeding ticket. They have to pay to help wipe out the Curse, and to help atone for whatever evil they did. And as for burning the houses, we do that partly so no one will wonder why the people disappeared, and partly just in case they had books or papers hidden somewhere inside that might tell some new owner about the Curse," she explained.

I could understand the thinking on that, too, in a grudging kind of way, so I let it go and changed the subject.

"So how do you do the thing? I mean, what do you have to do to get them into these bottles?" I asked.

"Oh, that's the easy part, Zach. If we can get close enough to touch them, that's all there is to it. It's getting close enough which is hard," she smiled.

"You just poke them with your finger or something?" I asked.

"No, we touch them with the rings," she explained, and held up her hand so I could see the ring on her middle finger.

"Very pretty," I commented.

"Yes it is. There are only six of them, and they've been passed down ever since we first started hunting *loup-garous*. I only got mine last year," she said.

"So what do you do with it?" I asked.

"All you have to do is touch the star to their skin. That's all. They turn to dust, and then we put them in the bottles and bring them here to sleep," she said.

"But what if you touch yourself with it, or somebody else that you don't want to put to sleep?" I asked.

"Oh, that doesn't matter. You have to wish for it to happen or it won't," she said.

"So you could turn me to dust right now, if you touched me with that ring and wanted it to happen?" I asked.

She half-smiled.

"Scary thought, huh? But yeah, I guess I could. Want to give it a try?" she asked mischievously.

I decided not to answer that.

"How many people are there in this place?" I asked, changing the subject again. The whole idea of turning people to dust was starting to seem kinda creepy. Especially when I knew that the girl standing next to me could do it to me, anytime she felt like it.

"I don't know exactly. A few thousand, I think. It's all in the files," she said.

"Okay then, just one more question; why do you keep them in these bottles at all, if you don't ever want to wake them up anyway?" I asked.

"We've always done it that way, ever since the beginning," she said.

"Yeah, but why?" I asked again, and this time she didn't answer me right away. When she did, it was only with another question.

"Do you think it's possible to believe in something, Zach, even though you can't see how it could ever be?" she asked. It didn't seem to have anything to do with what I wanted to know, but I went along with it.

"Sure," I agreed. That's what faith means, you know, the substance of things hoped for, and the evidence of things not seen.

"Then I'll tell you something we don't talk about a lot, and maybe you'll understand why we believe it," she said.

"Okay," I told her.

"Papa always said we keep them this way because someday we'll find a way to break the Curse forever and cure these people, and then we can set them all free before the End comes. We call it the Hope," she said quietly. She said it just that way, too, so you could kinda hear the capital letter when she spoke, like it was something almost sacred. I guess in a way it was.

"We don't all believe it, but some of us do," she added.

"Do *you* believe it?" I asked.

"Yeah. . . I don't think I could do this work, if I didn't believe there was any Hope," she said.

That put a whole new twist on things, and I looked at Jolie in a totally different light than I ever had before. In fact, I think looking back that's the very moment when I felt the first stirrings of love. I don't mean thinking she was hot or awesome or anything like that, either. I mean love; the real thing.

I read somewhere once that the only reason we ever love anybody or anything in the world is because they remind us of God in some way, like the reflection of the sun in a dew drop. I believe that with my whole heart, and when Jolie told me about the Hope of the werewolf hunters, how could I keep from loving her for that? It reminded me of something Justin told me once about why he loved Eileen so much, because her heart was even more beautiful than her face.

There was a long pause while I thought about all those things, and when I spoke again I didn't say a word about what I felt inside. It wouldn't have been the right time, and I still needed to think a while about what it meant. It was scary in a way, you know.

But however that might be, I decided it was high time to get back to the main problem.

"We still need to find out how to bring back your mom and dad and Cam and the others, though. *They* didn't do anything wrong," I said.

"Wait a minute. How do you know Cameron is asleep?" she asked.

I hadn't meant to tell her about that, but somehow it slipped out anyway. There was no point in hiding it anymore, though.

"Me and Justin found a bottle with his name on it at Jake's house, out in a shed in the back yard," I admitted.

"Yeah, that's where I found all the others, too. You should have told me sooner, Blue-Eyes; I could tell you were upset about something. I'm so sorry," she said, and put a hand on my arm.

"I'll be okay. I just want my brother back," I said.

It crossed my mind that I still had those two hundred bottles of sweet water sitting there in Miss Edith's basement, and I wondered for the first time whether I could use that to wake up Cameron and the others; it was supposed to make broken things whole, wasn't it? I couldn't think of anything much more broken than getting turned to dust.

I was afraid to take a chance without knowing for sure, though. It was Cam's life I was playing with, and that was no joke.

I decided to play it safe for now and wait a little while to see what Jolie was able to come up with. She was supposed to be the expert, after all.

"All I know is to ask my uncle Marc in France. He ought to know, and he hasn't been back to the states in years, so I know Jake didn't nail him too," she murmured thoughtfully, and I felt a surge of new hope.

"I guess it's too late to call him right now, isn't it?" I asked anxiously, thinking about the time difference. It was probably after midnight at Marc's house by then.

"Oh, he wouldn't talk about something like that on the phone, Zach. Only in person," she said.

"You mean we have to go to *France?*" I asked, when it finally sank in what that meant.

"Sure. Why not?" she asked, like it was the most ordinary thing in the world. Maybe to her it was, but certainly not to me. I'd never been farther away from home than Gulf Shores, and France was a whole 'nother ballgame. I'd never even been on a plane before. But after I got over the first shock of hearing it I couldn't honestly think of any particular reason not to go. I would have been willing to do a lot more than that, if that's what it took to save my brother.

"All right, then. I'm game," I told her, and she smiled.

"Come on, Zach. There's nothing else to see down here. The only time we visit this place is when we're bringing bottles to put away," she said.

She led me back outside, making sure to lock the door behind her and replace the vines in front of the passage so nobody could find it. Then she slipped the key back wherever it went behind the purple hydrangea, and we were done.

It was quiet in the big old house when we went back through, and for a long time we didn't say anything else. There were stacks and stacks of old and dusty books everywhere, and I stopped to glance at a few of them as we passed.

"Uncle John keeps all the records and histories and stuff for the family. That's his job, since he's too old for field work now," Jolie commented when she saw what I was doing.

She took a detour into the dining room, where she tapped on one of the stones beside the fireplace. It must have been fake, because it popped open on hidden hinges, and there was a metal safe in the compartment behind it. Jolie twisted the knob with practiced ease and opened it.

"You know the combination to your aunt's safe?" I asked, kinda impressed.

"Yeah, all the ring-holders know it, just in case. This is where we keep anything really important," she said absently, and then reached inside and pulled out a wad of cash big enough to choke an elephant with.

"Holy cow! You're just gonna take that?" I asked, wide-eyed.

"Yup. Aunt Sarah won't care, and we need the money if we're going to France, don't you think?" she pointed out.

"Well, yeah, I guess so," I admitted. I'd never seen that much money in my entire life, and I don't think I would have taken it without asking even if this had been Justin's house and I knew he wouldn't have cared. It seemed too much like stealing.

It was probably pocket change to Sarah Doucet, though, and Jolie certainly didn't seem to have any second thoughts about taking it. I decided if she thought it was okay then I'd just have to trust her that she knew what she was talking about.

She put the money on the mantel, and then she pulled five silver rings from her left pocket. They all looked a lot like the one she wore, and I guessed they were the ones that belonged to her sleeping family members. She put them in the safe, then closed the door and shut the panel. As soon as that was done, she divided the money into two rolls.

"Here, you hold on to half of this. That way if something happens to one of us the other one isn't stranded," she said, handing me one of the wads. I stuffed it in my pants pocket without a word, and she put the other half in her purse.

"Do you think it's a good idea to carry this much money around?" I asked.

"No, but we'll stop somewhere and get some of those disposable credit cards. That will be a lot better and easier to use, and it'll also save time because we won't have to convert all these dollars into euros once we get to Paris," she said glibly.

She made it sound like she'd done it hundreds of times and it was no more unusual than clipping her fingernails. Maybe she had, for all I knew; she might be used to flying to Paris every time she took a notion to go shopping, but that wasn't the kind of life I'd ever had or ever even thought about.

"Don't you have to have a passport to go to France?" I asked. I remembered that because Cameron had to get one last summer when he went to Jamaica on a short-term mission trip. I didn't go with him that time because I went to summer camp in Missouri instead.

"Well of course you-" Jolie started, and then groaned.

"You don't have one, do you?" she asked, shaking her head.

"Sorry. Never needed one before," I told her.

"Never mind. It can't be helped. We'll have to get you one before we can leave, and that will waste some time, but if we drive down to the passport office in Houston and pay extra for it I think we can get it done in two or three days," she said.

"Sorry about that," I said again, but she wasn't paying attention.

"Do you have your birth certificate at least? You'll have to have that at the passport office, you know," she asked.

"Yeah, I've got one. It's at home, though," I said.

"Okay then, we've got to swing by your house and grab that birth certificate, then cruise down to Houston and get your passport. I think we can get a direct flight from there. Maybe the same day, if we're lucky," she said, thinking out loud.

There didn't seem to be anything I could add to that. She was the experienced world traveler, so I was content to leave the planning up to her.

It had started misting rain just a bit when we left the house, but not enough to get us wet. I was glad for that, since we still had several blocks to walk before we got back to where the bug was parked.

It was one of those nights when it's awful quiet outside, and the traffic noises seem few and far away. There was no wind, and I remember the mist settled down on Jolie's hair and glistened in the light from the street lamps, and I thought to myself how beautiful and brave and amazing she was.

I didn't think she was cruel anymore, or heartless, or any of those other things that used to worry me so much at first. She was doing what she thought was right even though it was really hard sometimes, and I could respect her for that even if I didn't completely agree. She wanted to make the world a better place by getting rid of the pods, and if I knew of a better and truer way to do that then she was willing to listen. She'd said so herself.

On impulse, I reached out and grasped her hand, and she didn't seem to mind. She just squeezed mine back without saying anything. We walked the rest of the way back to the car like that, just holding hands and thinking our own thoughts.

I read something on the flyleaf of a calendar once about how you shouldn't measure your life by the number of breaths you take but by the number of moments that take your breath away. Yeah, I know it sounds cheesy and stupid, but there's some truth behind it, too.

I think walking with Jolie that night was one of those moments for me. Maybe it seems like it wasn't that important, and I know it only lasted for ten minutes or so. But nevertheless, as long as I live, when I think about Louisiana, I'll remember glistening mist on a Cajun girl's hair, and walking together under those live oak trees, and being happy.

Chapter Seven

We drove all that long weary way back to Texarkana, and I have to tell you, by then I was sick of riding in cars. I was just about ready to take a barge or a bicycle by then; anything but a car.

Justin and Eileen were not at home when we got there, and I guessed they'd probably gone out to dinner or something like that, because Eileen's car was gone. She has a bright red Dodge Neon, and they almost always drive that vehicle when they go somewhere together.

I left them a note on the kitchen table saying I'd be back in a few days, without particularly mentioning where I was going. I wasn't sure what Justin would think about me going to France alone, or even with Jolie for that matter. I more than halfway suspected he wouldn't like it much, but I was willing to risk getting in trouble when I got home, if things worked out the way I hoped they would.

I grabbed my birth certificate while I was in there, and before we left I took Cameron's dust out of Justin's glove box and looked at it again.

"I'll find a way to get you back, bubba; I promise," I whispered.

Oh, I knew he couldn't hear me. I was talking more for myself than I was for him, but sometimes you need to do that, you know. I put his bottle down deep in my bottom desk drawer, in the place where I keep all my most important things.

Maybe I'm just sentimental or mushy or some such thing, but I picked up his bullet necklace from where he always hung it on the side of the lamp, and I slipped it over my head. He hadn't worn it to school yesterday, and I wanted something with me to feel like he was close. That bullet was one of his favorite things, and I didn't think he'd mind if I borrowed it for a few days.

That done, we hit the road.

I'd only been to Houston a time or two, since we never had any reason to go that way much. Dallas is closer if we needed to go to the city, and if we wanted to go to the ocean we usually went to Gulf Shores or Destin because the beaches are nicer.

I did remember that it was a long drive, and you had to go through a bunch of little towns with unpronounceable names like Tenaha or Nacogdoches, or funny ones like Waskom or Appleby. I don't know why they struck me that way; I guess I'm easily amused.

We got to Houston pretty early the next morning, and Jolie drove us straight to the passport office. We had to wait in line for a long time, and then the agent hassled us about where we were going in such a hurry and why it couldn't wait a while and where my parents were, and similar hogwash. Sometimes I think government workers must get extra bonus pay if they annoy people.

But when all was said and done, and after we paid them triple the usual fee, I got my passport the next morning. Jolie already had us booked on a flight to Paris that afternoon, so it was none too soon.

I don't know what I expected, exactly. Being on a plane for the first time was a little bit nerve-wracking. Jolie didn't seem to mind at all, and I envied her.

Anyway, takeoff turned out to be kinda fun, actually. I could feel the engines roaring and it was almost like riding in a racecar, and it was amazing how fast we got up above the clouds.

After that came the dull part. You can only look at cloud-tops for so long before you've seen just about all you want to. We had to fly to Atlanta and then Boston before we crossed the ocean, but I don't remember much about all that. Jolie threaded us through the airports and I was just along for the ride.

It wasn't as cloudy out over the Atlantic, but you can only stare at water for so long before that gets boring, too. I guess I never realized how big an ocean really is until I had to cross one. It seems like there's nothing but water that goes on forever in the moonlight. I slept for a while, but I've never been able to sleep very well sitting up.

I do remember the first bit of Europe I saw. It was just after sunrise by then, and there were some dark gray rocks out in the middle of the water below us, with the wind thrashing whitewater up against them; I guess it must have been a blustery day down there. I looked them up later on an atlas and found out I was looking at the Aran Islands off the west coast of Ireland.

It wasn't long after that when we landed. It didn't feel like it ought to be morning yet when we got there, I guess because of the time difference; seven or eight hours ahead, I think. Jolie collected our stuff and bought us train tickets to Clermont and just generally took care of everything. She made me wonder why I was even there.

Except there was no way I could have stayed home and let her do it all alone, of course. It would have driven me crazy.

Clermont is way down in southern France, nowhere near Paris, and that meant another long ride to get there. We had our own compartment on the train and it was a nice one; first class, I'm sure, and I slept for another couple of hours until Jolie woke me up for lunch.

I don't know what it was we ate; dog toenails and fried monkey brains, no doubt. It was good, whatever it was, but I was already starting to feel the first twinges of culture shock, and I didn't want to make it worse by asking too many questions.

It's little things, you know. . . I wasn't used to hearing people speak anything but English, for one thing, and I don't understand French. There was other stuff too, though. The shape of the hay bales in the fields was all wrong, and the houses didn't look right, and the sunlight slanted down at the wrong angle, and a hundred other things like that.

All those minor bits add up, and they make you feel uneasy and out of place. You can never quite put your finger on what it is that bothers you unless you're paying close attention, though. Jolie had warned me to expect it before we left Houston, but knowing about it and feeling it are two very different things.

"So what's your uncle like?" I asked, to pass the time.

"He's okay. Maybe a little strange, but he's always been like that ever since I can remember. I haven't seen him in a long time, though. Not since he moved here," she said.

"What did he want to move *here* for, anyway?" I asked.

"I don't know, exactly. He used to be a history professor for a long time, and then about five years ago he quit his job and told everybody he was moving to Clermont. Everybody was kinda shocked at the time because it was so sudden, but. . . I told you he was a little weird," she explained.

"But he'll know what to do about the sleepers?" I asked.

"He should. I hope so," she said. She didn't sound as sure of herself as I would have liked, but if there was any chance Marc Doucet could tell us what we needed to know, then I was prepared to go visit him on the moon if necessary.

"Didn't you say that mountain was around here somewhere? The one where the dust comes from to curse the stones?" I asked.

"Mont Mouchet. Yeah, it's not all that far from where Marc lives. He never said so, but sometimes I think one of the reasons he came here was to keep an eye on that place and whoever comes snooping around over there," she said.

We got to the train station in Clermont not long before sunset, and for the first time Jolie seemed a little uncertain.

"I hope he's home," she fretted.

"Why wouldn't he be?" I asked.

"Oh, he goes off and disappears for weeks at a time sometimes, or at least he always did when he was still in Natchitoches. He likes to travel, and since he lives alone he can pretty much come and go as he pleases," she said.

That didn't sound too promising, but as it turned out we didn't have anything to worry about. Jolie took us to a long street lined with big, gorgeous houses, and walked up to the front door of one of them.

"Here we are," she murmured, and knocked. Nobody answered at first, and she knocked again a little louder. This time an old lady opened the door and said something in French which I couldn't understand, and Jolie answered her in the same language. I don't know what the conversation was about, but the result of it was that we got invited inside to sit down on a leather couch in the parlor.

"That's Madame Louise; she's Marc's housekeeper and cook. She said he's upstairs in his study and she'll go tell him we're here," Jolie explained.

We cooled our heels in the parlor for several minutes, and before long Madame Louise came back in and said something else to Jolie, which must have been an invitation to come up to the study. Jolie smiled.

"Merci, madame," she said sweetly.

Marc Doucet was older than I thought he'd be, when I first saw him. He was short and thin and his hair was almost completely white, and he wore horn-rimmed spectacles that made his eyes look too big, like a bullfrog. He was sitting in a leather chair behind a desk, and he looked up when we came in.

"Jolie, my dear! What an unexpected pleasure!" he said, with a broad smile that made him look even more frog-like. He came around the desk to hug her and then shake my hand; he must have just come in from outdoors, because I noticed he still had his gloves and jacket on. It was none too warm, even inside the house.

"Come in, come in! Sit down and tell me what everybody's up to. I'll have Louise bring some hot chocolate," he said.

"I'm afraid we're not here for pleasure, uncle Marc. There's a problem, and we need your help," she said, with a serious face. Marc nodded.

"I see. In that case we'd better discuss it right away, then," he said. He gestured for us to sit down on the couch in front of the fireplace, and then he shut the door and locked it before he joined us.

"Louise won't disturb us, but you can never be too careful. Now, what's on your mind, my dear?" he said.

"One of the *loup-garous* got hold of Angie's ring, and he used it against her and Papa and Mama and Uncle John and Aunt Sarah and Matthieu. He almost got me too, but I put him to sleep before he could do any more damage," she told him, getting right to the point.

"Did you secure the rings?" Marc asked immediately.

"Yes, of course. That was the first thing I made sure of. I put them in Aunt Sarah's safe in Natchitoches," she said. Marc breathed a sigh of relief.

"Good girl. And did you have a chance to speak to this *loup-garou* before you put him down?" he asked.

"No, there wasn't time. I had to get him while I could," she explained.

Marc smiled.

"Never mind, my dear. I'm sure you did the best you could in a difficult situation," he soothed.

"He did save everyone's dust, thank God. I put all the bottles in the storeroom before we left, till we get a chance to wake them up," she said, and a cloud passed over Marc's face when she said that.

"So what are you asking of me, child?" he asked quietly.

"Papa always said there was a way to wake up the sleepers, as long as we kept the dust. I hoped you could tell me how to do that, so I could wake them up when I get home," she said.

Marc hesitated, like he wasn't sure what to say to that, and I noticed he wouldn't make eye contact anymore. That was a bad sign.

"I'm afraid you wouldn't like what you would have to do, my dear," he finally said, and he sounded so serious that it scared me a little. I glanced at Jolie and I could see that it was scaring her, too.

"What must I do?" she whispered.

"If you would wake one of the sleepers, you must give them blood," he said.

"Blood?" she asked.

"Yes. All the living blood from one person, poured out onto the dust. Do that and the sleeper will live again, as if nothing ever happened. But the one who gave the blood would die, for no one can live without it," he said.

For once, Jolie was speechless.

"So you see, you may only trade a life for a life, and no more," he finished.

"There's no other way?" she asked, wide eyed and stricken.

"Not that I know of, unless by chance you might ask for a miracle from God. But otherwise, that is your choice," he said.

There are times when you feel cold even in the middle of a warm sunny day, and I had to grip the edge of my chair to keep from shivering. Jolie had bright tears in her eyes.

"So they're gone after all," she whispered.

"I'm so sorry, *chérie,*" Marc said, and he put an arm around her and proceeded to whisper something in French. I got up quietly and walked across the room to the big window, to leave them alone together for a few minutes. I didn't think it was right for me to be eavesdropping on a conversation like that, even if I couldn't understand it anyway.

And besides that, I had my own problems to think about. Mostly I thought about Cameron's dust, sitting cold and dark back home in my desk drawer, and how he might as well be dead if what Marc said was true, for I'd never see him again till the end of days.

I didn't want to believe it, at first. It didn't sound like it fit very well with what I heard from Jolie in the store room, about the Hope they had to set the sleepers free someday. They could never do that, if they had to kill somebody for each and every one they woke. Unless maybe that was also part of what they hoped for; some other way to wake them, without blood. That sounded like it might be true, and I think that's when Marc's words really started to sink in.

Sometimes there are things that hurt too much even for tears. I used to think that was just a stupid thing people said in hack novels, until I found out it's really true. I couldn't have cried right then even if I wanted to, even though I hurt so much inside that I could barely breathe from the pain of it.

Maybe you wouldn't understand, if you've never been that close to anybody before. But Cam was my brother and my best friend all rolled into one, and we were tighter than I was with anybody else in the world except maybe Justin and Eileen.

I couldn't let it end with that, no matter what. I grasped Cam's bullet in my left hand, and silently promised him I wouldn't give up till he was safe back home with us again.

We stayed with Marc for several days, mostly because we had no idea what to do next. Jolie cried a lot at first and it was hard to have a conversation with her that didn't end up with her in tears at some point.

As for me, I was strangely calm. I wasn't falling apart or even all that upset like you might think I'd be after I heard some news like that. I hurt, but I never cracked. Sometimes I envied Jolie and wished I could just cry it out the way she did, but I never could.

I called Justin the day after we got there to let him know where I was, and I was right about him being less than pleased. He had a few things to say to me, but truthfully I think he was more hurt than angry. He said he always thought we could talk about anything at all, no matter what, and when he put it that way I felt ashamed of myself. I told him I was sorry, and we made things right again.

There wasn't much to do in that big old house, and I ended up spending a lot of time in the study with Marc, believe it or not, listening to whatever he felt like talking about. He told me a lot about the Doucet family and how they got into werewolf hunting and all that kind of thing. I could tell he used to be a history teacher, just from how much he loved to talk.

I've said before that history is not my thing; never has been and never will be. But I never let on that my attention was drifting or that my enthusiasm ever slipped. I wanted to know *everything,* no matter how unimportant or stupid it seemed, because I still hoped I might learn something that could save Cam. That was worth listening to all the boring history lectures in the world, if only it would help.

That's the thing about hope, you know; somehow you can never kill it, no matter how black and evil the times may be.

I learned a few tidbits, for whatever they were worth. He told me the Doucets had been werewolf hunters since 1767, when a certain Michel Doucet joined the hunt for the great Beast of Gévaudan, who, I gathered, was an especially vicious and powerful *loup-garou* who terrorized that whole area around Clermont for several years.

So much so, in fact, that the King of France got interested and sent hunters and noblemen all the way from Paris to deal with the problem. Michel Doucet was one of those. He was what Marc called an *hoboreau,* a minor noble with no land or money who had to take whatever opportunities he could get, and the hunt for the Beast seemed like a good chance to make a name for himself.

But the things he saw and did in those dark forests on Mont Mouchet made a believer out of Michel Doucet, and he decided to devote his life to hunting werewolves, wherever he might find them. He even married the daughter of a local hunter who was the actual one who killed the Beast.

Those two fled France in 1790 during the French Revolution, since it wasn't a safe place to be for anybody with a noble title, no matter who they were. Michel and Marie Doucet spent time in Martinique and Haiti, and finally ended up in Louisiana. And there, apparently, they and their descendants had been ever since. Up to and including Jolie.

Marc wouldn't tell me where the rings came from or how the Doucets came to have them or anything at all about that subject, even though I was dying to find out. I guess it was a family secret.

That's the only thing I can remember him ever refusing to talk about, though. He seemed to have taken a liking to me for some reason; maybe because I was such a good listener. I've found that generally the more you keep your mouth shut and your ears open, the better people will enjoy your company.

He even took me out to Mont Mouchet one day after I mentioned I'd like to see the place while I was there. No particular reason, you know; just curiosity.

The mountain was covered in thick woods almost all the way to the top, and when we reached the summit it was a very desolate and empty kind of place. If you looked east you could see the Alps far away in the distance, and if you looked west I swear you could catch a glimpse of the ocean, though Marc said not. It was windy and cold up there, and I couldn't help thinking maybe the real reason the Doucets went to Louisiana was to find someplace warmer to live.

Marc picked up a handful of dust from next to his feet and let it slip through his gloved fingers. It didn't look like anything special; just dry, pale dirt with a few lumps and little flecks of stone in it.

"Take a handful of this dust, and sprinkle it on a piece of flat sandstone anywhere in the world, and a new pod is born," he murmured, half to himself.

"How far down from the top does it still work?" I asked, and he shrugged.

"Wherever it looks pale, like this. I don't think anybody ever checked to see how far down the mountain it goes. There's plenty of it near the top, after all," he said.

He was right about that; there was certainly no shortage of dust. As Jolie had said, it was a mountain, and there was no way of blowing it up or destroying it or getting rid of it or anything like that. It was just too dadgummed *big*.

But still. . .

"Nobody ever tried to get rid of this place?" I wondered out loud.

"No, the best we can do is to guard this place, and burn any book that has the secret in it, and stamp out every pod we can find. Hopefully in time we can put them all to sleep, but that remains to be seen," he said.

"You don't ever feel sorry for them at all?" I asked, appalled that he could say such a thing. I already knew from our talks that Marc didn't believe in the same Hope that Jolie and some of the others had. For him, dust was dust, and sleep was forever. Knowing that's what he thought, his words sounded cruel.

"Sometimes I'm tempted to, but never for long. Angie now, she took pity on a child, barely more than a *baby*, Zach, and left him with his grandparents instead of putting him to sleep as she knew she was supposed to do. You see what happened to *her* because she had too much pity. And if that wasn't bad enough, she nearly destroyed the whole family, too. Then, when all was almost lost, it fell to Jolie to finish that same work that should have been done ten years ago. So I ask you, to what purpose was her pity, except to cause more suffering than there would have been without it?" he asked reasonably.

I had no answer to give him, but in my heart of hearts I had a feeling he was overlooking something in all that. He almost seemed to be saying that having no pity was actually kinder in the long run, and there was no way I could bring myself to believe *that.* You can justify *anything* you feel like doing, no matter how cruel or wicked it might be, if you keep telling yourself it's all for the best in the long run.

But I didn't want to argue with Marc about it right then. I was pretty sure nothing I said would change his mind, anyway, if I could even think of the right way to say what I felt. Instead, I changed the subject and asked him something else that was a lot closer to my heart.

"Marc, are you *sure* there's no other way to wake up the sleepers?" I asked. I must have asked him that same question a thousand times already, and he didn't even answer me this time; just shook his head and clapped a hand on my shoulder.

I didn't say anything else for a while, just stood there and looked out into the blue distance and felt the wind whipping my hair. Whatever Justin might say and whatever Daniel Trewick might have thought, I didn't feel like much of a Curse Breaker right then. I felt alone and hopeless, six thousand miles and an ocean away from home.

I thought again about those two hundred bottles of sweet water in Red Lick. Marc didn't know about that; nobody did, except me. I still didn't know if all those people sleeping in the dust counted as a broken thing or not, but I could pray. There was nothing left to lose by trying it.

I decided that as soon as I got home, that would be at the very top of my list of things to do. I felt a little better after that; even a tiny pinch of hope is better than none at all.

There was one other thing I wanted to know about, though, while I had the chance.

"Is this the only place where you can find wolf dust?" I asked, and Marc seemed glad to slip back into his teacherly pose.

"Yes. We think there were other places, long ago, but this is the last one. It's been said that the Beast of Gévaudan destroyed all the others himself, because he wanted no rivals. He had an idea that he would be the king of all *loup-garous* in the world from then on, and he could have more control over them if they all had to come here to get the dust. So the others are all gone," Marc explained.

"Are you sure?" I asked.

"Yes. Every pod we've dealt with since 1767, we've been able to trace back here. There are no others left; we're sure of that," Marc said.

"But how did the Beast destroy those other places, then? If he could do it then there has to be a way," I pointed out.

"Who can say? He was the most powerful wolf who ever walked the world, and perhaps he had powers and knew things no one else knew," Marc shrugged. I didn't like hearing that, so I didn't answer him immediately.

"Yeah, I guess you're right," I finally admitted.

"It's a brave idea, Zach, but it wouldn't amount to much, I'm afraid. We'd still have to go on hunting down pods and putting them to sleep just like we always have, and they'd still have all the wolf-stones they've already got. So even if we did somehow destroy this place, it wouldn't be much use," he said.

I gave Marc a sidelong glance; he may not have been paying attention to what he said, but if they'd been able to trace every pod and every stone back to this place since 1767, then didn't that mean that when the Beast of Gévaudan destroyed the other places that it must have wiped out all the stones and pods that came from them?

In fact it *had* to mean that, or else there'd still be some pods out there which couldn't be traced back to Mont Mouchet. So if we found a way to crush this place, then it ought to wipe out all the stones and pods that came from it, too, shouldn't it? It was plain as a pikestaff, when you thought about it.

So the million-dollar question was, why was Marc telling me otherwise? Surely he couldn't have overlooked something that obvious.

I'm not dumb. Marc was either flat-out lying to me, or at the very least he was stretching the truth to discourage me from trying to do anything about Mont Mouchet. I just couldn't figure out why.

I didn't let out a peep that anything was wrong, though. If Marc wanted to lie to me for some unknown reason, then it was better if he thought it worked.

We didn't stay up there on the summit for much longer. The wind was too cold, and we were both ready to get indoors for a while.

When we got back to Clermont, Marc excused himself and went to lie down for a while, like he usually did in the afternoons. Jolie and Louise were nowhere to be found, so that left me all alone in the house.

That suited me just fine; I had some hard thinking to do. I went to the guest room where I was sleeping and laid down on the big four-poster bed where I wouldn't be disturbed.

Marc didn't want me to try to find a way to get rid of the curse on Mont Mouchet. That much was plain. There could be several reasons why he might think that way, of course; it was no use trying to guess what his motive might be.

But all the same, if he'd lie to me about one thing then he might lie to me about other things too, if it suited his purposes.

That meant I had to sift his words carefully before I trusted what he said.

I was pretty sure the part about the Beast of Gévaudan destroying the other mountains was true, since Marc would know I could simply ask Jolie about that part. I was also fairly sure the part about how every pod since 1767 could be traced back to Mont Mouchet was also true, since that's the very tidbit that got him caught lying in the first place. So if those two things were really true, then I was probably right that it would wipe out the curse everywhere in the world, if someone crushed the mountain.

If I understood it right. If I wasn't missing something important. I thought I had it nailed down, but like I've said before and like Justin and Eileen have told me more times than I could ever count, it's so very easy to be totally wrong.

What I needed was more information.

I left the house quietly and walked downtown to an Internet café, where I could do some research and maybe figure something out. The library didn't help me since I couldn't read books in French, but the net is the same everywhere.

I searched for the Beast of Gévaudan and spent most of the rest of the day reading everything I could find about him. It was interesting stuff, and I found some references to books I could read to find out more. Most of them were in French, but nevertheless, I wrote them down just in case.

I didn't tell Marc or Jolie what I'd been doing when I got back to the house. I didn't quite trust Marc anymore, at least not till I figured out what his game was and what made him tick. I probably could have told Jolie, but for some reason I didn't do that either. Sometimes you have a little warning voice deep inside that tells you not to do something, and I've learned to pay attention to such things. Your instincts tell you things that bubble up from stuff you don't consciously notice, but they're there for a reason.

So I kept my mouth shut about the Beast of Gévaudan and I didn't breathe another word about Mont Mouchet, or the sapphire rings, or anything at all that had to do with werewolves, or how curious I still was about all those things.

I don't think Marc or Jolie noticed too much. They were doing a lot of talking about whether she ought to stay in Clermont for a while or whether he ought to move back to Louisiana for a year or two, since she had no other family left.

The best I could tell, they finally decided that Jolie would stay in France for a month or so, until Marc could get his affairs in order and move back to Natchitoches. Somebody had to watch the storehouse where the sleeping wolves were kept, and they were talking about recruiting some of Jolie's cousins and more distant family members to take up the werewolf hunting game. She didn't mention asking me, and I didn't remind her.

But I couldn't stay in France for a month, so it was decided that I'd fly back home alone. That suited me just fine, because I already had that half-formed plan in mind for what I wanted to do with the sweet water and the sleepers, and it wouldn't work unless the Doucets were firmly out of town.

"I'm sorry it had to be this way, Blue-Eyes," Jolie told me that night.

We were sitting alone in the parlor after Marc went to bed, and watching the fire in the grate. It was a cold night, even inside the house, and Marc liked wood fires. The heat from the coals felt good.

"It is what it is," I shrugged.

"Yeah, no doubt. But I'm sorry for dragging you into all this. I know you didn't really want to," she said.

"It's always a pleasure to be of service to a lady," I said, with what I hoped was a cheesy smile. She smiled back a little.

"You're sweet, Zach," she said. She scooted over next to me on the big leather couch and snuggled up close.

"It's too cold in here; I just need some body heat," she said, and laid her head on my chest. I put an arm around her and she didn't object, and for a while we just sat there and looked at the fire together, thinking our own thoughts. She was warm, and she was right about the body heat. It felt good.

"Jolie?" I asked after a while.

"Yeah?" she answered.

"When this is all over, would you like to go see a movie sometime?" I asked. She laughed a little, and for a second my heart sank.

"I thought you'd never ask," she finally said, and snuggled a little closer.

"Awesome," I said, and meant it.

Chapter Eight

That's how me and Jolie got to be more than just friends. I only had three days left in Clermont before I had to go home, but they were happy ones. For a while, I almost managed to completely forget about *loup-garous,* and curses, and all that stuff.

Marc let us take his Jeep out driving, and Jolie took us to all kinds of places. This was France, after all, the home of Cinderella and Beauty and the Beast and all those other fairy tales, and she knew the stories behind all of them. She showed me the very castle (she said) where Belle fell in love with the Beast.

I can't remember where all she took me and I couldn't pronounce half the names anyway even if I did remember. I know she took me to the ocean once, somewhere close to Bordeaux, and we walked on the beach in our bare feet and felt the waves wash around our ankles. The water was cold, but neither of us minded that.

I remember looking out to the west across the Atlantic and thinking that home was somewhere that way, however many thousands of miles across the sea. I think that was one of the only times I felt a twinge of homesickness, but Jolie must have read my mind, because she kissed me just then and for a while I forgot all about it.

She was good at that.

It didn't seem like very long before I had to head back home without her. Maybe it helped that we both knew it wouldn't be long before she was back in Natchitoches, and then we'd see each other all the time. That's what I kept telling myself, at least.

I got home after what seemed like forever, and the place seemed a whole lot like it always did, except that Cam wasn't there. I could somewhat put it out of my mind when I was off someplace else, but at home there was no way I could do that.

Justin and Eileen had been feeling it worse than I did, I guess, since they'd been there the whole time. Maybe it helped a little, knowing for sure what happened to him; it would have been much worse if he was still missing, since it's always the not knowing part which is the hardest to handle. But not knowing if we'd ever get him back again was hard enough.

Oh, I know he was sitting there in that little plastic bottle, sleeping just as safe as he could be. But I didn't want a handful of dust. I wanted my brother and my best friend back, the way he used to be. I'd be glad to listen to him tease me about Jolie or anything else he wanted, if I could only hear his voice again.

But unless the sweet water worked or I found something else that did, I knew that might never be.

The next morning I took Cam's bottle of dust from my desk drawer and zipped it up in my jacket pocket so I wouldn't accidentally lose it, and then I got the truck keys and walked out to the back yard where the Dodge was parked. I looked behind the seat real quick, to make sure the bottle of sweet water was still there. I never did take it out after we came back from Natchitoches that first time, but I wanted to be sure nobody else had touched it. It was still there, wrapped up in the same old t-shirt.

You might think I'd want to try to wake up Cameron first, after everything I've said about that and how much it meant to me. But I had a good reason for waiting. I didn't know for sure what the water would really do when I mixed it with the dust; not until I tried it, and I didn't want to do experiments on Cam, just in case something went wrong. Maybe it was selfish of me to be willing to risk somebody else when I wouldn't risk him, but there it is.

Besides that, I also wanted to talk to a pod leader. I remembered what Jolie had said, about how pod leaders sometimes knew things, and I hoped one of them could tell me what I needed to do about breaking the curse on Mont Mouchet. There was only one place I knew of where I could find what I wanted, though, and that was in the storeroom in Natchitoches.

I hesitated, torn by indecision. I didn't want to wait any longer to head down there, but on the other hand, I was supposed to be back in school that day. I hadn't said anything to Justin and Eileen about going out of town, either. I remembered what Justin told me about being able to talk to him about anything, and I decided I'd better ask first, just in case.

He must have been out doing field work somewhere in the wild blue boonies that day, because I couldn't get hold of him when I tried to call, but Eileen was in the lab like she usually is.

"Hey Zach, what's up?" she asked when she answered the phone. She sounded a little bit absentminded, like she was in the middle of doing something.

"Eileen, I need to miss one more day of school," I told her.

"What for?" she asked.

"I need to go down to Natchitoches for a couple of hours. I think I found a way to get Cameron back," I told her. I halfway expected her to ask me why it couldn't wait till Saturday, being the ever-practical lady that she is, but for some reason she didn't.

"When would you be back?" she asked.

"Before bedtime, I promise," I said.

"Do you have money for a trip like that?" she asked.

"Yeah, I have some," I said.

"Well, I guess one more day won't kill anybody, since it's Friday anyway. Go do what you need to do. But no more skipping after today, Zach," she told me.

"Thanks, Eileen," I told her.

I stopped in Shreveport at a hardware store and bought a crowbar and some allen wrenches and anything else I could think of that a burglar might use, and then I went to the mall and got me some really nice clothes. I mean suit and tie type things, with black shoes that were so shiny you could see your face in them.

I felt a little bit uncomfortable spending Sarah Doucet's money for things like that, but I did have a good reason for it. People pay attention to clothes, you know. I was about to do some serious breaking and entering, in a rich neighborhood where people were always thinking about thieves, and I hoped if I looked like a rich boy then anybody who saw me might just possibly think I belonged there instead of calling the cops on me. Burglars don't usually wear suits and ties, you know.

As soon as I got to Natchitoches I spiffed up in my new duds and parked the truck in the usual place at the Piggly Wiggly parking lot. Then I grabbed the bottle of sweet water from the back of the seat, locked up the truck, and headed down the street for that big brick pile where John and Sarah Doucet used to live.

It was a quiet, drowsy day, and it felt hot in those scratchy clothes, even as late in the year as it was. Louisiana is a lot warmer than France, let me tell you. I could feel little beads of sweat popping up on my forehead, and I wished to myself that I could have worn a t-shirt.

There didn't seem to be many people around that day. I saw an old lady raking leaves in her front yard, but that was all.

When I got to the house, I opened the front gate and went inside just like I belonged there. But instead of going to the front door, I slipped around the side, intending to get to the back yard where the flower garden was. I didn't need to go inside the house at all for what I wanted.

That's when I hit a snag. About halfway past the side of the house, I bumped up against that high brick wall that surrounded the garden. I'd forgotten it was there, and I soon found that it blocked the entire space between the side of the house and the neighbor's fence. There was no gate, either, and it was much too high to climb.

I wasn't licked yet, though. I backtracked around the front and tried the other side instead. There *was* a narrow little wrought iron gate through the wall on that side, but it was locked with a padlock. And not just any padlock, either. It was one of those round kind that you can't break open with bolt cutters or even a hacksaw.

There was a little marble bench next to the wall, and I sat down for a few minutes to think. The only good thing about the whole situation was that nobody could see me behind all the ivy and bushes and other plants in the yard, so I didn't have to worry about neighbors getting suspicious while I tried to figure out a way to get through.

After a while, I noticed that one of the big pecan trees in the yard had a branch that hung over the wall into the garden. It looked mighty thin and wispy to hold my weight that far out, and pecan branches are notoriously brittle anyway. If you've ever climbed one then you know exactly what I mean. I had, lots of times, and I wasn't anxious to try it today.

But after a while I decided I'd just have to risk it. I couldn't think of any other options since I couldn't go through the house and I didn't dare try the neighbors' yards and I couldn't climb the wall.

I dragged the little marble bench up against the tree trunk, and then stood on that so I could reach the lowest branch. The dadgummed suit didn't help matters; if you've ever tried to climb a tree in church clothes then you know what I mean about that, too. I ended up having to strip down to my boxers before I could get up into the tree, but before I did that, I piled up the clothes and shoes and the water and the dust right next to the gate, so I could reach through the bars and get them from the other side.

If I ever made it that far.

It was a lot easier to climb without the suit on, and I made it up to the branch I wanted with no trouble. I can climb like a monkey when I need to. I hadn't done it much lately, but there are certain things you never forget how to do.

Then came the hard part. I started inching my way along the branch toward the wall, and for a while everything was fine. Near the trunk it was thick enough that I could crawl along without much risk of falling, but the farther I went the thinner it got, and the less there was to hold on to. I did my best to imitate a sloth, easing along and trying not to make any sudden moves that might snap the wood. It wasn't easy, but after a while I got pretty darned close to the wall.

That's when the branch broke. I heard it start to crack before it actually let loose completely, and I jumped for the wall while I still had time.

I caught the top of it, and the broken branch whipped back up and left a deep bloody scratch on my back. It stung like the devil, and I could feel blood running down and soaking my shorts, but I couldn't pay attention to that.

I heaved myself up onto the wall with my arms until I was lying face down on top of it, and then I slid my body off the back side until I was hanging by my arms again. Then I let go, praying I didn't twist an ankle when I hit the ground.

Well, I didn't twist an ankle, but I did land right in the middle of a big white camellia bush and that was almost as bad. I got cuts and scratches all over my body and a poke in the eye to boot, before I finally crawled out onto the flagstone path.

I wearily fetched my clothes and put them back on, and slipped Cameron's dust back in my pocket. Then I hit *another* snag. The dadgummed wine bottle wouldn't fit through the bars in the gate. I could get the neck through, but the body wouldn't quite slip past the iron.

I sighed. Who knew it could be that much trouble just to break into somebody's garden? I pity rabbits, if it's always that hard for them.

I managed to solve that problem fairly easily, though. There was a big steel trash can beside the patio, and after a little bit of digging I found a plastic Coke bottle in there. I washed it clean inside and out with the garden hose, and then I simply opened the wine bottle and poured the sweet water from it into the Coke bottle. It wouldn't quite hold all of it, but that was okay. It ought to be enough.

After I did all that, I made my way through the garden to the place where I remembered Jolie had hidden the key to the storeroom, behind the big purple hydrangea plant. I found it with no trouble, since it was the only one like it in the garden. I pushed the flowers aside and saw a crack in the brick wall where the cement had fallen out, and when I felt around in there I touched a chain. I pulled it out, and sure enough, there was the key.

It was a little harder to find the spot that hid the passageway, but even that didn't take too long. I slipped through the heavy vines and let them fall shut behind me so nobody would notice anything amiss, and for the first time since I parked the truck I halfway relaxed. Nobody would ever find me in there.

I went down the little passage until I came to the door, and then turned the key in the lock and let myself in. It was pitch black inside, and I fumbled against the wall for the light switch. There wasn't one, so I opened the door wide and waited for my eyes to adjust to the dimness. When they did, I finally found the switch behind the door, just about the last place in the world I would have expected it to be. It's always like that in strange places, you know; I think they must intentionally put every light switch wherever they think you're least likely to find it in the dark.

Anyway, the chandelier came on and I shut the door so nobody would catch a glimpse of the light. Then I started rooting.

I still couldn't figure out how the bottles were supposed to be organized, exactly. The only general rule seemed to be that the more recent ones were usually nearer the door and the farther back into the room you went the older they got. Some of them were downright ancient; I found one from 1798 at the back of the room, and I'm pretty sure even that wasn't the oldest one. They all had a name and a date, but that was it. I wondered how the Doucets ever managed to find anything in there.

I decided I might do better if I started with the filing cabinet instead of just browsing the shelves, so I went back there and opened a drawer at random.

The cabinet was much better organized than the bottles were, I have to say. Every pod in the room had a folder, and all the pods were numbered and arranged by year. The first page in each folder was an information sheet on each pod as a whole, which told things like where it operated and who the founder was and GPS coordinates for the wolf-stones it used and so forth. After that came sheets on each pod member, including the person's whole name, the date they were put to sleep, where they were from, how old they were, and quite a bit of other stuff, including where to find the person's bottle on the shelves. Finally, in the back of the folder there were usually lists of what had been looted from the pod and various notes and such.

It was while I was riffling through those folders that I found something I'll never forget. I was looking at the more recent ones when I came to pod number 391. The number didn't mean anything to me, but when I got down to the list of members it did.

Daniel Edward Trewick, Shreveport, LA, Oct. 29, 1863. . . it began, and I quickly read down the list of other names. Several were marked deceased, and then I got to names I knew.

Maralyn Marie Johnson, Anthony James Trewick, Jenna LeAnne Wilder, Lola Jane Trewick, Zachary James Trewick, Cameron Lee Parker, Laura Leigh Beckham, Logan Andrew Tygart. . .

I didn't need to read any more. All I needed to see were the dates, all of them this year, when each one of them had been brought into the storeroom. Each one had been initialed with the letters SD beside them; I guessed for Sarah Doucet. The only ones left with no dates or initials were me and Cam. It was all very neat and proper, in a creepy kind of way.

I couldn't resist flipping through the pages to see if I had my very own information sheet tucked away in there, and sure enough, I did. There wasn't much to see on it, except for a scribbled list of dates on the bottom of the page that meant nothing to me. Cameron had the exact same dates written on his, and all of them were initialed JD.

I remembered what Jolie had said, about how the Doucets never took any chances. They found a pod and they wiped it out, simple as that. Marc had said pretty much the same thing: no pity, no second thoughts, no loose ends. Anybody who was a member of a pod, or even knew the secret, they were all put to sleep and brought here to wait, and God could sort them out later. All neat and tidy.

I wondered if me and Cam were just loose ends to be tied up, just business as usual, and if that was the real reason why Jolie came and found us at the fair that night. Maybe she just wanted to find out whatever I knew that was useful before she put me in a bottle, too.

My mind jumped instantly to that old, old fear I had about whether she was just pretending to like me for her own purposes. The memory made a hard, bitter lump in my chest, and when I thought about how she said she loved me and snuggled up against me on the couch in Clermont, it stung my heart. Was it all nothing but lies and manipulation?

I didn't think I'd have the courage to go find them, but somehow I did. They were scattered out a bit amongst the newer bottles that had come in this year, but it didn't take me too long to find them all. Mama and Daddy and Lola were there, and Nana Maralyn, Cam's mother, and all the others too. Even Logan, who wasn't a *loup-garou* at all. Just for good measure, I guess. I found Jake Golden and his grandparents, too, and as an afterthought I went and found Jason and Charla.

I set all of them on the table in the middle of the room under the big chandelier, maybe twenty bottles or so, and for only the second time in my life I wanted to cry and couldn't do it. I don't know why. It felt like losing my family all over again, and losing Jolie, and I was full of a storm of savage feelings I couldn't even begin to put into words.

But presently I calmed down and tried to think what to do. Justin always tells me not to get upset because it doesn't help and the problem is still just as much there as it was before. I know that's true, but it's harder to do than you might think.

I decided I might as well go ahead and see if I could wake somebody up, since that was the main reason I was there in the first place. First things first, you know. With an effort, I pushed all that other stuff out of my mind to think about later. I needed to focus on what I was doing, and the first thing to do was to pick somebody to test the water on.

After mulling it over for a while, I decided to try Jason Golden first. He seemed to be a good choice because he was a pod leader, and also because I thought I knew enough about him to gamble that he'd be one of the milder and more reasonable ones. The last thing I wanted was to get in a fight with some vicious *loup-garou* who'd try to rip my head off the instant he woke up.

I was uneasy even about Jason, because even though I *thought* he was one of the milder ones because of what I found in his house, I knew I could be totally wrong about that. He might be dangerous. He might escape, or break bottles, or even hurt somebody. Namely me. I couldn't think of any way to tie up a handful of dust, though, and I had no idea whether he'd wake up instantly or be groggy for a while or even if he'd wake up at all for that matter.

I finally decided this was another one of those times when I'd just have to bite the bullet and take a risk. I could wring my hands over it for weeks and I'd never be any surer than I was now.

There was an old ashtray on the table which had a few pennies in it, and I dumped those out and wiped it clean with my new tie. I wanted something to hold the dust so I wouldn't lose any of it, just in case. Then I unscrewed the lid on Jason's bottle and carefully shook out the reddish dust into the tray. It made a little mound and gave off a spicy smell, sort of like nutmeg.

"Well, here goes nothin'," I whispered to myself, and poured a little bit of water from the Coke bottle into the ashtray. I hoped if it didn't work, I could just wait for the water to evaporate and then put Jason's dust back in the bottle with no harm done.

It didn't work out exactly the way I thought it would. I stirred up the mixture with a pen, and for a few seconds nothing happened and I was afraid I'd end up with nothing but a handful of mud in an old ashtray. But then it sort of shimmered and glinted and grew, and in the twinkling of an eye, before I could quite grasp what was happening, there was the body of a young man lying sprawled out on the table.

Buck naked, I might add, and I quickly threw down my suit coat to cover him. It was Jason Golden, no doubt about it; I recognized him from the picture I found at the burnt-out trailer in Fouke. He didn't look like he'd aged a single day in all these years. He was breathing very slightly, like he was deeply asleep.

I checked his fingernails and he was definitely a *loup-garou.* There was no mistaking that part, either. I was still a little uneasy about waking him, so I came up behind his head where it might be hardest to grab me if he woke up suddenly. Then I shook his shoulder.

Nothing happened, so I shook it a little harder. Still nothing, and I soon found that nothing I did could wake him up. He might as well have been a stone or a log lying there, except that he was alive.

This was a pretty pickle, I have to admit. There was no way I could carry him through the streets of Natchitoches like that, even if I found a way to get him over the wall outside. But I couldn't leave him there, either. Dust didn't need to eat or drink and it never got too cold, but a living body would. Jason would die for real if I just left him there like that.

I hadn't foreseen that particular problem, and I thought desperately to myself how to fix it. I had no ring to turn him back to dust, and I didn't know what else to do with him. I was in totally uncharted territory.

One thing was certain; there was no way I could wake up any of the others until I found a way to finish the job. They were better off in their little plastic bottles than like Jason.

"You can really get yourself into some messes, boy," I said to myself with a sigh.

I thought about what Marc had told me, about how it took living blood to wake a sleeper. He'd said it took all the blood from one person, mixed with the dust. But Jason wasn't dust anymore; he was already reformed or reconstituted or whatever you wanted to call it. He was only sleeping. So maybe just a little blood would do the trick.

I took my pocket knife and scraped open one of the scratches on my arm that I got from the camellia bush, until it bled freely. Then I held the scratch over Jason's chest so the blood could drip on his heart. I had no particular reason for that; it just seemed like the best place.

And you know, it was strange. Every drop that touched his skin disappeared instantly, like a raindrop into dry ground. But it wasn't long before a faint flush came to his cheeks, and the tone of his breathing changed, and when I thought I'd bled my last drop, I heard him take a deep breath. Then I saw his eyes open.

I don't know why it worked that way, and why the water by itself wasn't enough. Maybe there's no substitute for the sacrifice, even if it's a small one, and maybe unless I was willing to give up a little bit of my own life then I couldn't give life back to someone else. Maybe. All I know is, it worked.

Jason still looked half stoned, to be sure, but I guess that's not so hard to believe after you've just had a ten-year nap in a spice bottle. I'd probably feel cruddy after that, myself. He turned his head and his eyes partly focused on me, and then he groaned.

"Where am I?" he asked. That was about what I expected him to say, but I wasn't quite sure how to answer it, to tell the truth. How do you give a man a simple answer to an awfully complicated story?

"Everything's all right now. You're with friends," I said soothingly.

"What happened? Who are you?" he asked, trying to sit up and not able to do it.

"Don't try to get up or you'll fall. You've been asleep for a long time. Do you remember anything?" I asked, and he groaned again.

"I remember. . . somebody came to the door a while ago and I didn't know who she was. She made a fist and I think she hit me. How long was I out?" he said.

"You've been asleep for almost eleven years, Mr. Golden," I said bluntly. There was no way to soften it, and I didn't have time to make up a story even if I'd wanted to.

"Huh?" he asked, looking at me stupidly.

"That lady who came to the door. Her name was Angie Doucet, and she knocked you out. You've been asleep for eleven years," I repeated.

"You mean like a coma? Did she hit me that hard?" he asked, looking even more confused.

"Something like that," I said dryly. I didn't know how to explain the truth so he'd understand, and that was close enough for now. Then came the question I'd been dreading.

"Where's Charla? Where's Jake? Can I see them?" he asked.

"They're close by. You can see them shortly," I said, trying to be truthful without saying too much. But Jason seemed satisfied for the time being.

"Man, I feel like I got hit by a Mack truck," he said, rubbing his eyes. Then he seemed to really notice for the first time where he was, and he looked at me with a frown on his face and sat up on the table.

"Hey, this ain't no hospital. You ain't no doctor, either. Where am I?" he said, and there was a hard edge to his voice now.

I decided it was time to get tough with him, fast. He was still too weak to lick a stamp, but he might not stay that way for much longer.

"Look, I'll tell you exactly what happened, but you need to stay calm, buddy. I'm here to help, but if you get wild then I'll put you right back to sleep," I warned him sternly.

It was an empty threat, of course, but *he* didn't know that. He looked at me hard, but then he visibly got hold of himself.

"All right, then. I'm calm. Please tell me what's going on and where my family is," he asked.

"Good. First things first. I know you're a werewolf, so let's get that out of the way before we talk about anything else," I said, and I could have sworn he got a shifty glint in his eyes. He wasn't a very good liar.

"I don't know what you-" he began, but I cut him off.

"Look, I said I *know*. Don't waste time telling me you're not, because I'm not arguing about it," I told him.

"Think whatever you want to, then," he said. I was annoyed with him for trying to hide it when I knew dadgummed well he was lying, but I let it go.

"That lady who came to your house was a werewolf hunter. She found out what you are and where you lived, and she put you to sleep. You've been a pile of dust sitting in a spice bottle in a cave in Louisiana ever since. So has Charla," I told him.

He turned pale at that.

"Jake?" he whispered.

"Angie took him to Charla's parents' house, since he wasn't cursed yet and she felt sorry for him. But he grew up, Jason. He's sixteen now, and he must have found your wolf-stone, because now he's a werewolf too, and he tried his best to wipe out Angie Doucet and her family. But they got him too, and Charla's parents, and now all of them are asleep in the dust," I told him.

"No, I don't believe it," he said, shaking his head.

"Believe it," I told him forcefully, and then I added the lure.

"But it doesn't have to stay that way. I can wake them up, just like I woke you up, if you'll cooperate and tell me what I want to know," I went on. The look of misery on his face lightened just a bit.

"I'll do whatever you want, if you can bring them back," he said softly. I hated being that harsh with a man who was still so weak and sick, but this was one of those times when it had to be done.

"Good, let's start at the beginning. How did you first become a werewolf?" I asked. For a second he looked almost like he was getting ready to lie to me again, but then he seemed to have a change of heart.

"All right. I'll tell you, since you know so much anyway. My uncle Jack always used to tell me there was a big rock out in the woods by Boggy Creek, and if you went down there at the right time of year and knew how to do it, you could turn yourself into a werewolf. I didn't believe a word of it back then, but he showed me the rock and told me what to do with it. I didn't think nothin' about it for a long time, but then I got to talking to Charla about it one day for some reason and she thought it was funny. She likes wild and crazy things like that. It was the right time of year, so we went out there and did what we did. We just wanted to see what happened. We didn't really believe it," he repeated.

"And then?" I prodded.

"Well then I guess you know what then. It really worked, and then we didn't have no way to undo it after that. It was done," he said.

"Where's the stone you used?" I asked.

"Maybe a mile from the trailer, in the middle of a canebrake down by the creek. It's not hard to find if you know where to look," he said. I filed that away in my mind for future reference. As soon as I got a chance, I'd go cleanse that stone.

"How did your uncle know all that stuff?" I asked, and Jason shrugged.

"That I don't know. He passed away several years ago, and I never had a chance to ask him," he said.

I believed him, for what it was worth. Jason seemed like a careless bumbler who didn't understand what he was messing with, until it landed him in deep trouble. In fact, he knew even less about werewolves than I did. That might be better for him and Charla since it meant he wasn't one of the really evil ones, but fat lot of good it did *me*.

I sighed to myself.

"Let me ask you one more question, Jason. If you could, would you take it back?" I asked him. He hesitated again like he wasn't sure how much to say, and when he spoke he wouldn't look at me.

"I won't say I never liked it, and I won't say it wasn't fun sometimes. I like to hunt, and it's the wildest hunting I ever had. But it's not worth all this. So yeah, if I could then I'd take it back and never wish no more for it," he finally said.

I believed him when he said that, too. He might have been pulling my leg, just telling me what he thought I wanted to hear, but somehow I didn't think so.

Jake might be another story, of course, but I was hoping Jason and Charla could knock him in line. Bobby and Sandra too, for that matter.

I didn't have enough sweet water nor enough blood in my body to wake up all those people right then, and maybe it wouldn't have been wise to do it in the storeroom anyway. I still had to get out of there, and dragging a bunch of weak and sickly folks down the streets of Natchitoches without a stitch of clothes on was probably not the most ideal plan. I'd have to find a better time and place to wake up Jason's family like I promised.

As overjoyed as I was that I'd found a way to wake up the sleepers, I was also disappointed in a way. I didn't know a whit more about Mont Mouchet or the Beast of Gévaudan or the sapphire rings than I did before.

"Come on, let's go home," I said abruptly. There was nothing else Jason could tell me, and there was nothing to be gained by staying in the storeroom any longer, either. He looked surprised.

"Is that all you wanted to know? What about Charla and Jake?" he asked.

"I'll fix them as soon as we get to Fouke; don't worry about it," I promised him.

Chapter Nine

I found a plastic bag and put all the bottles from the Trewick pod in there, along with Charla and Jake and the rest of Jason's family. I couldn't think of anybody else I needed to take, right then. Cameron was still in my pocket.

I had to share clothes with Jason since he didn't have any, so I gave him the slacks and just wore my boxers; with any luck, nobody would look close enough to notice they weren't shorts before we could get back to the truck. I also gave him the suit coat and kept the white shirt for myself. Everything was too small for him and I'm sure we both looked ridiculous, but it was the only thing I could think of.

I cleaned up the storeroom before we left, then made sure to lock the door and replace the key in the crack behind the hydrangea bush. Marc or Jolie might notice that a few bottles were missing if they paid close attention, but I was hoping they wouldn't.

We found a wooden gate at the back of the garden that I hadn't noticed before, and to my equal disgust and relief, it wasn't locked. I could have spared myself the whole episode of having to climb over the brick wall, if I'd only known.

Or maybe not, come to find out. The gate wasn't locked, but it did have a latch that could only be opened from the inside. I guess that's why they didn't bother to put a lock on it; not many burglars are trying to break *out* of the house.

Before we left, I picked up a stick and wedged it in the opening just enough to foul the latch, just in case I needed to get back inside later. I didn't want to climb any more pecan trees unless I absolutely had to.

The gate opened into a narrow alley, and that suited me just fine. No prying eyes to see us traipsing along and wonder what we were up to.

The alley came out onto one of the side streets that crosses Hickory, and after a little more footwork we made it to the truck without incident.

Jason didn't talk much, except now and then he'd say something about how much gas cost, or how weird it was that everybody had cell phones, or some little comment like that which reminded me how long he'd been asleep. I guess I never thought about how much things had changed in ten years.

I stopped at a dollar store just outside Natchitoches and bought him some new jeans and a t-shirt and some tennis shoes; I felt like that was the least I could do. I got an outfit for Charla too, since I knew she'd be needing one when we woke her up. Jake and Bobby and Sandra all had clothes at their house, so there was no need to bother with something for them.

Jason slept for an hour or two on the way to Fouke, and when he woke up he seemed to feel better. He wanted to go to his old house as soon as possible, and I didn't object since I had an errand to do there, too. I wanted to cleanse that stone, and in the process see if Jason really meant it when he said he'd give it up.

I warned him about the fire, but he still seemed caught off guard when he actually saw what was left of his old place.

"She did this, too?" he asked.

"Yeah, I'm afraid she did," I agreed.

"Well, it don't matter. Things can be replaced," he said, with a deep breath.

"Show me where that stone is, if you remember," I told him.

"Yeah, I remember," he said.

Jason was as good as his word, and he led me down a weedy path into the pine woods behind the trailer. It was probably a little more than a mile before we came to a clearing in the middle of a canebrake, and a flat sandstone rock of the type I knew so well. I opened the Coke bottle and sprinkled some water on it and prayed over it to wash it clean, while Jason watched.

It didn't take long to finish that, and then I poured out Charla's dust on top of the wet rock, for lack of anywhere better to put it. I poured some water on it and mixed it to mud, then turned away before her body appeared. I told Jason what to do, and he pricked his thumb and dripped some blood onto her chest.

It wasn't long before she woke up, and it wasn't long after that before he had her dressed and made her understand what had happened to them. She cried and cussed and said some things about Angie Doucet that I won't repeat, but after a while she calmed down.

We made our way back over to the Lees' place to revive Jake and Bobby and Sandra, since that's where all their clothes were. There were tears, then, from just about everybody. It wasn't the kind of thing an outsider wants to see, but they didn't seem to mind.

Jason told me that if I ever needed anything, no matter what it was, I should never hesitate to ask them, and the others nodded. Charla kissed me on the cheek, and even old sourpuss Bobby shook my hand. But it was what Jake said that I remember best.

"Tell Cameron I'm sorry for what I did," he said, and I smiled.

"You can tell him yourself, when you see him at baseball practice one of these days," I said.

"I'll do that," he said, and then he hesitated, like there was something else he wanted to say.

"Come here a minute, Zach," he finally said, and I followed him down the hall to his bedroom.

"What is it?" I asked.

"There's something else you need to know," he said, after the door was shut. He spoke in a low voice, like he didn't want anybody to hear, and he seemed almost scared.

"What is it?" I repeated, more curious than ever.

"There's somebody else you need to watch out for," he whispered.

"Huh? What are you talking about? Who?" I asked, with a sinking feeling.

"He's an old dude with white hair. I don't know his name, but I met him just before school started this year. I was workin' at the truck stop for the summer, sweeping the parking lots you know, and he just showed up one day and started talkin' to me. He knew who I was and everything about me, it seemed like. He knew I was clumsy and he said he had a way to fix that so I could be strong and fast and maybe even rich someday, if I wanted to be. I laughed at first, till I saw him pick up the back end of a car with one hand. After that I kinda believed him, you know. He said he'd tell me how to do the same thing, if I'd help him," he said.

"Help him what?" I asked.

"Yeah, I wondered about that part myself. You know what they say about things being too good to be true and all that. But he started talking about what happened to my mom and dad when I was little, and he said he knew who did it and he wanted to get payback against them just as much as I did. He said he wanted me to help him steal some rings they had. That's all," he said.

"And so you went along with that?" I guessed.

"Yeah. . . I did. It was hard to turn down, you know. So he showed me where to find that wolf-stone down by the creek and how to use it, and I found out he was right about being strong and fast and all that. It was awesome, Zach. I'd never felt like that in my whole life," he said.

"I see," I said.

"Anyway, I was ready to do my part after that. So he met me at the park one afternoon and gave me a silver ring and told me how to use it, and then he gave me a list of names and addresses where the Doucets lived. He said he wanted me to go down to Natchitoches and turn them all to dust and collect it in little bottles for him. He said he'd wake them up later, he just wanted them out of the way until he got all the rings," he said.

"Wait. Did that ring he gave you have a name on it anywhere? Maybe on the inside of the band?" I asked.

"Yeah, it said Angela Doucet," he answered.

"So you're not the one who burned down Angie Doucet's house and stole her ring?" I asked.

"No, I didn't know anything about that till later," he said.

"All right. Go on," I said grimly.

"There's not much more to tell. I went to that place in Natchitoches where he told me to go, and I got in the house with a key he gave me so I wouldn't wake anybody up. There was an alarm system, but he gave me the code to turn that off, too. So I slipped in there and put the people to sleep in their beds without even waking them up, and picked their rings up off the floor where they fell. They never knew what happened," he said.

"And then?" I asked.

"Well. . . he said there were three people in that house, and the other one turned out to be Jolie. So I went to her room to put her down, too, like he told me to," he said, and then hesitated.

"So why didn't you, then?" I asked, curious.

"I don't know. She was lying there on her bed, and the moon was shining in the window, and she was so pretty I just couldn't do it," he said, turning a little red. I couldn't decide whether to laugh or cry at that, but I didn't do either.

"Yeah, I guess she is," I said at last.

"Anyway, I turned on the light and she woke up, and I think she was confused for a second about who I was. But I showed her my ring and told her if she ever wanted to see her family again, she'd come along quietly. She didn't try to fight me after that. Just asked me to turn my back so she could get dressed. I didn't trust her, so I left the bedroom door open and stood right outside instead and told her she had five minutes," he said.

"And she didn't try anything?" I asked, finding it hard to believe. I couldn't understand why she hadn't gone for her ring while she had the chance.

Unless she was afraid she wouldn't be able to reach it in time before he nailed her with *his* ring. That was possible; she would have known he was a *loup-garou* when she saw his hands, and she would have known he'd be much faster and stronger than her. He would have had a clear view of that spot where she hid her ring, too, if he was standing in the hall with the bedroom door wide open. So maybe she decided go along with him at the time and wait for a better chance later. That sounded like her.

But she also would have known that a *loup-garou* wearing one of the rings was an incredibly dangerous enemy, and she might never *get* a good chance to escape. So the last words she might ever get to say, she used them to tell me she loved me on the back of that picture, knowing I might never even read them. I'd be a liar if I tried to say that didn't touch my heart.

I didn't forget about the folder on Pod 391 that I found in the storeroom earlier, but people don't usually waste their last words on somebody they don't care anything about. But if she really cared about me, then why didn't she tell me about my family and what did all those dates mean on my information sheet? I was hopelessly confused again about what she really felt and thought.

"So she just went along with it, after that?" I finally asked.

"Yeah, sort of. She wouldn't tell me where her ring was, though, and that aggravated me. I couldn't look for it with her standing right there, so I tied her up so she couldn't get away, and then I brought her here and locked her in the bedroom downstairs, where I was sure she couldn't get out," he said.

"What did you think you were going to do with her?" I asked.

"I don't know, Zach. I wasn't really thinking that far ahead," he shrugged.

"So what happened next?" I asked.

"Well, I set the place on fire like I was supposed to, and then I went back down to Natchitoches a few days later and got the other three. That was easy, too. The lady opened the door and I got her before she even had a chance to say a word to me. The old guy was watching TV and didn't hear me when I walked up behind him, and the boy was asleep upstairs. So I collected the dust and the rings and went back home," he explained.

"You didn't burn that place?" I asked.

"No, I was supposed to leave that one alone," he said.

"And then?" I asked.

"Well. . . somehow or other Jolie must have got hold of her ring from somewhere, because I opened the door to bring her some breakfast and that's the last thing I remember," he said.

There were a lot of things I wanted to ask Jake right then, but the one thing that interested me the most was who that shadowy old man was who started the whole thing. I already had a sneaky suspicion, but I couldn't be sure unless I found out more.

"Do you know anything about that old guy that might help me figure out who he is? Anything at all?" I asked.

"I don't know, Zach. Maybe. He was short and thin and he had a funny accent, and he always wore gloves and big horn-rimmed glasses that made him look like a frog," he said.

That clinched it. There was only one person who fit that description and who might have known all the things he told Jake, and that was Marc Doucet.

It was almost impossible for me to believe it at first; Marc was supposed to be a werewolf hunter, wasn't he? He was the last person on earth I would have suspected of spreading the curse and betraying his own family that way.

But there it is. What else could I think, after what I'd just heard? He must have become a *loup-garou* himself at some point; he wouldn't have been able to pick up a car bare-handed otherwise. That's probably why he wore those gloves all the time, too; to hide his claws.

Maybe he'd been alone over there in Clermont for too long, studying the Beast and thinking about him all the time, until finally he'd started to envy him instead of hating everything he stood for. It happens that way sometimes, you know; the things people hate the most can often end up being the very things they fall in love with, strange as that sounds. No wonder Marc didn't want me to find a way to get rid of Mont Mouchet.

The more I thought about it, the better it all fit together. Marc was in a perfect position to wipe out all his most serious enemies before they even realized it, and then he could have his own pod *and* all six rings. Who would dare to fight him, after that? He'd be just like the Beast himself; the most powerful *loup-garou* in the whole world.   And if I hadn't decided to wake up Jake, he might even have gotten away with it.

In fact, he still might. Jolie was still over there in Clermont with him, not suspecting a thing, and he could do anything to her if he took a notion. There are lots of ways to get rid of people other than turning them to dust. I was terrified he might do just that.

Although maybe not, when I got to thinking about it. Jake had thrown a pretty big monkey wrench into the plan by not putting Jolie to sleep when he was supposed to, and that had given her a chance to escape and take the rings back and lock them up in Sarah Doucet's safe.

I remembered Jolie telling me that only the ring-holders knew the combination to that safe, so that meant right now she was the only one who could open it. All the others were asleep. Marc might decide it was better to wait a while and let her open it for him instead of having to crack it, as long as he was sure she didn't suspect anything. Sarah Doucet undoubtedly had the best safe that money could buy, and cracking it might be tough.

That made me feel a little better when I thought about it, but still, she was in an awfully dangerous situation. So was I, for that matter, and so was Jake and his family.

"You know, it might be best if y'all went away for a while, at least till things calm down. I think I know who that old man is, and he might come after you if he finds out you're awake again. *Especially* if he figures out you told me all this," I warned him.

"I know, and I think maybe the old guys out there are planning something like that, anyway. Things will take some getting used to for all of us since Mom and Dad are back now, and getting away might be a good way to work on that. Do you have any idea how weird it is to have parents who are barely older than I am?" he said.

"Yeah, I guess it *would* seem strange," I admitted.

"But seriously, thank you, Zach. I won't forget what you did, and if you ever need me for anything, I'm here," he said, and shook my hand.

I said good-bye to the Goldens and went home not long after that. I was anxious to get there and wake up Cameron since I knew how to do it now. I couldn't wait to tell him everything that happened.

As soon as I got home, I gathered up some of his clothes and took them out to the barn, and then mixed his dust with the last bit of sweet water in the bottle.

It wasn't long before his body appeared on the ground, and I bled my blood out onto his chest. It seemed to take more this time than it did with Jason, and I was light-headed by the time I saw Cam's eyes open.

Maybe I was just imagining the light-headedness, or maybe it's because I don't like the sight of blood, but in any case all was well. Cameron slipped into his clothes and I helped him to his feet.

"What happened?" he groaned.

So I explained everything while we walked back to the house, and if he was surprised he didn't act like it. He just took it all in and didn't say much. By the time we reached the kitchen door he was pretty much carrying his own weight and didn't need my help anymore.

"So Jake was the Boggy Creek Monster, huh?" he asked, with a hint of his old goofball smile.

"Yeah, it seems that way," I said.

"Well, you caught the monster and rescued the princess. What's next on the list?" he asked. I couldn't tell if he was teasing or serious.

"Yeah, well. The princess has a habit of getting herself into trouble, so she's not rescued yet," I said moodily. I expected Cam to have something snappy to say about that too, but for once he didn't seem inclined to comment.

"Sounds like you've got a full plate, bro," he finally said.

"Don't I always?" I asked with a laugh.

"True 'nuff. Well, we see how much help I've been so far, but you know if you need me, I'm here," he said.

"Yeah, I know. I love you, bubba," I told him. I don't say that very often, but sometimes it needs to be said.

"Yeah, I love you too, bro," he said.

There was a pause, and we didn't say anything else about all that.

"So seriously though, what's next?" he finally asked.

"I don't know, Cam. I need to find a way to break the curse on Mont Mouchet. That's the only way this whole thing will ever end for good. I know there has to be a way, because the Beast of Gévaudan wiped out all the other places. I just don't know how to find out what he did," I said.

"Have you thought about asking him?" he suggested.

"Are you crazy? That was two hundred years ago and more. How would I ask him?" I pointed out.

"Well. . . what happened to him? Is he there in the Doucets' storeroom?" he asked.

"No, he was killed by somebody with a silver bullet," I said.

"Really? Who was it? If you can't talk to the Beast, then somebody who knew him is the next best thing," he said.

"Um. . . hold on a second. I don't remember," I said. I went to the computer and looked it up real quick, and since I already knew where to look for it the search didn't take very long.

"Looks like it was a man named Jean Chastel, on June 19, 1767," I said.

"Well you can't talk to *him,* I don't guess," Cam said, pointing out the obvious.

"You think not?" I asked dryly.

"No, probably not. But you might could talk to some of his family, if you could find any of them. Or maybe he wrote a book about what happened," he pointed out.

That wasn't such a bad idea, truthfully, but there was something about that name that niggled my mind, like I'd heard it somewhere before. I just couldn't quite put my finger on when or where.

"I think I've heard that name before, somewhere," I said out loud.

"Can't remember where?" Cam asked.

"No, can't say that I do. But I know I have," I said.

I tried to think back over all the stuff Marc told me while I was in Clermont. It was a good bet he might have said something about Jean Chastel, since he'd talked about the Beast so much. But try as I might, I couldn't remember. Marc had said so *many* things, and they were all a jumble in my mind. And then too, I had to wonder now whether any of what he said might have been lies meant to mislead me. Sometimes I wonder why life has to be so complicated.

"Maybe he was some relative of Jolie," Cameron suggested.

"Possibly," I agreed, and I was struck with a vague memory of reading something like that, somewhere. I looked at that old family tree file that I scooped off Angie's burnt-up hard drive to see if I could find him, and sure enough, there he was. Jean Chastel, the first name in the list, killer of the great Beast of Gévaudan. It was one of his daughters who married Michel Doucet and took up the werewolf hunting business. Simple enough, when you knew where to look.

But there was something else, too. Angie had stuck an attachment to the file at that place, and when I tried to open it I couldn't get anything but the first few lines and then nothing but gibberish laced with a few words or sentences here and there.

It was apparently the story of how he killed the Beast, pasted whole from some other document. I skimmed through the little bit I could read, and the only interesting thing I found was that it mentioned star sapphires in one place. I would have given a lot to be able to read the rest of that paragraph, but it was hopeless.

The only thing it told me was that Jean Chastel had something to do with those rings the Doucets used, and that wasn't much. I knew he hadn't used them himself, because he shot the Beast with a silver bullet. If he'd had a ring, he wouldn't have needed anything like that.

It crossed my mind that there might be *one* place where I could find out everything I needed to know, if I could find a way to get in there, and that was in John Doucet's library in Natchitoches. If there were secrets to be found anywhere, that's where they'd be.

I didn't look forward to going back down there again. I'd been back and forth to Natchitoches so many times I was beginning to feel like I could drive that road blindfolded with one hand tied behind my back.

But there was nothing else for it, so I went to the living room and told Justin what I had in mind.

"How will you get in past the alarm system?" he asked immediately.

"That's one thing I wanted to ask you about. I don't know," I admitted.

"And you thought I would?" he asked.

"I don't know. It was worth asking," I shrugged.

"I'm a geobiologist, Zach. I know about rock formations and the environmental conditions around oil well pads. I don't do electronics," he reminded me.

"They don't use alarm systems at the oil company?" I asked.

"Well, yeah, but I don't work on them, Zach. I just use them," he said.

"So you don't know anything about them at all?" I asked.

"I know the one we use at the lab works by making an electrical connection when the door or the window or whatever is shut, and then if it opens it breaks the circuit and sets off the alarm. I think most of them work that way, more or less," he said.

"So if I don't go in through a door or a window, it shouldn't set off the alarm, right?" I asked.

"Maybe not, but how else would you get in? You can't just bust a hole in the wall," he pointed out.

"No, but I'll figure somethin' out," I said.

After that I put it all out of my mind, and me and Cam did something normal for a change. We made popcorn and watched a movie. All four of us seemed to have a tacit agreement not to talk about anything having to do with wolves, at least for one night.

We just watched the show, and for a while it seemed like old times. Nobody said anything about Cameron biting the dust, so to speak. Least of all him.

But I know it was on their minds, because Justin and Eileen both kissed him twice before he went to bed, and that was sorta unusual nowadays.

After we were lying down on our beds, I couldn't resist asking him a question.

"Cam, what was it like?" I asked.

"What do you mean?" he asked.

"I mean when you were. . . you know. Dust," I said.

"I don't remember anything about it, Zach. I remember talking to Jake that afternoon and him offering me a ride home, so I got in the truck with him and we talked about Jolie for a while. I remember crossing the interstate, and after that the next thing I knew I was waking up on the floor of the barn. Nothing in between," he said.

"So it didn't hurt or anything?" I asked.

"Nope. I felt kinda bad for a few minutes when I woke up, but that's all. Don't think I'd want to do it again, though," he said thoughtfully. There was a long silence after that, and I thought he'd gone to sleep.

"Zach?" he asked.

"Yeah?" I answered.

"What do we do about Mama, and your family, and all those other people?" he asked.

"I wish I knew, Cam," I said heavily.

I'd been thinking a lot about that very thing, but the more I thought about it, the more I realized it was a lot more complicated than just waking them up.

For one thing, they'd all be penniless. If the Doucets followed their usual pattern, then as soon as they turned the pod members to dust, they immediately looted anything and everything they wanted or could use and then burned the rest. If I woke up Mama or Daddy or Janell or any of the others right now, they'd have nothing. No home to go to, no car to drive, no money, no job, not even clothes on their backs. And who would believe them, if they tried to get any of it back? Wolves are not generally the type of people to have close friends they could call on, either; they had too many secrets to keep.

So what could we do with them? Let them sleep in Justin's barn? Send them to a homeless shelter? Drop them off at the deer camp in Caddo Gap, if it was even still there? None of those choices seemed like very good ones.

And it wasn't just them, either. However hard it might be for them to get things back together after a six month nap, it could probably still be done. But what about the people who'd been asleep in the dust for decades or even centuries? How would somebody who fell asleep in 1798 ever adjust to the world as it was today? That was a lot to think about, you know.

And then there was the fact that some of them were dangerous and wicked people who might hurt somebody if we turned them loose, and I had no way of knowing which ones were which. Those files in the storeroom were awfully spotty. They gave a lot of information about some of the pods, and for others there was almost nothing except the bare bones of who, when, and where. I didn't dare just guess.

What to do with the sleepers was turning out to be almost as tough a problem as how to deal with the curse on Mont Mouchet.

We left town early the next morning, hopefully so we'd have more time to work before the dark caught us. It was my second Saturday in a row of not going to see Miss Edith, and I reminded myself to call her later and let her know what was up.

I racked my brain all the way down there for some way to get around that dadgummed alarm system. Justin was right about not being able to bust a hole in the wall, but surely there was some other way.

There was no need to dress up or climb the wall this time; we just went down the alley and used the wooden gate at the back of the garden. The little stick I'd put in there yesterday to hold it open was still in place.

Getting inside the garden was the easy part, though. After that we had to figure out how to break into the house without getting ourselves hauled off to jail.

I thought about shutting off the power at the outside breaker box, but then I decided not to. The alarm system surely had batteries or some kind of backup power to handle anything *that* simple. So how could we get in, if we didn't dare touch a door or a window? What other way was there?

I looked at the house with a critical eye, but it was Cameron who came up with the best idea.

"What about that?" he asked, nudging me and pointing at the chimney.

"Are you nuts?" I asked, but after I looked at it a little closer I reconsidered. I remembered the fireplace in the dining room, and it was a monster. That chimney was huge, too, and it was possible we could fit down through it if we were careful.

Maybe.

"Let's go look and see," I finally said.

Chapter Ten

We found a ladder in the gardener's shed, and then gingerly climbed up to the roof. I don't like heights, and roofs are worse than most places because you know all the time if you lose your footing you're probably going to roll all the way down the slope and off the edge.

I remembered what it felt like falling off that brick wall into the camellia bush yesterday. I still had scratches from it, in fact. I didn't want to try falling three times that far onto a concrete patio. So you better believe I crawled. Cam didn't seem to mind at all, and he walked over to the chimney like it was nothing. I envied him.

But eventually we both made it, and I cautiously stood up beside him. I could hold on to the edge of the brickwork there and not feel quite so apt to fall.

There was a steel cupola over the top of the chimney, to keep rain out, I guess, and there was a metal grate bolted in place below that; probably to keep out birds and squirrels and such. Both of them were held on with four big rusty bolts. The mouth of the chimney below the grate looked blacker than tar and deeper than a well, and just about as inviting as one, too.

"Aw, this doesn't look too bad," Cam said brightly. I had a different opinion, but I bit my tongue and didn't say anything. If he could handle it then I could too.

"Come on, I know I saw some rope and some tools and stuff in that shed. We'll have to take these bolts off and then we're good to go," he said.

"Yeah, I guess," I agreed grudgingly, thinking about having to cross the roof and climb the ladder again. Cameron looked at me and sort of smiled.

"On second thought, why don't you stay up here and wait for me while I run down and grab that stuff?" he asked.

"Sure," I agreed, not wanting to admit how scared I was. Cam already knew, of course, but he was kind enough not to tease me about it for once.

He was back in just a few minutes with the tools and a can of WD-40, which we sprayed on all the bolts to loosen them up. Then he took a big crescent wrench out of his pocket and adjusted it to the right size, and we got to work.

The first bolt wasn't too hard. It turned pretty smoothly and when it finally came out it was longer and thicker than my finger. We got two more of them out without much trouble, but then we came to the hard one.

Have you ever noticed when you're working with bolts that one of them always has to be a booger to come out? We pulled and sweated and sprayed it with more lubricant and beat on it with the wrench and did everything we could think of, and that danged bolt would *not* come loose. Maybe if we'd had a jackhammer we could have gotten it out, but not with anything less than that.

"This ain't workin', dude," Cam finally sighed, putting the wrench back in his pocket.

"It's only one bolt. Maybe we could swing the grate around and get it open that way, even if it's still attached," I suggested.

So we tried that, and after some of the hardest heaving and shoving and pray-and-try-again I've ever done in my life, we pushed the grate and the cupola far enough around that we could squeeze into the mouth of the chimney.

"Whew," Cam said, breathing hard from all the work.

"Yeah, I know. But come on, time's wastin'. Let's get down there," I said, trying to sound cheerful about it. To be honest, I think I would almost rather have cut off my left hand with a rusty steak knife than crawl down that chimney, but I knew it had to be done.

Cameron tied the big rope in knots about a foot apart all the way down so we'd have something to hold on to while we climbed, and then he tied one end of it to the heavy steel grate. There was no way it was coming loose from that. Finally he tossed the other end down the chimney.

"Better let me go first," he offered.

"All right, then. After you, Santa Claus," I said. He laughed and climbed up onto the edge, then swung his feet around and put them on one of the knots before he grabbed hold of the edge of the grate and carefully slipped inside. He slid down until he had his back against the brick wall and the rope in his hands, and then he headed down. I waited for a minute till he was a body length or two ahead of me, and then I followed him.

I think climbing down that chimney has got to rank right up there as one of the worst experiences of my life. It was dark and stuffy and I felt like I was about to fall the whole time. Even worse, I couldn't tell how far it was to the bottom or what might be down there. Not to mention the soot. It got all over us before we'd gone ten feet, and it kept falling on us and getting in our eyes and noses when we knocked it loose from the walls. I soon learned to keep my mouth shut and not try to talk.

"Uh-oh, that's not good," I heard a muffled voice say from below me. A second later I almost kicked Cam in the head with my shoe. He was standing on something, and I dropped down beside him. It felt like metal below us, and there was barely room for us to stand side by side.

"What is it?" I asked.

"There's a firebox or a fireplace insert or something we're standing on. End of the road, bubba," he said.

"You mean we did all that for *nothing?*" I cried.

"No. . . wait a minute. There are some vents here on both sides. They're not too big but I *think* we could slip through, if we knock the cover loose," he said.

"You *think?*" I asked.

"It's either that or climb back up and try somethin' else," he shrugged.

"Yeah, but what if we get stuck?" I asked.

"Let's not think about that, okay?" he said. Then he balled up a fist and hit something. I heard the vent cover pop loose with a hollow *bong* and then hit the floor outside the chimney.

"There. Now let's see what happens," he said. He wormed his way into the vent, and if he hadn't been such a wiry kid I don't think he could ever have made it through. I know I couldn't have. As it was, it was such a tight fit that I had to give him a hard shove from behind to push him the rest of the way through. I heard him fall into the room and knock over something that clattered and banged on the floor.

"Are you okay?" I asked.

"Yeah, I'm fine. I knocked over the poker and hit my shoulder on the corner of the hearth, but I'm okay," he said.

There was a pause.

"I'm not sure you can make it through there, dude. That was tighter than granny's girdle," he went on.

"No, I wouldn't even try it. I'm surprised you could even do it. But I can't just stay in here, though," I said.

"Well. . . hold on a sec. Let me check somethin'," he said. He disappeared for a minute and I heard him making noises around the fireplace.

"Climb back up the rope a little bit," he said in a muffled voice. I climbed back up about a body length, and not long after that I saw the top of the firebox swing up and open, and Cam's soot-black face appeared.

"Come on down," he said.

"Be right there," I told him.

I climbed back down and Cam moved the logs out of the way so I could squeeze out through the fireplace. It wasn't long after that before we were both standing in the dining room. We were both covered in soot and ashes and filthier than I can ever remember being in my entire life, but we were inside.

"Well, that was fun," Cam said.

"Yeah, it was totally awesome, but let's get to work," I said dryly.

"Don't you think we should wash off some of this soot before we handle anything? It'll get all over the books and the seats and everything else if we don't," he said.

"Yeah, let's wash our hands at least. We can't help the clothes. We'll have to not sit down anywhere," I said.

We took off our shoes and left them on the hearth so we wouldn't track soot everywhere, and then we washed our hands and faces in the kitchen. I was careful to make sure we didn't leave any black stuff in the sink for somebody to notice later, and then we got started on the books. It looked like it might take a while, because the house was full of them. We found three whole rooms on the second floor that were crammed floor-to-ceiling full of bookshelves, not to mention the ones scattered here and there elsewhere.

John Doucet might be the family librarian, but I still think he wasn't worth diddly as an organizer. Those bookshelves sort of reminded me of the way the storeroom was set up, and I wondered if John was the one who handled both places. Maybe he was one of those freaky people who remembers where everything is even though nobody else could find it in a million years.

We came across a lot of interesting stuff. Anything you ever wanted to know and were afraid to ask about werewolves, that would have been the place to go. But we didn't have time to read it all. The best we could do was skim through and hope we found something.

Even so, it was hours and hours later before we came across anything really useful. There was a red leather book in the dining room that told the story of Jean Chastel and the Beast of Gévaudan, written by his daughter Marie in 1769. I think it was a copy and not the original, but I didn't care about that part. I wasn't there to collect rare books; I was there to find out things. Unfortunately, it was written in French and I couldn't understand more than a word here and there.

That frustrated me, but I decided to take the book with me and see if I could find a way to read it later.

It was about to get dark by then, and since we didn't dare turn on any lights, it was time to get out of there.

"Come on, Cam, let's hit the road. It's getting dark, and if there's nothing in this book then we can come back another day if we absolutely have to," I said.

We backtracked everywhere we'd been to check for soot marks and clean up any of them we could find, and Cameron put the vent cover back where it belonged. Then we both climbed back through the fireplace and up the chimney.

We left the lid of the firebox open, just in case we needed to get back in later. It wasn't the kind of thing anybody would notice right away, and if they *did* notice then they'd probably just think somebody left it open by mistake.

I have to say, it was a lot harder climbing back up than it was going down. We had to stop several times to rest, and in fact I don't think I could have made it back up at all with that heavy book if I hadn't found a stash of plastic Wal-Mart bags in the kitchen. I triple-bagged the book to make darned sure it wouldn't poke a hole through the plastic and fall out while I was climbing, and then I slipped the handles around my belt so I didn't have to hold it. It was still cumbersome, and I had to cinch my belt tight to keep the weight from pulling my pants off, but it worked.

At long last we dragged ourselves back out onto the roof, and then we pulled the grate back around as far as we could. We couldn't get it quite far enough to put the bolts back in, but it was close enough that nobody on the ground would have noticed anything different. Then Cam untied the rope and we wearily put away the tools and the ladder.

We were just about to leave the gardener's shed when Cam put out a hand and stopped me.

"What is it?" I asked, and he thumped my chest and made a hushing sound. Then he pointed to the house.

There was a light on in the kitchen.

"Did you leave that light on?" I whispered.

"No, I didn't turn on anything while we were in there. Did you?" he asked.

"No," I said.

Not a second later, we saw the shadow of somebody's head move behind the curtains. Somebody was definitely in the house, and if we'd stayed in there even fifteen minutes longer we would have been caught.

"Let's wait till it's dark outside and then we'll slip out the back gate," I whispered, and Cam nodded.

We lurked in the shed for what seemed like forever. Then, to our horror, the back door opened and we saw Jolie herself walk out onto the patio and sit down in one of the lounge chairs. She didn't look like she meant to leave anytime soon, and we hardly dared breathe for fear she'd hear us. The gardener's shed was barely ten feet from where she sat.

She didn't seem to be doing much besides looking up at the sky, though. I couldn't tell if she was watching the stars or just lost in thought. It looked like she'd just come from taking a shower, because her hair was wet and she was wearing a bath robe.

I couldn't help thinking how beautiful she was and how much I'd love to go sit with her and talk to her right then, soot and grime and all, but I knew I didn't dare do any such thing.

She pulled out her cell phone after a while and punched in somebody's number, and she was close enough that we could hear her side of the conversation just fine.

"Hey, just wanted to let you know I'm back home. Everything's fine. The house is still locked up and nobody's been here. Talk to you soon," she said, and hung up. I guessed she was talking to Marc's voicemail, and I was relieved to find out he wasn't there, too.

She played with her phone a few seconds, and then she opened it up again and started punching in another number.

"Turn your phone off," Cam whispered urgently, and it was none too soon, either. I barely had time to switch it to silent before it started ringing. I knew it was her without even looking.

"Hey, Blue-Eyes. I'm home now. Call me whenever you get the message. Love you," she said. It's kinda strange listening to somebody talk to you when they think you're not there, I have to say.

It was a long time before she went inside after that. I was starting to get hungry and I had a horrible thought that she might hear my stomach growling and come find us. And then what would I say to her?

So I thought desperately about juicy cheeseburgers and pepperoni pizza and every other kind of food I like. That's the best way to keep your stomach from growling, you know. If you think about food then you fool it into believing you're about to eat something, and then it doesn't need to remind you anymore.

Eileen told me that. I didn't believe her the first time I heard it, but I've got to admit that it works.

It doesn't work forever, though, and I knew it was only a matter of time before we'd make some kind of noise. If not a growling stomach, then we'd breathe too loud or accidentally scuff the ground with a foot, or some such thing. You can't be totally silent for very long. Try it sometime if you don't believe me.

But that didn't happen, and eventually she got up and walked inside. We waited a few extra minutes to make sure she wasn't coming back out, and then we saw a light come on upstairs. I guessed she was fixing to go to bed. It probably felt a lot later to her, because of the jet lag. It would have been past midnight already in Clermont.

"Come on, Cam. Let's get out of here," I whispered. I opened the door with infinite care, and then shut it behind us. It was almost pitch dark in the garden by then, and the moon wouldn't be up for another couple of hours. We tip-toed through the darkness, and then the very thing I'd been dreading would happen, happened. I bumped into the steel trash can in the dark, and it tipped over and hit the brick walkway with a horribly loud crash.

We gave up on secrecy and ran for the gate. A light came on downstairs, and just as we slipped out into the alley I caught a glimpse of the back door opening and flooding light across the garden. I prayed Jolie would just think it was a raccoon after food.

Whatever she thought, she was cautious enough not to follow us into the alley at least. We got back to the truck and didn't stop anywhere until we were miles out of town.

"You really know how to play it close to the edge, bubba," Cameron commented.

"Yeah, no doubt. I just hope that stupid book was worth it," I said.

"I hope so, too. I don't know how much more cloak and dagger stuff I can take," he joked.

"Me neither, bubba. Me neither," I agreed.

After church the next day, I was finally able to sit down and relax for the first time in I couldn't remember when. Me and Cam took some chrome polish and spent a couple of hours making the truck all nice and shiny, and for a while it seemed like just an ordinary day.

Jake texted me and said he was gone to Galveston for a couple of weeks with his family so they could sort things out. I was glad to hear it, since it meant Marc wouldn't hear anything.

It started to rain about three o'clock, so I went back inside and opened *Jean Chastel et la Bête du Gévaudan* to page one and started typing it into a website that does automatic translations from French to English. It was tedious and time-consuming, but it went faster than I thought it would. The book was handwritten, and that always takes up more space on paper than print does. It's also harder to read, of course, but whoever copied the book had pretty nice handwriting, actually.

The translation software wasn't all that great, but they say you get what you pay for, and free is about as cheap as you can get. It got the job done; that's about all I can say for it. The final result was full of words it didn't recognize and sentences that didn't make sense and all that. But on the whole, I could read it well enough to get a pretty good idea of what was going on. If any section seemed important enough, I could always work on it a little harder if I needed to.

So, about ten thousand hours later, I managed to read the whole thing. Part of the story I already knew, about Jean Chastel killing the Beast with a silver bullet and all that. But what I didn't know, and what interested me very much, was that after he killed the Beast he and his son-in-law tracked it back to its lair on Mont Mouchet and looted the place before anybody else got there. I guess that was a family tradition that went way back, too.

I probably wouldn't have cared too much about that part, except I found out that's where the six rings came from. They belonged to the Beast. The book said he wore three on each hand and he used them to get rid of any of his pod members who got out of line, as an example to the others.

I wondered at first how they could possibly know all that, but then I read about how Michel Doucet caught one of the Beast's underlings and squeezed the info out of him under threat of torture if he didn't tell everything he knew.

But anyway, when the Beast was killed several of his followers scattered out and went into hiding, so Michel took the rings and swore to finish destroying the rest of them, and that's how *that* got started. I couldn't help thinking he hadn't done too great of a job, if his descendants were still at it two hundred years later.

Then I read something that changed the whole way I looked at the problem. Marie Doucet started talking about the curse and how it worked, and explaining how new pods were formed and all that. More stuff they learned from the squealer they caught, I guess; I'm not sure where else they could have heard it. I already knew most of that stuff, but then she mentioned that as long as any of the sapphires existed, the curse would endure.

I guess Michel knew that too, way back when, and maybe he decided it was necessary for the curse to endure a while longer, till he hunted down all the rest of the werewolves first. Those ones back then were some tough customers, I gathered. The kind who ate people and terrorized whole villages and stuff like that. And probably back then he didn't know for sure if breaking the curse would wipe out all the wolves there were, or just keep there from being any new wolf-stones. And maybe he felt like he needed every tool and every bit of help he could get, at the time.

So maybe he thought he had a good reason for putting off destroying those rings. I don't know that I would have blamed him for thinking that way, if I'd been in his shoes. I might have done the same.

And maybe, as time went on, the Doucets found that they couldn't keep up with all the new pods, and they didn't dare throw away their only weapon. Maybe they kept meaning to do it someday, and then someday just never came. And besides, like I said before, it's hard to lay aside the thing you've fought for and worked at for centuries. It's hard to come to the point where you can say you're finished and move on to something else. It's also hard to turn away from the thing that makes you rich and gives you purpose and holds your family together. That's a lot to give up. Especially when you can always tell yourself that you'll do it someday, when all the pods are gone and there's no more danger.

And then there was the fact that they had some pretty hate-filled and vengeful enemies that might come after them, too, and people don't have to be werewolves to do *that*. The rings were good protection. I could see how so many generations of Doucets might decide it was too risky to give them up.

Or I could be generous and say maybe they didn't even know about it anymore. Maybe none of them had read that book in a hundred years and they'd completely forgotten about all that stuff. It sure didn't look like anybody had opened it recently.

But whatever *their* case might be, I wasn't in that situation. It was my job to break the curse if I could, and that's what I meant to do. When you see something evil then you crush it if you can; you don't sit around wondering whether crushing it might cost too much or turn out to be harder than you thought.

I was fairly sure all the stones and pods would be wiped clean when I broke the curse on Mont Mouchet. But if not, then I still had two hundred bottles of sweet water at Miss Edith's house to destroy their stones with. It might be the work of a lifetime to find them all and wipe them clean, but at least I'd know there would never be any more new ones.

As for the people who were already cursed before I could reach their stones; well, that was between them and God. I knew He wouldn't abandon any of them who wanted to turn away from that choice, and if they didn't want to turn away from it then that was their choice, too.

So the next question was, how did I go about destroying those rings?

It didn't take me much more reading to find the answer to that one, too. The ring itself was nothing; it was just a cradle for the sapphire, to make sure it didn't get lost. The jewels were what held the power, and all I had to do was crush them, and then sprinkle the dust on the summit of Mont Mouchet. That was all.

For a while I couldn't believe it was that easy, and I kept reading to try to find a catch somewhere. But the rest of the book had nothing else to say about it.

I wondered what Jolie would have to say to the idea of crushing her precious family heirlooms like that. I was guessing she wouldn't like the idea very much. But she was the only one who could open that safe, and unless she agreed to help me I was out of luck.

As fate would have it, she called me again that very night, pleased as a pig in a mudbog.

"Hey, Blue-Eyes! What's up?" she asked, in a chirpy, bubbly voice that she only used when she was at her happiest.

"Oh, nothin' much. How's France?" I asked.

"Oh, did you not get my message? I'm back home already. I just got home last night. I tried to call you but all I got was your voicemail. It's all good now, though," she said.

"You mean you're back in Natchitoches?" I asked, pretending I was surprised.

"Yeah, I'm staying at Aunt Sarah's house for a while. Marc got to thinking it wasn't such a good idea to leave the storeroom and everything alone for so long, so we decided I'd come back here just to keep an eye on things. He'll be here in two or three days," she explained.

"Yeah, that makes sense," I said.

"Anyway, that's not important right now. Why don't you come see me?" she asked.

"Just name the place and the time, and I'm there," I said smartly, and she laughed.

"Come pick me up at Aunt Sarah's house at six o'clock tomorrow evening. Do you remember where it is? The address is 337 Hickory," she said.

"I'm sure I'll find it," I promised.

"Well, if you get lost then just call me and I'll meet you somewhere," she said.

"Sure thing," I agreed, putting as much enthusiasm into it as I could manage.

"All right, then, Blue-Eyes. I'll see you tomorrow. Love you bunches," she said.

"Love you too," I said softly. That at least was true, in spite of everything, but I couldn't bring myself to say it very loud.

Cameron noticed my lousy mood when he came in from the barn.

"What's up, bro? Why the long face?" he asked.

"I don't know," I said, and that was such an outrageous lie that he laughed.

"Aw, don't tell me that. You know exactly what it is. You just don't want to tell me," he said.

"Yeah, I guess so," I admitted.

"Well if you change your mind, I'm here," he said. And with that, he laid down on his bed and started reading a book. Cam likes to read true crime novels, which isn't my taste at all, but he never seems to get tired of them. He was reading something about the Green River Killer in Seattle, and seemed totally absorbed.

After a while I decided I really did want to talk to somebody.

"Cam?" I asked.

"Yeah?" he asked absentmindedly, still wrapped up in his reading.

"I've got a problem," I admitted. He dog-eared his book and set it down on his night stand, and got up on one elbow to look at me.

"Yeah, I figured you did. So what is it?" he asked.

"Jolie wants me to come see her tomorrow, and I don't know what to do," I said.

"What's so hard about that? Do you want to go see her or not?" he asked.

"No, it's not that. I want to go see her a lot," I said.

"So what's the problem?" he asked.

So I explained the whole thing to him, about how I wasn't sure if I could get Jolie to go along with crushing the rings and how there was no other way to break the curse. He listened till I was done, and then he asked me a question I wasn't expecting.

"Do you really love her, Zach?" he asked. I hesitated to answer that, knowing Cam like I do, but he seemed dead serious for once.

"Yeah, I think maybe I do," I finally said, in a small voice.

"Yeah, I thought so," he nodded.

"Why are you asking me that?" I asked him.

"Because I don't think it's really the rings that are bothering you so much, bubba," he said.

"They're not?" I asked, raising an eyebrow.

"Nope. If that was all it was, you wouldn't be tearing yourself to pieces inside the way you are. You'd just go and ask her. But that's not your real problem," he said.

"So what's my *real* problem, then?" I asked.

"Your real problem is that you're afraid she's just stringing you along and using you for her own purposes and sooner or later you'll get hurt if you trust her, even though you want to. That's why you don't want to ask her about the rings; if you trusted her then you wouldn't think twice about it," he told me.

I hadn't thought about it quite like that before, but I wasn't quite ready to admit he was right. Not yet.

"Maybe," I shrugged.

"You know I'm right, Zach," he went on.

As I've said before, it's not like Cameron to be so philosophical. I looked at him suspiciously.

"Where'd you read all that?" I asked him, and he laughed.

"Justin told me to tell you that, as soon as you felt like talking about it," he said with a grin. I couldn't decide whether to feel pleased that Justin was paying attention or annoyed because he could read me so well. The psychiatrist strikes again, I thought to myself.

"Y'all are too nosy," I said sourly.

"No we're not, Zach. We just love you, that's all, and you're not too hard to figure out, you know. Justin didn't know exactly what your problem with Jolie was, but he's not stupid, and neither is Eileen, and neither am I. So we sat down and talked about it earlier, and between the three of us we pretty well had it figured out before I even came in here," he said.

"I see," I said, for lack of anything better to say. It's hard to realize you're so transparent.

"So go talk to the girl and see what happens," he told me.

"I'll think about it," I said.

"Good," Cam said cheerfully, and that was all we said about it. He went back to his book on serial killers, and I went back to my brooding.

And you know, after a while I decided they were right. I needed to at least give Jolie the chance to listen to what I had to say, and then hear her out. I made up my mind to have a long heart-to-heart talk with her tomorrow, whatever else happened.

I felt a lot better about things after that, and I went to sleep in a much better mood.

Chapter Eleven

The next day dragged by, like it always does when you're waiting for something. I dropped Cameron off at home after school and made it to Natchitoches right about when I was supposed to.

I'd never had the time or interest to notice it before, but it's really a pretty town she lives in, you know. I don't know what it was like in 1790, but maybe that's why the Doucets had decided to settle there. Maybe it reminded them of home.

Anyway, I pulled up in front of Sarah Doucet's house right at six o'clock and parked right in the no-parking zone, tickets be danged.

Justin had warned me never to expect a girl to be on time, so I was prepared to wait a little while just in case. But surprisingly, she came out right away, and I have to say she looked really nice. She had her hair down and some gloss on her lips and just a bit of perfume that trailed after her.

And you know, for a minute I forgot all about serious conversations and big plans and just wrapped her in my arms and held her. I think I could have stood there on the sidewalk with her for centuries and not gotten tired of it. But she finally laughed and pulled away, still holding both my hands.

"I'm so glad to see you, Blue-Eyes. It seemed like forever," she said.

"Yeah, it did," I agreed, still in that mood where all I wanted was to be near her and drown myself in her eyes. She didn't seem to mind, and for a while we just stood there looking at each other. I'm sure anybody who walked by on the street would have thought we were half-wits, but at the time I didn't care.

"Come on, baby-doll. Let's get out of here," I finally said, and we did.

What can I say about an evening like that? She scooted over and sat next to me in the middle of the truck seat and I put my arm around her while I drove, and we listened to country love songs and sang along with the ones we knew and laughed at the parts we didn't know.

We ate at someplace downtown that I can't even remember, and I was in such a warm glow all evening that I think I could have walked across burning coals in my bare feet and not noticed it.

Then we went mudbogging in an old cornfield down in the bottoms by the Red River just outside of town, and I got the truck so splattered and coated with red clay you couldn't even tell for sure what color the paint was underneath all the mud.

We ended up parked on top of the levee with the tailgate down, just sitting there looking down at the water slipping past. There was an almost-full moon shining down on the far shore, and it left a trail of rippling silver across the river. It was such a perfect moment, it was like something I read in a book somewhere.

"I didn't know you were such a country girl," I told her, and she laughed.

"Yeah, I can be sometimes," she said, and squeezed my hand.

We were quiet for a while, just enjoying each other's company, and she snuggled up next to me.

"I guess you'll have to be headed home pretty soon," she said wistfully.

"Yeah, I guess so. Don't want to, though. I wish I could stay here with you, just like this, forever," I said.

"Yeah, I love you too, Blue-Eyes," she said, and I laughed.

"That's not what I said," I told her.

"Sure it is. There are a thousand ways to say I love you," she said.

I thought about that later, and I guess she's right about that. You can say you love somebody without ever needing to say the words, if they know that's what you mean. I'd just never thought about it that way before.

But at the time, I just felt warm all over and felt like I would have done anything for her if she asked me. I didn't want to spoil the mood, but I knew there was no time left to dawdle, and we needed to have that talk.

"Jolie, there's something I need to tell you," I began.

"What is it, Blue-Eyes?" she asked, turning to look at me.

"I've been doing some reading, and I know about Jean Chastel," I told her. She laughed again.

"Oh, Blue-Eyes, is *that* all? You had me worried for a minute," she said.

"Have you ever read about him?" I asked doggedly.

"Well. . . yeah, some. I know the basic story about him killing the Beast and all that, if that's what you mean. Why do you ask?" she asked.

"Did you know he took those rings y'all use from the Beast's lair?" I asked.

"Yes, I've heard that," she said, and I swore I detected a note of wariness now that hadn't been there before, like she was sizing me up.

"Did you know there's a way to break that curse on Mont Mouchet?" I went on.

"No I didn't. How would you do that?" she asked. She was definitely wary now, and I hated it, but I had to finish telling her.

"You have to crush those sapphires that came from the Beast, and scatter the dust on the mountaintop," I told her.

"And how do you know all this, pray tell?" she asked. That was the question I'd been dreading.

"I read it in Marie Doucet's book she wrote," I told her grimly.

"So it was *you* that broke in the house while I was gone," she accused, sitting up straight.

"Yeah, it was me," I confessed.

"I *knew* somebody had been in there. I can't believe you did that, Zach. Why didn't you just ask me?" she demanded.

"I didn't dare," I said miserably.

"What do you mean, you didn't dare? It was you that broke in the storeroom too, wasn't it?" she asked.

I couldn't figure out how she knew about that, since I'd been so careful not to leave anything out of place when I left. But apparently I'd missed something, and it was no time to lie about it now.

"Yes, that was me too," I admitted.

"Were you afraid to ask me about that, too? How could you do that to me, Zach? You went behind my back and pilfered through my aunt's house with no good reason that you can give me," she said.

"I had a reason," I said softly.

"Care to tell me what it is?" she asked.

"You want the truth?" I asked, looking her right in the eye. I think that unnerved her just a bit, but she didn't back down.

"Yes, I do," she said.

"All right. I went to the storeroom because I thought I found a way to wake up the sleepers without anybody having to die. I wanted to try it first before I said anything to you, just in case it didn't work," I said.

"Go on," she said.

"Well, it worked," I said simply. It took a second for the full impact of that to sink in, and then her mouth fell open.

"It did? You woke up one of the sleepers?" she asked, with wide eyes.

"Yeah, I did. But that's not all," I said. I thought she'd want to know who I woke up and how I did it and all that kind of stuff, but it turned out she wasn't interested in that at all. There was something else on her mind.

"So. . . we could wake up Papa, and Mama, and Aunt Sarah and Matthieu and the others?" she whispered.

"Yeah, we could, but-" I started, but she didn't care what else I had to say.

"Oh, I love you so much, Blue-Eyes. I'm sorry for blowing up at you like that. I should have known you had a good reason for whatever you did," she said, and kissed me before I could stop her. Her anger had vanished like a soap bubble, and her forgiveness was just as complete. I was sorely tempted to let it go at that and just bask in the warmth of her excitement and love, but I knew better. There was something else that had to be said.

"Jolie, calm down. There's more," I told her, and she contained herself.

"What is it, Blue-Eyes?" she asked.

"While I was down there in the storeroom, I found my family," I said, and that silenced her for a minute.

"I'm sorry, Blue-Eyes. I wanted to tell you about that, but Aunt Sarah said I couldn't," she finally said.

"So you *did* know about it," I accused, getting angry myself.

"Yes, I knew. But it was already done even before I met you. There was nothing I could do about it, and Aunt Sarah told me it would only hurt you if I said something," she said.

That was probably true, when it came right down to it, and I cooled off a bit. I couldn't stay mad at her for long, anyway. But I still didn't like it.

"You should have told me anyway. I thought. . ." I said, but she put a finger to my lips.

"I'm pretty sure I know what you thought, Blue-Eyes, but don't say it. You thought you were next on the list, didn't you?" she asked. I couldn't say it, but I nodded.

"All right then. No more secrets between you and me. You *would* have been next on the list, if you'd still been at home with your parents, or even if you hadn't broken those stones like you did. But Aunt Sarah found out all about you while she was collecting all the others in that pod, and she decided you and Cameron were special, and she left y'all alone because you gave it up and fought so hard against it. That's the *only* reason you and Cam are not both sitting in a bottle in the storeroom right now. But she wanted to be sure, and she wanted to know how you did it, and that's why she sent me to watch both of you for a while and get to know you, if I could. She thought since we were all the same age I might stand a better chance of getting one of you to talk, and I was already up there in Texarkana with Angie all the time anyway. But then there was that whole thing with Jake Golden and the Fouke pod that blew up in our faces like it did. Nobody saw that coming, and so you got dragged into all this in a way nobody ever meant to happen. So. . . here we are," she explained.

"I see," I said, not able to think of any other reply to all that until I chewed on it for a while.

"Aunt Sarah really likes you, though," Jolie went on.

"You could have fooled me," I snorted, remembering how unfriendly she'd seemed when I talked to her.

"Oh, she can be starchy and old-fashioned sometimes, but you can't let that pull the wool over your eyes. She's a sweet lady when you get to know her. She was the one who wanted to offer you the job as a werewolf hunter," she said.

"Really?" I asked, finding it hard to believe.

"Yeah, really. You have to be strong and fast and you've got to have sharp eyes and ears and quick wits to do this job. It's too dangerous not to. You're an all-star baseball player and a pretty brilliant thinker, so you seemed like a good choice," she explained. I didn't know how to answer that, so I let it be.

"There's one other thing you need to know, Jolie," I told her, changing the subject.

"Ah, more deep dark secrets. I don't know if my heart can take any more," she said, with mock seriousness.

"Jake wasn't alone," I said.

"Well, I know his grandparents were helping him, but-" she began, and then trailed off when she saw my face.

"I'm not talking about them. I'm talking about somebody a lot more important than they are," I said grimly.

"Then who? If you know something, tell me," she said.

"It was your uncle Marc. *He* was the one who wanted to get rid of all the werewolf hunters and keep the rings for himself. He's the one who taught Jake how to become a *loup-garou* and told him where you and the others lived and how to get to everybody. He's the one who burned down Angie's house and took her ring and gave it to Jake and told him how to use it. He's a traitor, Jolie," I said.

Jolie looked utterly shocked speechless, but I have to give her credit; she didn't fall to pieces. It took her a minute to compose herself, but when she did she was dry and matter-of-fact.

"How do you know all this?" she asked first.

"Jake told me himself. I woke him up," I said.

"I see. And you don't think he might have been lying?" she asked.

"No, I don't think so. And besides that, he knew too much. He knew how to make the ring work by wishing it. He had a key to y'all's house and the access code for the security system. He knew where everybody lived. He couldn't have guessed all that just from watching Angie put his parents to sleep when he was a little kid, Jolie. Somebody had to tell him, and the only people who would know those things are your family. You and Marc are the only ones left, and I know *you* didn't do it. It had to be Marc; there's no other explanation," I said.

She thought about all that for a long time, and pulled her legs up under her to hold her knees, the way she did when I saw her sitting on the bed in Jake's basement.

"I hear what you're saying, and I know you're probably right. I just can't believe it," she finally said.

"Believe it," I told her earnestly.

"But why would he betray us like that? What was there for him to gain?" she said.

"I think he's a *loup-garou* himself, Jolie. I think he has been for a long time, and that's why he moved to France, to be away from everybody who might find him out. I think he wants to be like the Beast, and rule all the wolves in the world. He'd have to have the rings for that," I said.

"That's crazy," she said.

"No it's not. Don't you remember how he always wore gloves? I bet he did that so we couldn't see his fingernails," I said. I could see in her face that it was starting to sink in.

"When did you figure all this out?" she asked.

"Not till after I talked to Jake and thought about it a while, and after I read the book I found in your Aunt Sarah's house," I admitted.

"All right. So the next question is, why didn't you tell me sooner?" she asked.

"I was afraid he might do something to you, if he thought you knew anything. I didn't dare breathe a word of it to you while you were still in France with him," I said.

She sighed.

"I guess you have a point. It's just hard, you know," she said.

"Yeah, I know," I agreed.

"The only thing I can't understand is, why did Jake not put me to sleep when he had the chance, if that's what he was supposed to do?" she wondered.

"Uh. . . he said you were so pretty he couldn't bring himself to do it," I told her. She looked at me for a second like she couldn't believe I was serious, and then she burst out laughing.

"No way," she finally said.

"Yeah, that's what he said. He was right, too," I told her, and she laughed a little bit again.

"Well, I'm flattered. . . I guess," she said. She leaned over against my chest again, and I put my arms around her, and for a little while we didn't say anything else. It was quiet except for the lapping of the water against the bank, and the rattle of the breeze in dead leaves.

"Do you know why I kissed you that day at the fair?" she asked suddenly.

"Wasn't it to make sure nobody noticed what you told me?" I said.

"Well. . . that, too. But not mostly," she said.

"Then why was it?" I asked.

"Just because I wanted to, that's all," she said, and I laughed a little.

"Really?" I asked.

"Yeah, really. I'd been watching you since March, you know; it was my job to find out all about you. I used to come to your baseball games and watch you play, and I read your website, and I followed you out to Red Lick and saw you mowing the grass for that old lady, I listened to some of your conversations. Things like that. You never knew I was there, but I liked you, Zach. I just didn't want you to know it yet, so I had to think of some other excuse to kiss you," she admitted.

That explained a lot, I thought to myself.

"I'm glad you did," I said, and held her a little tighter.

"That's why I said I loved you on the back of that picture when Jake caught me. I wanted to say the words, just once at least, and I didn't know if I'd ever get another chance," she murmured.

There was another long pause after that, but silence is not always a bad thing, you know. Sometimes it's just warm and sweet and makes you feel close to someone. This silence was like that.

"What should we do now, Blue-Eyes?" she finally asked. I was kinda surprised she asked *me* that queston, but maybe she didn't know where else to turn anymore. Her whole family was asleep in the dust, and the only one left was a thrice-proved traitor. She was pretty much alone now, except for me.

"I want to go break the curse on Mont Mouchet," I told her.

"Yeah, I thought you might say that," she said sadly.

"Isn't that what you want too? Isn't that what the Hope is all about, to break the Curse forever and set the sleepers free?" I asked. She didn't answer the question directly; just offered one back.

"You know how much you're asking from me, don't you?" she asked.

"Yeah, I do. But you see what nearly happened with Jake and Marc. When you play with fire you always get burned sooner or later. It worked out all right this time, but if I hadn't been here. . ." I shrugged.

"That's true, but if we do this and it doesn't wipe out all the pods, then it'll be awfully hard for me to explain why I did it after we wake up the others," she said.

"I know. But I think it will; Marc told me every pod in the world nowadays can be traced back to Mont Mouchet. That must mean when the Beast destroyed the other places that it wiped out all the pods and stones that came from them, right? And wouldn't it be worth it, if it *did* wipe out all of them?" I asked softly. I desperately wanted her to say yes, but I knew it was no sure thing.

"But what if it doesn't? What if it leaves all the pods and their stones still out there, including Marc? We can't know for sure that it won't. They could still do a lot of damage, and we'd be helpless against them," she pointed out.

"No, we're not. I have a way to wipe out those stones, if any of them are left. I've got two hundred bottles of sweet water locked up at home. It might take a long time, but we could do it that way if we had to," I told her.

"You mean the holy water you told me about in the car that day, that you and Cameron used to wipe out the Trewick pod?" she asked.

"Yes. I didn't know there was any left, but there is," I said.

She played with the ring on her finger for a few seconds, and I could guess some of the thoughts that were going through her mind. But not all of them, apparently, because what she finally said was not what I expected.

"If I do this, will you promise me something, Zach?" she finally asked.

"What is it?" I asked.

"Promise me you'll keep your word, and break all those stones if they still have any power. Then I could show everybody that it was worth it, and I wasn't a fool for trusting you," she said.

"I promise," I said.

"And promise me one other thing," she went on.

"What's that?" I asked.

"Promise me that no matter what happens, you'll let me come with you and help you until it's done," she asked. That was a little bit more personal kind of thing than the other one, but it was a promise I was glad to make.

"I promise that, too," I said, and she smiled.

"Then let's do it," she said.

For a second, I was dumbfounded that she actually agreed. The safest and most reasonable thing for her to have said right then would have been no. Even I know that much. We could have woken up her family, given them their rings back, they could have dealt with Marc, and then things could have gone right back to the way they'd always been before. No sweat and no loss.

Instead, I was asking her to risk everything for a wild scheme that might not even work, and I honestly don't know what I would have said if I'd been in her shoes. Like she told me, it was an awful lot to ask.

In fact, I'm almost sure it wasn't anything I said to her that convinced her to do it. I think she did it mostly because she loved me, you know. Girls are like that sometimes. They have this wonderful ability to have faith in people they love, in spite of all the logic and reasons in the world. Justin told me that when I was too young to understand what he was talking about, but that night on the levee with Jolie was the first time I really saw what he meant.

I didn't tell Jolie all that, of course. When somebody makes a huge sacrifice for your sake, you don't go picking apart why they did it. That's rude and ungrateful. The only thing you can say is thank you.

So that's exactly what I did.

"Thanks, Jolie," I said, and she laughed.

"No problem, Zach," she said.

After that, we drove back to her Aunt Sarah's house from the levee. We went inside for a few minutes so she could grab some clothes and some extra cash and the other rings from the safe. It would be better if Marc didn't know where they were.

It was late when we got back to Texarkana, and Justin and Eileen and Cameron were long since in bed. I was so sleepy my eyes were starting to blur, but I didn't want to wait any longer.

We went out to the barn where my work table was, and Jolie took off her ring and gave it to me without a word. I don't think she could bear to watch while I crushed them, because she waited outside while I went to do it.

I pulled out one of the rings to look at it one last time. The sapphire shone like a star in the deep blue evening sky, and I could well believe that I'd never seen any jewel more beautiful.

They say a star sapphire is good luck to the one who wears it, even after he doesn't have it anymore. Even if he sells it or loses it or gives it away, it still brings him luck just because he had it for a little while. Maybe even if he crushes it and scatters the dust on a mountaintop in France.

Maybe that's true. Or maybe the Beast of Gévaudan just had a superstitious streak a mile wide. I'm not sure which.

I put the ring on my finger, just for luck, and to see what it felt like. It was Matthieu's, I think, because it was the only one that fit me.

"The last werewolf hunter," I said to myself, and laughed a little. It was kinda true, in a way; I was the last person who'd ever wear one of the rings.

I took out the others, and they were all just as perfect as the first one. Something about me hates to destroy beautiful things, you know. But nevertheless, I grabbed a screwdriver and broke the settings, and took the gems out of the rings so they were just loose stones. The rings themselves I put back in my pocket, just in case Jolie might want them. They were only ordinary pieces of silver now, nothing special about them, but I figured she might be sentimental about them.

There's a vise bolted onto the corner of my workbench for holding things, and that's what I meant to use to crush the jewels. Buster was chewing hay and pricked his ears up when I rattled the vise.

"Well, old boy, it's been a long day, hasn't it?" I asked him, and he neighed at me in a way that seemed to mean he agreed. You probably think I'm loony for talking to a horse, but sometimes it helps, when you can't talk to anybody else.

Cameron's bottle was still sitting out there on the table, empty, and I decided that was as good a place as any to store the dust. So I put one of the jewels in the vise and held it there with my fingers until it was just tight enough to stay in place by itself. Then I held the bottle right underneath it and started turning the handle.

It was surprisingly easy. First the stone cracked, then it shattered, and finally it pulverized. I was careful to catch all of it in the bottle, and then I unscrewed the vise and swept the leftovers in there too. I didn't want to miss a single particle of it. I shook the bottle to make the bigger pieces come to the top, just in case, and there were none bigger than a pinhead, if even that. Good enough. Then I crushed another stone, and another, and another.

Jolie's was the last one, and I hesitated and almost didn't have the courage to finish. Once it was gone, Marc would have a huge advantage over us, and we both knew it. But on the other hand, we'd also be sure that none of the rings would ever fall into his hands, no matter what happened to us.

I slid the last stone into the vise and quickly crushed it before I had a chance to change my mind. Finally there was nothing left, except some bluish-white powder in a plastic spice bottle.

Just like that.

When I was done, I came out and handed the powder to Jolie, and she turned it over a few times and watched it slide around inside the bottle.

"Well, that's that," she said, and handed it back to me. I slipped it in my pocket and zipped it up, and we said no more about it.

It was much too late to think of taking her anywhere else for the night, so she slept on the couch in the living room. Justin and Eileen and Cam would no doubt be surprised to see her there in the morning, but they'd almost surely be up and long gone before either one of us even woke up.

I was so tired I slept almost till noon the next day, and I woke up feeling heavy and bleary-eyed and just generally not so great, just like I did the last time I stayed up all night. Like I said before, I am *not* a night owl by any stretch of the imagination.

Jolie was already up and moving around, fresh as a squirrel and bright-eyed as a cat. She'd already had time to shower and change her clothes and put on make-up and all that stuff, and when I walked into the kitchen I found her cooking breakfast. Scrambled eggs with bacon and cathead biscuits, in fact.

I was mildly astonished. Anybody who can stay awake till three a.m. and still get up in the morning with that much energy to burn has got to be a robot; there's just no other possible explanation. I wanted to go pinch her and see if she had metal skin.

"I didn't know you were up," I said, lamely.

"Oh, yeah. I've been awake for a couple hours. You were sleeping like a baby and I didn't want to wake you, but I had nothing better to do so I decided to make breakfast. Sit down and have some with me," she said.

I went to the bathroom sink and washed my face so I'd look halfway presentable, and then I came back to the kitchen and had breakfast with her. It was nice, actually. We talked and ate and I was pretty impressed with her biscuits, as a matter of fact. They were the home-made kind that you make from flour and bacon grease and whatever else goes in there. I'd seen Eileen make them before but I hadn't paid enough attention to remember the whole recipe.

We washed the dishes when we were done so Eileen wouldn't have to do it later, and then I took Jolie out to the barn to meet Buster. Horseback riding was one thing she'd never done before, so I put his saddle on and took her for a ride around the lake. She sat behind me and laced her fingers together across my stomach to hold on, and I don't think Buster minded the extra weight too much. He's pretty strong.

We decided there was no benefit in waiting any longer to head back to France, so Jolie booked a flight for us that very evening. She had to pay almost double to get the one she wanted, but she didn't gripe about it.

We decided to take Cameron with us this time, too. Jolie felt naked and weak without her ring, and the more people we had with us the safer we felt. Like I said before, he already had a passport from that Jamaica thing he did last summer, so there was no need to bother with that.

"It's pretty here," Jolie told me while we were on the trail by the lake.

"Yeah, I like it. I still miss the mountains sometimes, though," I said.

"Do you?" she asked.

"Yeah, but it's not that far to go when I get to missing them too much. Me and Cam drive up to Beaver's Bend or Albert Pike and spend the weekend sometimes. Justin and Eileen have a cabin up there on the Roaring Fork River, and they like to go whitewater rafting and stuff like that once in a while. Sometimes we climb up on the ridge tops and shove boulders off just to watch them crush trees on the way down," I said, laughing a little.

"Sounds like fun," she said.

"Yeah, well, I guess everybody has a destructive streak somewhere inside," I said.

"So what else do you do for fun?" she asked.

"Aw, I don't know. Sometimes we go ride horses at Eileen's parents' place in Magnolia; they have four hundred acres out there to roam around on. Sometimes we go shoot bottles or hang out at the mall or work on the truck or go fishing off the dock by the lake, or just whatever we feel like doing," I said.

"I used to do beauty pageants sometimes, and my dad took me trout fishing in Colorado once in a while. I caught a real whopper one time; it was so big it took two of us to lift it. But here lately it seems like I don't have much time for that stuff anymore. Always working," she said regretfully.

"Justin always tells us you should never be too busy to stop and enjoy things, cause you only live once and you better make it count," I said, remembering how many times he'd told me that very thing. She laughed and hugged me a little bit.

"He sounds like a wise man," she said.

"Yeah. . . I guess he is," I agreed.

"He reminds me of you in a lot of ways," she commented, and I remember thinking that was the nicest thing anybody ever said to me.

Chapter Twelve

Cameron pulled into the yard not long after that, and we were ready. I'd already called him at school and told him what was up, so he was ready to go too. I think Justin was more worried about the whole adventure than he was willing to admit, but he didn't tell us not to go.

There isn't much to tell about the rest of the trip to France. Second time was old hat, you know. Besides that, I was too worried about Marc Doucet and what he might be doing to pay much attention to the scenery. I had no idea whether he knew what we were up to or not, or what he might try to do about it if he did know. Jolie hadn't heard from him since that night in the flower garden. That may not seem like very long, but I've learned that an awful lot can change in a *very* short period of time.

We got to Clermont a little after noon, if I remember right, and after a bit of hassle, Jolie was able to buy a cheap car. Sometimes it amazed me all over again, the way she threw money around.

I worried the whole time we were there; Marc knew too many people and had too many ways of hearing things in that town. He might even drive by and see us, and then what could we say to him?

It was a lot colder in France than it was in Texas, that's for sure, and we soon found out that the heater in the car didn't work. We had to sit bundled up in our jackets, shivering the whole way.

It had snowed sometime recently, and that didn't help matters, either. The highways were not too bad, but when we finally got to the foot of Mont Mouchet, things changed for the worse. The road that led up to the summit was covered in ice and snow, and it was pretty steep and curvy in places, too.

Jolie has a lot of wonderful traits, but she's also a Louisiana girl and therefore a winter driver she certainly is *not*. I thought my fingernails would end up permanently attached to the dashboard from gripping the vinyl so tight.

She crept along at less than ten miles an hour, but even so, every once in a while I could feel the tires sliding across the ice, and my heart came right up into my throat. It was a long way down in some places, if we slid off the road. Cameron was sitting in the back and couldn't see as well as I could; I envied him.

We were less than a mile from the summit when we ran into trouble.

"Hey, there's a car behind us," Cam said, and I looked back. I couldn't see much because the back glass was too foggy, but I knew we hadn't seen a soul on the road since we left Clermont.

"Uh-oh. I think that's Marc's car," Jolie said, glancing at it in the rearview mirror.

I rolled down my window so I could stick my head out, in spite of the cold, and I saw that Jolie was right. The other car was a black Jeep 4x4, just like the one Marc drove, and it was gradually creeping closer and closer to us. Nobody drives that fast on icy roads unless they're crazy or they have a darned good reason, not even with four wheel drive.

Marc must have found out what was up, somehow. I don't know who told him or how he figured it out, but I knew that's who it was behind us. Nobody else would have been out on the mountain that day, especially not driving like that. Jolie didn't dare go any faster, so there was nothing to do except wait and see what happened.

The Jeep got closer and closer, and before long it was so close I could almost have reached out and touched it.

Marc put on a sudden burst of speed and crashed against our back bumper. The car fishtailed on the ice and Jolie had to fight the wheel to get control of it again. She did, just barely, but it wasn't even a minute later when the Jeep smashed into us again. This time the car hit a patch of ice and slid crazily across the road. We hit a wooden guardrail and punched right through it, and for a second I thought we were goners. I could hear Jolie screaming beside me, or maybe it was me and I just didn't notice.

The car slid down a steep slope into a ravine and hit a pine tree with a bone-jarring crash. I hit my head against the window hard enough to shatter the glass, and everything went black.

It must have knocked me out for a second, because I woke up feeling dazed and sick at my stomach, but aside from some blood in my mouth from a split lip and a nasty bruise on my head, I seemed to be all right.

Jolie was stunned, too; I guess from hitting her head against the steering wheel, but I could see her breathing. Cameron was groaning in the back seat, and I tried to turn around to see what was wrong with him. I couldn't do it because of my seat belt, and when I fumbled for the latch I couldn't get it to open. I finally gave up.

"Cam, are you all right?" I called to him instead.

"Zach, remind me never to go anywhere with you ever again," he groaned. I quit worrying about him after that; if Cam still had his sense of humor then he couldn't be too bad off.

Jolie was still knocked out, but she was beginning to come around. I shook her, and she made a garbled sound I couldn't understand and lifted her head up.

My mind was beginning to clear by then, and I realized we couldn't stay there in the car. Marc wouldn't be content with just running us off the road. He'd show up soon to see if we survived or not, and then we'd be in serious trouble. It might take a little while for him to find a way down to the bottom of the ravine, but we needed to be long gone from there before that happened.

"Cam, Jolie, come on. We've got to get out of here, *now*," I said.

They didn't ask me why, so they must have been clear-headed enough by then to remember the need.

Getting out took a little more doing than I thought at first, though. I had to cut my seatbelt apart with Cam's pocketknife before I could get loose, and besides that, the car was almost completely buried in snow. It was so deep we couldn't get any of the doors open, and we had to crawl through my smashed window instead.

When we finally got out, draggled and soaking wet from melted snow, we had to think what to do.

I ached all over my body, and I was freezing cold and more tired than I can ever remember being, and I was sure the others felt just the same or worse. But we couldn't give up yet.

"Come on, guys; it's less than a mile to the summit," I told them.

"Yeah, with a nutcase chasing us the whole way," Cam muttered.

"That's one good reason why we've got to get away from this car," I reminded him.

"We can't take the roads; that's the first place he'll look after he finds out we're not here," Jolie said. My heart sank when she said that, but I couldn't argue with her.

Struggling to climb a mountain through waist-deep snow right after coming through a car wreck didn't sound like my idea of fun, to say the least. But there didn't seem to be a whole lot of choice, so we pulled ourselves together and got moving before we got caught.

There was a little creek at the bottom of the ravine which flowed down from somewhere higher on the mountain, so we followed that upstream since we didn't dare climb back up to the road. It was the right direction, and at the very least it would hide our tracks a bit.

After thirty minutes or so we'd made it considerably higher up, and Jolie suddenly stopped me with a hand on my arm.

"Look!" she hissed, pointing back to where the car lay buried far below us. Somebody was moving around down there, checking inside the car and probably trying to figure out which way we went.

"That's Marc; I know it is. He wears a jacket just like that," she whispered.

We started climbing again with redoubled energy, in spite of the ice and the cold. If Marc was really a *loup-garou* then he could probably follow us faster than we could run away, as soon as he spotted us. We had to get as big of a lead as we could before that happened.

It wasn't easy. We slipped and fell more than once, and Jolie tore her knee open fairly badly on a sharp rock. But she refused to limp in spite of the pain, and we kept going.

Not long after that I heard a faint cry from down below, and then a shot rang out. He must have seen us!

We quickly ducked out of sight behind a snow bank, but we all knew we couldn't stay there very long.

I've only ever been shot at one other time in my life, and that was back when me and Cameron destroyed the wolf-stone in my parent's apple orchard in Tennessee. I don't think I've ever been so scared in my life as I was then, and being pinned down by rifle shots in that freezing cold ravine on Mont Mouchet brought back every bit of the terror I felt that other time. Bullets are not something you ever get used to, believe me.

"We can't stay here, Zach. He'll follow us up the ravine and catch us if we don't move," Jolie said. She seemed fairly cool about the whole thing, but then again she'd probably been in a lot more bloody fights than I ever had. She was used to it.

"The road is right above us. If we get up there then we can make pretty good time while he still has to climb out of the ravine," Cameron suggested. It sounded like a good idea, but Jolie shook her head.

"No, we don't dare. We'd be in open view the whole time, and even though it's not far he'd still have plenty of time to pick us off before we could reach the road. We've got to stay under cover," she said.

"What about that?" I said, pointing about forty feet away. Another little creek came down through a culvert under the road to join the ravine we were climbing, and it looked big enough for us to climb through, if we squeezed a little. There were enough trees and snow that I was pretty sure we could make it there without showing ourselves, with a bit of luck.

"We don't know where it goes, Zach. We could get trapped in there with no way out," Jolie pointed out.

"Do you have a better idea?" I asked.

"Well, no, I guess I don't, if you put it that way. All right, let's risk it. Come on," she said.

We picked our way quickly through the snow to the lip of the culvert, where a trickle of water was flowing out. The opening wasn't more than two feet high, and it was dark as coal inside there. But we had no choice, so I crawled into the echoing tunnel first, followed by Cameron, and finally Jolie.

I hated it. It wasn't quite as bad as climbing down the chimney in Natchitoches, but it was almost as bad. It was nearly pitch black, and we had to crawl on our hands and knees through ice cold water, never knowing if there might be a drop off or a wild animal right in front of our noses.

I don't know how long we shuffled our way through the dark. I know it seemed like forever. After a long time, I started to notice gray light filtering in from somewhere outside, and eventually I glimpsed the other end of the culvert.

"Thank you, Jesus," I muttered under my breath.

After that, it wasn't long before we all climbed out on the other side of the tunnel. The little stream came down from somewhere up above, and it looked like there wasn't much more mountain left. We had to be almost at the summit. It had started snowing again at some point while we were underground, and the air was full of swirling flakes.

"Do you think we're close enough to the top to scatter the dust?" Cameron asked, shivering, and as much as I would have liked to say yes, I had to shake my head.

"I don't know, but we can't risk it. We've only got one shot at this thing, and we better make it count. It's not that much farther to the top," I said.

There didn't seem to be anybody following us, and the road was only about thirty feet above our heads.

"Come on, let's try to make it up to the road," I said, and for a little while we went back to struggling uphill over icy rocks and sliding snow.

We crawled out onto the pavement like a trio of waterlogged rats, and then hightailed it up the last lap toward the summit. I hoped the snow would keep Marc from tracking us, at least till we could get the job done.

As soon as we came out on top the east wind caught us, strong enough to freeze us half to death in our wet clothes.

The sun was nearly setting by then, and by some strange fluke it had dropped below the edge of the clouds in the west, flooding the mountain with dim reddish light. It was beautiful, in a lonesome kind of way.

We didn't have time to appreciate the view, though. Before I could even grab the bottle from my pants pocket, I heard the sharp click of a rifle behind us. We all three froze.

"Stop right there, all of you. Keep your hands up and turn around slowly," I heard someone say. It sounded like Marc, but I couldn't have said for sure. He must have guessed where we were headed and gone directly to the summit to wait for us while we were crawling through the pipe.

We all three turned around slowly, and sure enough, there he was, with a smile on his face and a twinkle in his eye that only comes from excellent good humor.

"Jolie, *ma chére,* how wonderful to see you again!" he said heartily, "and Zach, and Cameron I believe it is. Well met, my friends."

"We're not your friends," I said scornfully, but he only laughed.

"That's such a pity. I could use a few good lieutenants," he said with mock sadness, shaking his head.

"It'll never happen, Marc," I told him.

"No, probably not, but there are no shortage of others who'd be glad to fill the position," he said.

"How could you do this, Marc?" Jolie said, and I could almost swear she had tears in her eyes. Maybe it was just from the icy wind whipping against our faces, or maybe it was because she truly couldn't understand. Marc might have winced at the question, just a little, or maybe not. I couldn't say for sure. But he didn't answer it, either way.

"Enough talk. Which one of you has the rings? Give them to me, and I'll let you go. Cause me problems, and I can pick them out of your pockets after you're dead just as easily," he snarled.

He doesn't know we already crushed them, I thought to myself, and swallowed hard. There was no way we could give him those rings even if we wanted to, and that meant he was about to kill all three of us, if I didn't think of something fast.

I started to wonder if that was really how it all ended, there on a freezing cold mountaintop thousands of miles from home. No one would ever find us, and even if they did, they'd never know who we were. Marc couldn't have picked a better spot, if he wanted to get away with killing somebody.

Sometimes you find yourself in a position where the only thing you can do is to spend your life as dearly as you can, you know. I started to wonder if there was any way I could save Jolie or Cameron, or at least break the curse, even if it meant I never made it home myself.

You think about things like that, when you're staring at the mouth of a gun. It tends to remind you that life is short.

Justin told me once that there are only three questions a man ever needs to ask: What is the nature of God, what things are worth living for, and what things are worth dying for. And the answer to all three of those questions is the same: only love.

Well then. If love was worth dying for, then maybe I could live with dying, so to speak. If I broke the curse for love of God, and if it gave my girl and my brother a chance to live, then wouldn't it be worth the very real possibility that Marc might shoot me when he saw what I was doing?

I had only a few seconds to decide if I really believed all that, and I prayed under my breath for God to give me courage. Then I took a deep breath before I could change my mind.

"I have them," I said loudly, and Jolie and Cameron both turned to look at me with wide eyes. Maybe they thought I'd flipped my lid, but I knew exactly what I was doing. If I could only get Marc to let me stick my hand in my pocket for just a second.

"I thought you'd come around and see things my way. Give them to me. Now," he ordered.

I slowly reached my hand into my pants pocket, and he watched me closely. The lid was already loose on the bottle, and I quickly finished twirling it off with my two front fingers. Then I pulled out the bottle, hiding it inside my fist so Marc couldn't see what it was.

"All right. Here they are," I said, and held out my hand. Marc smiled and lowered his rifle just a bit as he started walking toward me, and I knew the time had come.

I thought about all kinds of things at that moment. I thought about what a long and winding road it had been to lead me to that place. I thought about Justin and Eileen and Miss Edith, and hoped they'd be proud of me if they could see me right then.

I thought about Jason and Charla and Jake and wondered if what I was about to do would really set them free or not.

I wondered about all those people sleeping the years away in that storeroom in Natchitoches, and if anyone would ever wake them up.

I thought about the Doucets, and what they might do with their lives if there were no more werewolves to hunt.

I wondered about Cameron, and if he'd finally have the kind of happy normal life he always wanted.

I wondered about me and Jolie, and how that would have worked out.

I wondered if I was finally done with this curse-breaking work that God wanted me to do.

I wondered what was really going to happen when I tossed that dust in the air.

Most of all, I wondered if Marc was about to shoot me when he saw what I'd done. If he did, I hoped it would give Jolie and Cameron enough time to get away.

But there was no use in waiting any longer. With a swift flick, I threw the dust up into the air with my blessing.

The wind caught it instantly, and it blew away in a glittering shower where the setting sun touched it. Marc seemed frozen in horror for a split second; that's a look which is easy to spot on somebody's face.

It didn't last long, but it was long enough for Jolie. Without a word, she moved faster than I would ever have believed possible and tackled him from the side.

Me and Cameron hit the ground as a spray of bullets filled the air, but they were wild shots that came from the rifle when it hit the ground and skittered across the bare stone. Marc must have dropped it when Jolie tackled him. Neither of us got hit, and the gun vanished into a crevice.

Jolie and Marc were fighting like cats and dogs, and in spite of the wreck and the cold and the climb, she was getting some hard licks in. I'd always known she was strong, but I'd never realized she could fight like a bar room brawler.

But Marc was also getting in a few hits, and he wasn't pulling any punches because she was a girl, either. She had a bloody nose and he'd torn out a handful of her hair, too. In fact he was quickly getting the best of her, in spite of everything. If he hadn't been a *loup-garou* he might not have been so strong and tough, but even a *loup-garou* is not Superman, and when me and Cam piled on top of him too, it turned into a fairly even match.

Still, it was all we could do to hold the old bird down. He smacked me hard on the side of my head with his fist, on the same side where I busted out the car window earlier, and it hurt so much I saw stars and wanted to throw up. I was beginning to be afraid he might actually beat all three of us down.

Just then the sun winked down below the horizon, and Marc seemed to have a sudden convulsion. He thrashed and kicked and foam mixed with blood flew from his mouth. He was too strong even for all three of us to hold him down at that point, and we backed off to let him alone. It went on for a good five minutes before he was still.

"What's wrong with *him?*" I whispered.

"I don't know," Jolie said. Her nose was still bleeding, and she wiped it clean with the sleeve of her jacket. After a while, when he didn't move, she cautiously went up to check on him.

"He's still breathing," she said, after feeling his chest.

There was a pause, and if any of us had had the sense of a golf ball, we would have left that place faster than a cat could lick its tail. But we didn't, for some reason. We just stood there looking at each other, like we couldn't quite believe it was over. That Arctic blast of wind soon reminded us not to linger, though.

"All right, we're done here. Let's go," I finally said, and we started back down the road. Marc's Jeep was parked somewhere down there, and that was our only hope unless we all wanted to freeze to death on that mountaintop. Me and Cam took turns carrying Marc on our backs, and if he'd been much heavier I'm not sure we could have done it.

Jolie didn't have a lot to say, and I guess it was an emotional moment for her just as much as it was for me, even if it was for different reasons.

We walked for almost a mile before we found the Jeep. Marc had parked not far above the place where he ran us off the road, and the only good thing about the situation was that it was downhill all the way. The wind slacked off a little after we dropped below the summit, but it never stopped completely, and my feet and hands were so cold they burned and hurt.

All three of us were hurting from the fight, too. Cam had a black eye and I was pretty sure I had a couple of loose teeth, aside from Jolie's bloody nose and torn hair. We all had scratches and bruises in more places than we could count.

As soon as we got to the Jeep we heaved Marc into the back seat as best we could, and then Cameron drove us back down the mountain. He didn't scare me nearly as bad as Jolie did on the way up, but maybe I was just too tired to pay attention and too sore to care by then. I think anybody's driving would have been scary in a place like that.

We stopped in Clermont just long enough to leave Marc at the hospital and call Madame Louise to come stay with him. They wanted to ask a lot of questions about what happened and who we were and all the usual things, but Jolie just said we'd found him in the woods and she didn't know him. Maybe in a way it was even true. You can think you know someone, and then find out you never really knew them at all.

The folks at the hospital weren't really satisfied, but it was enough of an explanation to let us get out of there. We hit the road running and didn't stop again until we got to Paris. Unlike that old junker we bought earlier, the Jeep had an excellent heater, and we were grateful for that. I don't think I've ever been so cold in my entire life.

For a steep fee, we were able to get a flight to Houston that same night, and Jolie paid it without so much as a quibble. We were all exhausted and ready to be home.

I wondered what would happen to Marc and if he'd be okay. He was an old man, and he might not survive an ordeal like that. Of course, I barely knew him and I guess it mattered more to Jolie on a personal level than it did to me or Cameron, but I couldn't help wondering.

My phone has no service in Europe, so when we landed in Houston early the next morning I wasn't surprised that I had fifty thousand text messages and a dozen missed calls waiting on me as soon as we entered the terminal.

I was too busy to read them until we were on our way out to the parking lot, and that's when I saw that I had three messages from Jake. They were all identical, and they were all sent yesterday. And all they said was:

"My claws are gone!"

I suppressed the surge of hope and excitement that immediately swept over me when I read that, and I calmed myself enough to call him.

He answered on the third ring, and I soon found out it was the same with Jason and Charla. Their claws had disappeared, too.

Jake said he felt a shock run through his whole body while he was eating lunch, so strong that he stumbled and almost fell, and after we accounted for the time difference, we figured out that it happened at almost exactly the same time Marc had his convulsion, or whatever it was; just as the sun was going down on Mont Mouchet. Jake hadn't noticed his fingernails for an hour or so after it happened, but when he did, he knew instantly what it meant.

The curse was broken.

* * * * * * *

And it was broken completely, too. Over the next few weeks me and Jolie and Cameron tracked down several active pods from the files in Natchitoches, and all of them were cured. All we had to do was check their fingernails and we knew without even asking.

We also checked at least a dozen wolf-stones in different places, and all the ones we looked at were just plain old rock. When we broke Mont Mouchet, we broke everything, just like I'd hoped and prayed we would.

Oh, not everything was peaches and gravy, to be sure. We still had a storeroom full of sleeping people we had no idea what to do with, and we still had to deal with her family, and mine.

We woke up the Doucets first, and even though I can't say they were exactly *pleased* with what we did, they accepted the fact that it had been Jolie's decision to make. They were horrified when they heard about what Marc had done, and I think that went a long way toward making them accept things.

Marc survived the convulsion he had on Mont Mouchet that night, although last I heard he wasn't in very good health. The rest of his family won't even speak to him anymore, but I guess he has Madame Louise to take care of him. Maybe he'll have time to ponder his actions and repent of them someday, but that's between him and God.

We also woke up my family, and that was hard on a lot of different levels. They knew I didn't have to do it, and they know they owe me big time for that. But they also know the curse is broken everywhere and for always, and I guess they probably still blame me for that. They didn't have any choice but to talk to me when they first woke up, and even though I can't say things are exactly *good* between us, we do talk now and then. . . a little bit.

They had nothing left in Tennessee anymore after Sarah Doucet got done with them, so they ended up moving back to Texas to start over, to Sulphur Springs, in fact, where Daddy grew up. It's not so far that I can't go and visit sometimes, if we ever get to that point. For now, they've thawed out enough to be civil and even talk on the phone once in a while. I have to be careful what I talk about, but I'm hoping time will make it better. Lola never had any reason to hate me in the first place, so it's usually her I talk to anyway. Mama even broke down and started talking to Justin again, if you can believe that.

I've never asked which one of them shot at us that day, because I'd really rather not know. None of them have even dropped so much as a hint about wanting me to come back to live with them or anything like that, but to tell the truth I'd just as soon stay where I am. It's better that way. All that stuff may sound like little baby steps, but I'm hopeful.

And then there's that, of course. Justin and Eileen's baby was born just before Christmas, and life has been different around here since he came along. They named him Josiah, after one of the righteous kings of Judah in the Bible, but we usually call him Joey.

At first I sorta thought having their very own kid might change the way Justin and Eileen thought about me and Cam, but I don't think it has. They love us both just the same as they always did, and that's a big relief.

Jake had a lot of problems at first, getting used to having Jason and Charla back again, but after a while they seemed to work things out. He also lost all his speed and strength when the curse was broken, so he went right back to being clumsy, goofy old Jacob again. I'm not sure he liked that part so well, and besides that he felt guilty for all the bad things he'd done and he almost never smiled.

I tried to talk to him sometimes and be friends with him as much as I could, but it wasn't until Cameron sat down and had a long talk with him one day that he really brightened up. I never did find out what they said to each other, but whatever it was, it worked wonders. After that he and Cam became pretty close friends, much to everybody's surprise. I don't think the guys on the team ever did figure that one out.

Miss Edith passed away in January, about three weeks after her hundredth birthday, and I was surprised to find out that she'd left me her old house in Red Lick. She also left me a letter telling me to be glad for her and to use the gift wisely while I had it. I don't think anybody else would have known what she meant, but I did.

All in all, it was a fairly busy and unsettled time for a while, and I was kept too busy to do much thinking about what it all meant in the bigger scheme of things. You have to chew on things for a while before you really understand what they mean and how they fit together, and that takes time.

In any case, things smoothed out and settled down after a few months, like they always do, and it wasn't until spring that I started to figure out some things.

Epilogue

It's hard to know what to say, here at the end of all things. I feel like my whole life has been wrapped up in werewolves and curses, and now that the curse is really and truly broken, I'm not quite sure what to do with myself anymore. When you put so much of your life and who you are into something, it's hard to let it go and find another purpose.

Justin says I'll find it someday if I look for it, and I'm sure he's right. But in the meantime, I think I'd kinda just like to be a kid for a while, you know. I almost can't remember what that feels like anymore.

He also told me I needed to set aside some time to simply be, to praise God in silence like the rocks and the trees and the clouds in the sky do, so that you get closer to Him and see with His eyes. If you spend all your life running hard, then you never have time to grow. Maybe so.

It sounded like good advice, and in spite of how busy my life has been these past few months, I've tried to spend at least a little time every day just be-ing. I sit down on the dock and toss pebbles in the water to watch the ripples wash the shore, and sometimes I go down there to see the full moon rise in a blaze of liquid silver.

It's very beautiful, you know. . . the moon. I never used to notice that before; I guess because it always reminded me of everything I was afraid of. But not anymore.

Sometimes Cam is with me, sometimes Justin or Jolie or Eileen or even Josiah, but as often as not I'm alone with God and my thoughts.

I haven't decided yet what to do with that cellar full of sweet water in Red Lick, if there's any left after waking the sleepers. I remember what Miss Edith told me about keeping it safe and using it wisely, and I'm trying to do that. I know I can't heal all the hurts of the world, but I hope I can make a pretty deep dent in them.

Me and Jolie are as close as two people can be, and every weekend I'm either down in Natchitoches or she's in Texarkana. She's the most amazing person I ever met. Some people would sit back and relax for a while, after they just fulfilled the deepest Hope of their family and broke a curse that was centuries old, but not her. She's already looking forward to even bigger and better things, if you can believe that. She has this great and wonderful faith, you see, and when I'm with her I can almost have it too. She makes me a better person than I could ever be without her, and I love her for that.

I've thought a lot about what Marc said, about how pity isn't worthwhile and just leads to greater suffering. At the time I didn't argue with him, but I've decided he was wrong about that. If Angie hadn't had pity on Jake, then Marc would have had to find somebody else to do his dirty work, and then the chances were a thousand to one that I could have ever figured out what happened to Jolie. Probably no one but Jake would have left her awake, nor given her the time to leave that Boggy Creek picture on the dresser as a clue. Yet because of that one little thing, in the fullness of time, the whole curse unraveled.

I don't know all that for *sure,* of course, since nobody ever knows what *might* have happened. But I'm willing to lay pretty good odds on it.

I think a lot about that whole episode up there on Mont Mouchet, too. I know I was closer to death than I've ever been before, and when something like that happens, it tends to make you look back on your life in a whole new light. I'm grateful for the time I've been given, and I don't think I'll take it for granted ever again.

I can remember when I was a scared little twelve-year-old, running from the dark for reasons I didn't even completely understand at the time, and sometimes I can hardly believe the way things have turned out for me.

Back then, I thought it was foolish to cry for the moon, to long for the impossible, to wish for things that can't be so. But God often has a different idea of what's possible than I do, and like Justin has told me so often, He never plants dreams to no purpose. All of mine have come true, in ways I never would have imagined just a few years ago.

But that doesn't surprise me anymore, you know. God is love, even to the lost, and to know Him at all is to know this. I hope that because of everything I've gone through, I've learned to be a little more like Him, to see with His eyes, to feel with His heart, and to carry inside me just a bit more of that Light more golden than day.

No other wish is worth having, and no other gift is more precious.

Blessed be He.

The End

Truesilver
The Last Werewolf Hunter, Book Four

With the Lord one day is as a thousand years,
And a thousand years as one day.
-2 Peter 3:8

Chapter One

I thought we were done with curses and wolves. I'd had more than enough spookiness like that to satisfy me for a lifetime.

It was the first of summer, right after we got out of school, and the long days stretched ahead of us full of freedom and promise. Me and Cam had a job baling hay and building fences for old man Barling on his cattle ranch, and we were playing Dixie League baseball with a good chance of making it to the world series later in the year if all went well. In other words, I had nothing to look forward to except good times and a fun break.

Or so I thought.

When Jolie asked us to come down to Natchitoches to help wake up all those sleeping people in the store room, it didn't seem like such a big deal at first. Just an extra pair of hands in case somebody woke up rowdy, you know. I was cool with that.

So we drove down there early one Friday afternoon to get started on the project, and the house was quiet when we got there. John and Sarah Doucet were out of town for the weekend, on a mini-trip to Cancun from what I heard. Lifestyles of the rich and famous.

The store room was just as dusty and dank as I remembered, with the same old shelves of bottles filled with dust, and the same rough wooden table under an incongruously fancy chandelier. It was me and Cameron, Jolie, and her cousin Matthieu. He's nineteen years old and sort of reminds me of a street thug, honestly. He's got the dark brown hair and eyes that Cajuns often have, with a sparse little goatee and some serious muscle. Definitely not the kind of dude you'd want to meet in a dark alley late at night, even though I'm sure he'd laugh if I ever told him that. He's really one of the nicest people you'd ever want to know; he just doesn't look like it.

"So, what do y'all think? Who's first?" Matthieu said out loud, rubbing his hands together while we all stood and stared at the dusty bottles.

"Just grab one, Zach," Jolie finally told me, since I was the one standing closest to the shelf. I shrugged and picked a bottle at random; there was really no way to be scientific about it. One bottle was as good as another.

"What about this one?" I asked. It looked just like all the others, and all it said on the label was *Joan Rusk, December 23, 1864.*

"All right. Hold on a sec, and I'll see if I can find her. Then we'll decide if she's a good pick," Matthieu said. He went to the big metal cabinet against the back wall and started thumbing through files till he found the one we needed.

"Um. . . here it is. Joan Rusk. Two-member pod, operated out of Titus County, Texas, from 1863 to 1864. Nailed that one pretty fast, didn't we?" he remarked, reading from the file.

"Only two members?" I asked.

"Yeah, that's a little bit unusual, isn't it? But it looks like the ringleader was a young one; only seventeen years old when we caught her," he said.

"Still just a kid, then," I said.

"Apparently," he shrugged, still looking at the file.

"So what's it say? Is she good to go or not?" Jolie asked after a while.

"Hmm. . . could be. There's not much in here about her. The case worker didn't seem to have much trouble catching her, or the sister either. Not very rich. In fact it looks like she didn't own anything but a horse and the clothes on her back. Doesn't say if she attacked people or animals or what. Let's see if there's anything about the sister," he said, riffling through the pages.

"Okay, the sister's name is Annabelle; sixteen years old. Looks like she was never a wolf, though. Just got caught up in the crossfire, apparently," he said.

"So we've got her, too?" I asked.

"Supposed to. Can you grab them off the shelf, Zach? Might as well get them both done at the same time," he said. I looked, but I saw neither hide nor hair of a bottle with Annabelle Rusk on it.

"Well, dang it, she's not here," I said after a minute of searching the bottles.

"She probably got misplaced, that's all. I'm sure she's there," he said.

"So does that mean we go ahead and wake up this one anyway, or should we find a different one?" Cam asked.

"Oh, I guess she'll do. Let's go ahead," Matthieu said.

He emptied the bottle into a green ceramic ashtray on the table and then poured a little bit of sweet water on top of it. He stirred up the muddy mixture with a pencil, and then it didn't take long before the old girl was laid out on the table, seemingly not much worse for the wear.

Jolie dressed her while the rest of us turned away; we hadn't known what size clothes she might need, so we'd done the best we could with some stretchy sweat pants and an extra large t-shirt. It wasn't the prettiest outfit in the world by a long shot, but we could always find her some better clothes later on.

"Okay, guys, she's decent," Jolie said from behind us, and we turned around. Cameron whistled, and I might have done the same thing if Jolie hadn't been standing right there. But it's kind of tasteless (not to mention dangerous) to do things like that in front of your girlfriend, so I bit my tongue and kept quiet.

"She's pretty," Cam said, pointing out the obvious. And so she was, in an old-fashioned kind of way. What I mean is, she looked like she'd never cut her hair a single day in her life, or plucked her eyebrows, or shaved her legs, or done any of those things girls nowadays like to do so they'll look nice. She had the kind of tan you get from spending a lot of time outside, but not the kind you get from tanning beds or laying in the sun on purpose. She had some faint freckles across the bridge of her nose and her brown hair was flecked with gold here and there. She was also short; probably no more than five feet tall at the most. But nevertheless, she was nice looking.

"Yeah, I guess she's okay," Jolie agreed, brushing it aside. Cam pricked his thumb and smeared some blood on the girl's forehead, and that seemed to be enough. After a few seconds she breathed deeply and opened her eyes, which were green as spring leaves.

"Joan?" he asked, and she moaned.

"Where am I?" she finally replied. Not surprising; that's almost always the first thing you want to know when you wake up in a strange place.

"You're in Louisiana. There's been some trouble but we're here to help you," he told her.

"Who are you? What happened?" she asked, rubbing her eyes and looking around. I don't think there was anything in the cave that would have looked too outlandish to her 1864 eyes, but then again I'm not a trained historian, either. Evidently there wasn't, because she didn't say anything.

"My name's Cameron, and these are my friends. I'm afraid it'll take a little while to explain what happened and how you got here, but just bear with us for a few minutes and we'll tell you everything," he promised.

Joan didn't say much to that, and I noticed her eyes roving the room again. There was an old letter-opener lying on top of the file cabinet at the back of the room, and as soon as I saw her gaze fix on it, I knew there was about to be trouble.

"Hey, she- " I started, but that was all I had time to say before the girl leaped off the table and snatched up that letter opener faster than you would think anybody could possibly move, especially somebody who just woke up from the dust sleep. I'd seen what *that* did to people, and I was amazed she could get up on her feet that fast. She was one tough cookie.

"Nobody come any closer!" she yelled, brandishing the letter opener like it was a dagger. Nobody moved an inch; somehow none of us doubted she was really good with a knife.

She was breathing hard and didn't look like she felt very well, but she wasn't letting that get in her way. She started edging her way towards the door, and we realized she meant to run if she could.

"Listen, Joan, you don't know what it's like out there. Things have changed. It's not like what you think it is. Please, let us help you," Jolie said.

"I'll help myself, thanks. Y'all just stay back," she said.

"Look, we don't mean you any harm, and we won't keep you from leaving if you really want to. But Jolie is right. It's a different world out there than anything you ever saw before, and it's dangerous, too. Go look and see, but then come back and let us help you," Matthieu told her.

"Why should I believe anything you say?" she demanded, jerking the letter-opener at us. She was still inching her way toward the door, and we were carefully backing away from her at the same time.

"You don't have to take our word for it. Go see for yourself that we're telling the truth, and remember we never tried to keep you from leaving. We'll help you if you'll let us," Matthieu repeated.

I thought I saw a flicker of doubt in her green eyes, but then again maybe not. However that might be, she made a sudden dash for the door and yanked it open, and then she was gone before any of us could say another word.

"Come on!" Matthieu yelled, and we all ran outside after her. What she thought about the flower garden I don't know, but it didn't take the girl five heartbeats to find the back gate and disappear into the alley behind Sarah Doucet's house.

"Great. We've let a lunatic loose on the world," Jolie hissed in frustration.

"Don't worry about it. Let her go," I said.

"We can't do that. She won't know *anything*. She might walk right out in front of a car and get killed," Matthieu said.

"Yeah, I know, but that's the thing. We told her we wouldn't stop her from leaving if she wanted to. So let her leave. Maybe she'll see that we meant what we said and then she might come back and let us help her," I explained.

"She didn't seem too keen on getting help from anybody, much less us," Cam pointed out.

"Yeah, but I bet she'll change her mind, though. Just wait a few minutes, till the first time she sees a car. She'll come back," I said.

"And what if she doesn't? What then?" Matthieu demanded.

"Well, in that case she'll just have to do the best she can. We can't help her if she won't let us. She looks like she's pretty good at taking care of herself when she needs to," I said.

"Yeah, that she does," Matthieu finally agreed with a sigh.

We all went to the patio to wait and see if Joan would come back. We had a pretty good view of the back gate from there, and it was better than going back inside the store room where she might not remember how to find us. After a while, Matthieu and

Jolie went inside to fetch some lemonade and sandwich materials from the kitchen, and me and Cameron stayed out on the patio to watch the gate.

"You really think she'll be back?" he asked in a low voice, and I shrugged.

"No way to tell. I *think* she will, but I guess you never know," I said.

"It's been almost thirty minutes," he pointed out.

"Yeah, but all we can do is wait and see," I said. There was a pause, and then he must have decided it was time to change the subject.

"She was a little spitfire, wasn't she?" he asked, grinning. It hadn't seemed very funny to me at the time, back there in the store room with her holding us off at knife-point (or letter-opener-point), but I guess it's amazing what you can laugh at in hindsight.

"Yeah, I guess she was, at that. But it takes all kinds to make a world, they say," I agreed, smiling a little bit myself.

Matt and Jolie got back with the lemonade and the cold cuts right about then, and for a while all of us were busy fixing our food. It seemed like a normal day, almost. But all of us kept glancing at the back gate while we ate, and whenever anybody tried to start up a conversation it always petered out before long. We ended up eating our sandwiches in silence. We waited most of the afternoon to see if she'd come back, but finally I had to confess that I'd been wrong about her.

"Guess she's not coming back after all," I finally admitted.

"Don't worry about it, Zach. Like you said, she'll just have to handle things on her own. We did the best we could," Matthieu sighed.

"I was so *sure* of it, though," I said.

"So what do we do, write that one off and try again? We've still got four or five hours worth of daylight left," Cameron asked.

"Yeah, let's do that. We can't let one setback stop us," Matthieu agreed, and we adjourned to the store room and got ready to start over.

"Maybe we should pick somebody from not so long ago, this time. They might not freak out quite so much," Jolie suggested.

I was closest to the shelf again this time, so I carefully picked up one of the bottles closest to the end.

"What about this one? Andrew Garza. Not even two years ago," I said, holding up the bottle for them to see. Then I noticed that Jolie had turned ashen-faced.

"What's wrong?" I asked.

"No, Zach. We're never waking *them* up. That's the New Mexico pod," she said, like she expected me to instantly recognize the significance of that. I vaguely remembered her mentioning a particularly bad pod in New Mexico, but she'd never told me any details.

"What's so bad about them?" I asked.

"That was one of the worst pods we ever had to fight. They almost killed Matthieu before we finally nailed them," she said.

"Well. . . yeah, but the Curse is gone, now. It shouldn't matter anymore at this point, should it?" I asked, confused.

"There are a lot of people in the world who don't need a werewolf curse to make them do awful things. For them, that's just icing on the cake," she said.

"What do you mean?" I asked.

"There were four of them, three brothers and a sister, and they used to kill people they caught on the highways out there, all over southern New Mexico and west Texas. It went on for years before we caught them. Andrew Garza was more than just a wolf; he was a sorcerer, too, and even a pretty intelligent scientist, I might add," she said.

She went on to tell us more than I cared to know about the Garza pod. Sometimes there are things that feel like they put a weight on your soul that will never go away however long you live. The stuff the Garzas did was like that, and I'm not going to darken anybody else's heart by repeating what I heard that night. It's enough to say that I understood completely what it was that made her face turn white when I first mentioned them.

Not all the monsters in the world are cursed ones, that's for sure.

Dr. Garza (that was Andrew) apparently had his finger in a lot of different pies. He was a physicist at the White Sands Missile Range and a professor at New Mexico State University in Las Cruces, among other things. His sorcery ran toward the destructive side; fire and lightning and explosions. Not to mention curses and speaking to the dead and some really bad stuff like that. It reminded me of the things Daniel Trewick used to talk about in his journal, only ten times worse. Andrew was no amateur, and the worst thing of all was that he was a necromancer.

That is, he could take dead people and turn them into zombies who would do whatever he told them to. That's one reason he killed all those people, since apparently the bodies had to be fresh and he needed to kill them slowly.

See what I mean about not wanting to know?

I don't think I would ever in a million years have imagined a professional scientist who also practiced magic on the side; the two things seemed like such glaring opposites.

"That's a strange combination to be involved in," I said.

"It might seem like that at first, but not really when you think about it. Dr. Garza was all about power. He'd do anything he had to do to get it. Science, magic, curses. . . all those things were just means to an end, as far as he was concerned," she said.

"Means to what end?" I asked.

"Power to hurt people and get away with it. He enjoyed watching people suffer, Zach, in every possible way you can imagine. All four of them were like that, even though he was the worst. In fact we never *did* catch the sister. If the Garzas got out, I don't know what they might do. Is that enough? Don't ask me any more!" she said.

"All right, then. Why don't you put his bottle in the file cabinet, so nobody grabs it again by mistake," I suggested.

"Good idea. Grab Gabe and Orem, too; that's his brothers," Matthieu said. Those two turned out to be easy to find, and soon they were safely stashed away in the bottom of the file cabinet. Then I picked through the bottles again till I found another recent possibility.

"What about Ashley Dolan?" I asked.

"Hmm. . . I don't remember her. Let me look real quick," Matthieu said, and after a few minutes of rummaging through the files he pulled out another manila folder.

"Okay, here she is. Ashley Dolan, four member pod out of Sarasota, Florida, brought in three years ago. Looks like it was Ashley, her husband Henry, and their two daughters, Daisy and Suzanne. She's a nurse, he's an optician, and the girls are still in high school. Notes only mention hunting cattle. They ought to be all right," he said, scanning over the information.

"Sounds like a dull bunch of wolves, if you ask me," Cameron muttered.

"Yeah, well, dull is good right now," Matthieu reminded him.

I fetched the other three Dolans from the shelf, and set them on the table.

"Do you think we want them knowing about this place? Maybe we should take them somewhere else first, before we wake them up," I suggested. I hadn't thought of that with Joan, but better late than never.

"Nah, I'm not worried about it. Nobody would believe them anyway, even if they said something. Besides that, they've got good reasons to be grateful to us for waking them up," Matthieu said.

"Yeah, I guess," I replied, thinking to myself that gratitude can be an awfully unreliable thing to depend on.

So we woke them up, one at a time, and dressed them and fed them and explained things to them, as best we could. And you know, in that particular case, Matthieu was right. They were too grateful to be alive again to ask too many questions. He bought all of them a plane ticket back to Florida, and then we had to drive them to the airport in Shreveport.

That took several hours, and by the time we saw them off and made it back to Natchitoches, it was way past dark.

"Why don't y'all just stay here tonight? There's no reason to drive all that way back to Texarkana tonight," Matthieu suggested.

"Sure, why not?" Cam said, answering for both of us. We were both supposed to go to work for Jeb Barling the next afternoon, but that still left plenty of time to get back as long as we didn't stay too late in the morning.

So that's what we did. The Doucets had plenty of room in that big house for ten people to spend the night if they'd wanted, but with all of us there and Matthieu's parents out of town it reminded me of an oversized slumber party. We sat on the patio for a while after we got back, I guess still vainly hoping that Joan might show up.

"Well, at least one of them went pretty well," I said.

"Yeah, I guess so. I think the Dolans will be all right, once they settle down. But I think in the future you might have a point about not waking them up in the store room, though. It might be better to take them wherever they live, first, and do it there," Matthieu said, and I nodded.

"We can think about it tomorrow," I told him.

"Which reminds me, I better go lock the store room before everybody goes to bed. Don't want anybody snooping around in there after everybody's asleep," Matthieu said.

"You mean Joan?" I guessed.

"Well, yeah, among others. I don't *think* she'll be back, and even if she does there's probably not much harm she can do, but I'll still feel better with it locked," he explained.

"I wonder where she ended up. She's got a hard life ahead of her, all alone like that," I said. I wasn't especially interested in Joan anymore, honestly; I'm not too fond of people who pull knives on me when I'm trying to help them. Not even beautiful 150 year old girls. But I did feel sorry for her a little bit.

"No telling," Jolie shrugged.

We all walked over to the store room with Matthieu, and it was already pitch black inside the tunnel when we got there.

"Hold on a sec," he said, pulling a mini-flashlight out of his pocket. I was about to say something funny about how he was always prepared for anything, but then he clicked on the light and we all gasped.

The door was standing wide open.

Chapter Two

"This is *not* good," Matthieu said, and I couldn't have agreed more. He might not have locked the door when we left, but I knew darned well he'd shut it.

"Uh. . . you don't think Rob or Celine-" Cameron began, and Matthieu cut him off with a brisk shake of his head.

"I doubt they'd come over here, and even if they did, there's no way they'd leave the door open like that. In fact, they'd probably jump all over me for being careless and leaving it unlocked even while we went to Shreveport. They're real strict about things like that. But come on, let's go see what's up," he said, heading straight for the door.

One thing I have to say about Matthieu; he's fearless. Sometimes a little too much so, for my taste. I grabbed his arm and held him back.

"Hold on a second. Let's grab something to fight with, just in case we need to," I said. There wasn't much to be had, but we all grabbed sharp sticks from the garden. Better than nothing.

Armed with those, we slowly crept closer till we reached the door. Matthieu cautiously flipped the light switch on, and we all sighed with relief when we saw that the room was empty.

"Nothing here," I said, lowering my toad-sticker. Then I noticed an anomaly. We'd left the Dolans's bottles sitting on the table, along with the half-empty jug of sweet water. Now there were *seven* empty bottles, not four, and the water jug was dry as a bone.

My throat went dry, and I swallowed hard before I could speak.

"See that?" I whispered, nudging Matthieu's arm and pointing at the table.

"Come on. Let's find out who they are," he said, surprisingly calmly. I got to the table first and picked up the first bottle I could reach.

"Orem Garza," I said, reading the label aloud. My heart almost stopped in my chest, and even Matthieu's face went pale. He quickly snatched the other two bottles from the table.

"Gabe and Andrew. But *how?*" he hissed, setting the bottles back down. I would have loved an answer to that question, myself.

"Come on, let's go," Matthieu said, almost as soon as he put the bottles down.

"Go where?" I asked.

"Back in the house. It might not be safe out here with *him* loose again," he said.

I didn't say a word while he locked the door and marched straight across the garden to the back door. As soon as we were all inside, he set the alarm system immediately.

"It was Joan; it had to be," Jolie said immediately.

"But that doesn't make any sense. How would *she* know what to do, and why *them?*" I objected.

"Those are some really great questions, Zach. I'd love to find out what the answers are. But in the meantime, I think Jolie is right; who else could it have been? It was nobody in this house, and it wasn't my parents or Aunt Angie or Rob or Celine. Marc is still in France, and nobody else even knows about the store room. It *had* to be her," Matthieu said.

"But *how?*" Cameron asked.

"I bet she came back while we were busy with the Dolans. If she was quiet enough she could have heard us talking in there and figured out what to do," I suggested. It seemed unlikely that she could have been that stealthy, but it was the only idea I could think of that made any sense at all.

"Yeah, but that still doesn't explain the why part. Why would she want to wake up one of the sleepers anyway, much less one of *them?*" Jolie objected.

All I could do was shrug at that; I didn't have a clue.

"That's not important right now. The only thing that matters is that they're loose, and if she's the one that woke them up then it won't be long before she's a dead girl. Plain and simple. They won't thank her for helping them," Matthieu said. All of us were silent at that.

"So what do we do?" I asked, and the question kind of hung there in air, unanswered. The Garzas might not be werewolves anymore, but they still had their sorcery and Andrew at least still had his brilliant mind. Those things were more than enough to make them very dangerous enemies. But on the other hand, we couldn't let them escape, either.

"Come on," Matthieu said decisively, leaving the kitchen.

"What are we doing?" I asked.

"Just wait; you'll see," he said, and we all followed him to a locked room in the center of the house. It looked like an office inside, but as soon as he opened the door he immediately went to the back wall and tapped out a code with his fingers, in a spot which didn't appear to be anything but bare wallpaper. But as soon as he finished, a panel popped open that you never would've guessed was there.

Inside was a rack of pistols and a shotgun, all of them polished and ready to use at a moment's notice. Matthieu grabbed one of the pistols for each of us, expertly checking to make sure they were loaded before handing them out. He acted like he'd been born with a gun in his hand, he was so casual about it.

As for me, yeah, I'm a pretty good shot with a rifle, but I've never had much call to use a pistol before. It felt heavy and lethal in my hand, and I hoped it didn't show how unfamiliar I was with it.

I noticed that it was loaded with silver bullets; a leftover from the werewolf days, no doubt. But that was okay. It's not like regular humans are immune to silver bullets or anything.

"What are we doing?" I asked again.

"We've got to find them before they get too far away. I know Andrew too well; he was my case to start with. The first thing he'll do is run as far from Natchitoches as he thinks he's got time for, and then he'll go to ground someplace where he can lay hid for a while. If he does that we'll never find him, and then you can kiss Joan goodbye. He *might* keep her alive till then, if he thinks she's useful as a bargaining chip or maybe as a distraction to throw us off his trail. But once he finds a good hiding place he won't need her for those things anymore. She'll be more trouble than she's worth at that point, and then he'll write her off without a blink. Mark my words," Matthieu said coolly.

"And she had to pick *that* one to wake up," I muttered again.

"Maybe that's not so surprising, you know. She didn't seem to like us much, if you remember," Cameron said.

"What difference would that make?" Jolie asked.

"Well, I don't know. Now that I think about it, maybe she got scared after she saw all this freaky modern stuff, and she thought we were the ones who brought her here, and she overheard us talking about the Garzas. Maybe she figured anybody who was an enemy of ours must be a friend of hers," he said. Matt frowned, but he must have been thinking it over seriously, at least.

"That's a lot of maybes, Cam," he finally said.

"True, but we can't do anything right now but guess, anyway," Cam said.

"Which is the most sensible thing I've heard anybody say all evening. We're wasting time trying to guess what Joan's motives could've been. We need to figure out what to do right this minute, or pretty soon there'll be nothing we *can* do," Jolie said flatly.

"Not so fast. It'll be dangerous without the rings. We'll have to be careful and stay hid for as long as we can and then hit them fast and hard," Matthieu said. Nobody questioned that; when it came to tactics he was an expert, and we all respected him.

"So what do we do, then?" I asked.

"First let's try to figure out where they went and how long it's been. We left here with the Dolans about five o'clock, so we have to assume she woke up the Garzas not much later than that, if we're right about the whole idea of her overhearing us. It wouldn't make sense for her to hang around twiddling her thumbs," he went on.

"Makes sense. Okay, let's say they left here about five thirty. The first thing they'd have to do would be to find some clothes. They couldn't walk through town naked for very long without attracting attention," Jolie said.

"They'd have to break into somebody's house for that, and I bet I know exactly which one, too," Matthieu said.

"Which one?" I asked.

"The Tolberts. They're right across the alley from our place, and they're out of town for three weeks. That would have been the perfect place for them to hit," he said.

"Do they have an alarm system?" Cameron asked.

"I don't know, but it's still my best guess. We better go over there and check it out. Andrew's smart, though; he may have set up a diversion to waste our time, or even a trap for us to fall into. Keep your eyes open," Matthieu said, and the rest of us nodded.

As soon as we got our weapons in order, Matthieu led the way across the back alley to a dark house that must have been the Tolberts' place. The back gate was open when we got there, and he stopped.

"See what I told you? I *knew* they went this way," he whispered, pointing at the gate. Nobody said a word while he crept up to the gate and then swiftly stepped inside, swinging his pistol around to cover the whole yard just in case there might be somebody lurking there.

I had to admire the way he did it, I admit; it reminded me of the kind of thing you see on cop shows.

But the yard was empty, and as soon as he was sure it was safe he motioned for the rest of us to come ahead behind him. We did, and the next clue we found was a garage window busted out with a rock.

"Never mind. I think they're already gone. Mrs. Tolbert's car is missing," Jolie said when we got inside.

"Are you sure they're the ones who took it?" I ventured to ask.

"I don't know who else would have. Orem is handy that way; he would have known how to break open the ignition switch and get it started without a key. And I bet they found some old clothes out here in the garage, too. Worse and worse," Matthieu said.

"Any idea where they might have gone from here?" I asked.

"No telling. Like I said, the first thing they'll do is find a place to hole up and hide for a while. They might even split up, for that matter. Andrew knows he's not strong enough to fight us off yet; not without his zombies. I'm sure he thinks we still have the rings at this point," Matthieu said.

"So where's the most *unlikely* place they'd go?" Cameron asked.

There was a pause, and we all glanced together at the Tolberts' house right behind us. It was funny in a way that we all had the same thought at the same instant, and I might have laughed if things hadn't been so serious.

"There's no way they could still be in there. The other car's gone," Matt said in a low voice, looking out at the street.

"Yeah, but we don't know for *sure* it was them who took it, remember? The Tolberts could have taken both cars for some reason. Maybe they had to drop one of them off at the garage to get it fixed or something like that. We don't really know," I pointed out.

Matt frowned, considering the idea.

"Yeah. . . maybe," he finally said, doubtfully.

"We're wasting time. Let's get in there and check it out," Jolie said, and we all nodded.

"Come on, then," Matt said, lowering his pistol and walking back into the garage.

There was nothing much to be seen in there, just a bunch of junk like you'd see in anybody's garage; half empty paint cans, a few tools, a deep freeze, some shelves with various uninteresting things on them. Nothing particularly helpful.

But there were three doors, and those were where we immediately zeroed in. One of them led into the main house, and one of them went upstairs to the guest house on top of the garage. The third one looked like it might be a closet or a storage room, but I wouldn't have sworn to it. Matthieu checked that one first, and inside we found nothing but shelves and boxes full of more junk. We didn't waste ten seconds on it.

The door that led upstairs to the guest house was locked, and it didn't look like anybody had messed with it recently. The one to the main house had nine small panes on the top half of the door, and as soon as we got close enough we noticed that one of them was broken out. It wasn't easy to tell, because whoever broke it had carefully removed all the glass shards to make it look as close to normal as possible.

There was a yellow muslin curtain on the inside that kept us from seeing what was past the door, but Matthieu went up close to the door and listened. There was nothing to hear, so he slowly and carefully tried the knob. Locked.

He quickly slipped his hand through the broken pane just like the Garzas must have done, and turned the knob from inside. Then he opened the door quickly and covered the room with his gun.

Inside was a kitchen; a completely deserted one.

We methodically worked our way through the house, letting Matthieu lead since he was the one who knew what he was doing. But the house was empty and silent, and the only things we noticed were an open drawer in the bedroom and a half-eaten box of granola bars left sitting on the coffee table. Neither of which necessarily meant anything.

"I know they were in here. The door proves that. I bet they took some clothes and ate some food and then left either on foot or in the car," Matthieu said.

I couldn't help thinking there was something we were overlooking, but I couldn't put my finger on what it was till we got back to the kitchen and were just about to leave.

The Tolberts had one of those key holder things hung up on the wall beside the door, with little labels above each hook so you'd know what they were for. Nothing unusual about that, at least not till I noticed the GSTHSE key was missing from its place. As soon as I saw it, I put a hand out to stop Matt.

"Hey, look at that," I said in a low voice.

"What?" he asked.

"The guesthouse key is gone. I bet they took it and that's why we didn't think anybody broke in there," I said. He glanced at the key holder long enough to make sure I was right, and then he nodded.

"All right, makes sense. Let's go find out," he said.

So that's what we did, but almost right away we ran into a problem. The door was locked and the key was missing, and if the Garzas really *were* up there, then we definitely didn't want to let them know we were coming.

"Never mind, I can handle this," Matthieu said. He trotted back into the main house, and soon returned with a handful of Mrs. Tolbert's bobby pins. We all watched in fascination as he expertly picked the lock, but then I guess you have to learn a lot of unusual things when you hunt werewolves and evil sorcerers for a living.

As soon as the door was open, he raised his pistol and took the lead again, opening the door slowly so there wouldn't be any noise.

Right inside the door was a narrow staircase leading steeply up to the guesthouse, and together we slipped our way up there to see what we could see.

It was dark and shadowy inside, and deathly quiet. Matthieu and Jolie went first, and then Cameron came along behind me to make sure we didn't get attacked from the rear. As soon as we made it to the top of the stairs, we immediately saw Joan tied up and gagged on the bed.

But I didn't have time to think about that, because all of a sudden a sword came slicing down on Matthieu's upper arm, knocking the pistol out of his hand and cutting him pretty badly. He staggered backward, knowing he couldn't defend himself against something like that without a weapon, and the dude who swung the sword stepped out of the alcove he'd been hiding in and raised his blade to finish the job.

Maybe he didn't realize there were several of us, but he caught the drift soon enough. Matthieu stumbled into Jolie, knocking her off balance and nearly making both of them fall head over heels down the stairs, right on top of me and Cam. Jolie was in no position to aim very well, but she still had the presence of mind to fire her pistol at the man.

She missed, of course, but the noise was deafening in the hallway and he must have decided the odds weren't in his favor without a gun of his own. He cursed and leaped back behind the doorway so we couldn't see him.

As soon as Jolie caught her balance she quickly fired again three times right through the wall, down low where she might hit the man's legs instead of his body, and we all heard a snarl of pain, followed quickly by the heavy thump of something hitting the floor. She must have nailed somebody pretty good.

Jolie whipped around the corner to cover the man, with me and Cam close behind her. Matt had slumped down against the wall and yanked his t-shirt off to wrap up his bleeding arm with, but he was out of commission.

I don't know which one of the Garza brothers it was, but he was lying on the floor glaring at us, still holding the sword in his hand while he tried to put pressure on a bullet wound in his calf. Where in the blessed world he got hold of a sword I'll never know, unless maybe it was some decorative item Mr. Tolbert had put up on the wall or some such thing. I guess anything will do as a weapon in a pinch.

Just then, I felt something crash down on my upper back. I didn't know what it was, but it hurt worse than anything I can ever remember. For a second I thought it was another sword, but whatever it was, it knocked the breath out of me and I fell face-down on the carpet, gasping for air.

I was a little bit dazed after that and I don't entirely remember what happened, but I gathered later on that Gabe had been hiding in the bathroom and he'd come out and hit me with the shower curtain rod. Cameron tackled him from the side and they crashed to the floor, causing the curtain rod to hit the carpet six inches in front of my face.

I couldn't help him, and neither could Jolie for that matter. She had her hands full with the wounded one on the floor. He seized the moment of distraction to go for Matthieu's dropped pistol and

Jolie had to blow another hole in the floor beside his arm to make him back off.

Cam is no weakling, but then again neither was Gabe, apparently. He must have decided we had the upper hand, though, and that's when I got my first taste of the Garzas' sorcery. Gabe tore Cam loose and hurled him across the room with no hands at all, slamming him into the wall beside the bed. Then he took off down the stairs, abandoning his wounded brother. None of us was in any position to stop him, but the upshot of the whole thing was that we collared Orem, at least. Apparently Andrew had never been there to start with. All that takes a long time to tell, but it didn't take more than a few minutes to actually happen.

"Where's Andrew?" Matthieu demanded, after he'd bandaged his arm and got his pistol back. Orem didn't say a word, except to spit on the floor right by his feet.

"Let it alone, Matt. We'll find him sooner or later, anyway. Wherever he is, it's obvious he's not here," Cameron said. He'd earned his share of lumps from the fight; he had a split lip and his nose was bleeding from where his face hit the wall.

"Yeah, I guess you're right. At least we saved the idiot who woke them up in the first place," Matthieu said sourly. He's not usually like that, and I could tell he must have been in considerable pain to make him that curt. I could sympathize; my back was still throbbing from that smack with the curtain rod, and I was sure I'd have a bruise from one side to the other by morning.

I glanced at the bed, where Joan was still bound and gagged. Cameron was already over there from when Gabe had flung him across the room, and since Jolie and Matthieu were both occupied at the moment, I painfully got up and went to help him cut her loose.

She must have been awake the whole time, and I guess she'd probably had a rough few hours. The Garzas had probably been pretty cruel jailers. Her face was dirty, and there were tear streaks where she'd cried and not been able to wipe it away. Some of them looked pretty fresh, in fact, and her eyes were shut when we got to the bed.

"Joan, I know you're awake. You're safe now. Nobody wants to hurt you. I've got a knife and I'm just fixing to cut you loose if you'll be still. If you want to leave after that, you can. We won't try to stop you. But we'd really like to help you if you'll let us," he said.

I saw a tear well up and slide down through the dirt on her cheek, but she nodded. He cut the gag off first.

"There, that's better, now isn't it?" he said soothingly.

Then he cut the girl's hands and legs free, and put his knife away. Joan sat up and opened those leaf-green eyes, looking at the four of us in turn while she rubbed her wrists and ankles.

The full version of
Truesilver
Is available now at your favorite retailer.

Author's Note

As Zach himself said, it's hard to know what to say, here at the end of all things. In writing this series, I have watched him grow up from a precocious boy to a deeply thoughtful young man.

But as he also said, when speaking about Jolie, she finds herself already dreaming of even bigger and better things someday, not looking to the past. I hope he does the same, and if he grows into the man I think he will be, I'm sure that's where his heart will lead him. I myself would love to see where that desire may take him someday.

I wrote this series with several aims in mind. For one thing, I have found a sad lack of modern adventure novels for young adults with Christian characters who take their beliefs seriously and try hard to live by them. There is such a thing as real evil in the world, and, as C.S. Lewis once said, since it is so very likely that our children will meet cruel enemies, at least let them have heard tales of heroes and saints who have faced the Devil and the World and overcome them through Christ our Lord. That, it seems to me, is the best lesson any story could ever hope to teach. Better yet, let those heroes be ordinary boys and girls who found themselves thrust into extraordinary circumstances by no choice of their own. Let them be normal people who sometimes make mistakes, sometimes have doubts and fears, even about God, so that in the end they may find their way to deeper faith and stronger love.

When all is said and done, I hope that will be the strongest memory that my readers carry away from Zach's tale. . . that of a normal boy who faced heartache and fear, and suffered great loss, but who never gave up until he fulfilled the task God had given him, and in the process learned what truly matters. If I could be certain that even one reader was inspired or uplifted by this story, then I would be a happy man indeed.

The next book in this series, *Truesilver,* will continue to explore the theme of good vs. evil and the ways that a Christian young person (or anyone, for that matter) should approach those kinds of issues and the sometimes thorny problems they raise.

Like all of us, Zach is more thoughtful at certain times than others, and he'll actually be too busy in the next book to do quite as much thinking as he did in this one. This happens to all of us, which is precisely why it's so important to decide what we believe and be certain of those things while we can, so that when the time of testing does arrive and there's no time to think, we already know what to do and have the strength to stand firm in our convictions.

That said, there will be some major changes coming up in the next book, and some long-hinted connections made to other books which readers may not even be aware of. *The Last Werewolf Hunter* series will continue, of course, but there will also be some related stories told about characters off to the side who don't really hold a central place in the storyline, such as Cody and Tycho McGrath and Brandon Stone. I hope readers enjoy these other tales, too.

William Woodall
June 20, 2013

Discussion Questions

1. After first meeting Jolie at the fair, Zach comments that things are not always what they seem. Has there ever been a time when you experienced something which wasn't what it seemed to be at first?

2. When Jolie first offers him the job as a werewolf hunter, Zach is thrilled and longs to say yes, but later has second thoughts about the idea, partly because he isn't sure it actually has anything to do with breaking the Curse. Have you ever felt a calling from God to do something? If so, what was it and how did it make you feel?

3. After visiting the Goldens' mobile home, Zach feels sad and can't understand why anyone would want to do them harm. Have you ever felt sorry for someone you didn't know? If so, talk about that experience.

4. Zach talks several times about how much he loves baseball and hopes to play for the Texas Rangers someday, and maybe then become a writer. What are some things you hope to do someday?

5. For a long time, Zach is uncertain about whether Jolie really likes him or whether she might simply be using him for her own purposes. Why do you think he feels this way? Are there any events in his past which might affect the way he sees things?

6. After a while, Zach begins to think that perhaps being a werewolf hunter is almost as bad as being a werewolf. Do you agree with that opinion? Why or why not?

7. At one point, Zach mentions that the only reason we ever love anybody or anything in the world is because they remind us of God in some way, like the reflection of the sun in a dew drop. Discuss this idea and how it might apply to people you know and love. Do you agree with this idea, or do you think there are exceptions?

8. Marc Doucet grew up among werewolf hunters all his life, and yet chose to betray them and become a werewolf himself. Why do you think he might have done this?

9. On Mont Mouchet, Zach says that there are only three questions a man ever needs to ask; what is the nature of God, what things are worth living for, and what things are worth dying for. He adds that the answer to all of them is the same; only love. What do you think about this statement? Can you think of other questions that might be necessary to ask, in order to have a meaningful life and be happy? What might those questions be?

10. Cameron is unhappy with the idea of fighting werewolves again, and says that all he wants is a normal life. Yet he chooses to help Zach anyway, in spite of how he feels. Has there ever been a time when someone you loved needed you to do something you didn't like? How do you think it might have changed the story, if Cameron had refused to help?

11. When he first gets to France, Zach talks about culture shock and how all the little differences add up to make him feel uneasy and out of place after a while. Have you ever visited a place that made you feel uncomfortable like that? If so, where was it and what were some of the differences you noticed?

12. Things don't always turn out the way Zach hopes they will. Give some examples of times when you've been disappointed, and tell how you were able to handle the situation.

13. In the end, Zach still has hundreds of bottles of spring water that Miss Edith gave to him. What do you think he might do with that water in the future? What would you choose to do with it, if you were the one Miss Edith had given it to?

14. There are still thousands of sleeping ex-werewolves to awaken. What are some of the problems you think these people might face when Zach brings them back to life? What problems might Zach and the others have to deal with?

The Curse-Breaker Books
By William Woodall

Long ago, there was a Godly woman named Marybeth Trewick, who for various reasons found herself married to a rich but wicked man named Daniel who practiced all kinds of evil. She could only watch helplessly as her five sons grew up to become just as wicked as their father, and as her only daughter was forced to flee for her life lest she be killed.

But in the midst of her despair, God sent Marybeth a dream that after seven generations had passed, there would be five boys born to replace and redeem the ones that she had lost. These five would be breakers of curses and fighters against all things wicked and evil, and each of them would have the same vividly blue eyes, the same color as Marybeth's.

And even though the Curse-Breakers are each called to very different tasks in the world, the basic goal of fighting evil and loving God is always the same. These are their names and stories.

Brian Stone: The oldest curse-breaker, Brian's task is to save his brother's life and to remind men of Heaven by showing them the beauty of what could have been if the world had never fallen.

Cody McGrath: Two years younger than Brian, Cody is called to break the power of a dangerous sorceress. He's a dreamer of true dreams and a healer of the lost and broken-hearted.

Zachary Trewick: Four years younger than Cody, Zach is called to destroy one of the worst remaining aspects of his ancestor's wickedness; the werewolf curse which most of his family still embrace wholeheartedly.

Cameron Parker: Cameron and Zach are the same age, not to mention third cousins and best friends. Cameron has a big role to play in the struggle against the wolves, and later becomes the leader of all the survivors of Earth.

Brandon Stone: Brian's little brother, Brandon is three years younger than Cameron and Zach. He has a gift to know the meaning of dreams, and he is called to defend the weak and to uphold all that is righteous and true.

The Curse-Breaker Books form a collection of related stories about these five boys and sometimes their children. Each series tells the tale of a different Curse-Breaker (or sometimes more than one), but they also fit together in ways you wouldn't expect, in order to form a single unified storyline. It's helpful to read the books in order if possible, but it's not strictly necessary. You can read more about each series on the following pages.

The Last Werewolf Hunter Series
By William Woodall

Zach Trewick always thought he'd become a writer someday, or maybe play baseball for the Texas Rangers. What he never imagined in his craziest dreams was that he'd find himself dodging bullets and crashing cars off mountainsides, let alone that he'd ever be expected to break the ancient werewolf curse which hangs over his family.

But Zach is the last of the werewolf hunters, the long-foretold Curse-Breaker who can wipe out the wolves forever, and he's not the type to give up just because of a few minor setbacks. . .

Cry for the Moon: What would you do, if your family wanted you to become a monster? What if they wouldn't take no for an answer? When 12 year old Zach faces questions like these, he seems to have only one choice; *run.* Thus begins a long search for refuge, and perhaps redemption also.

Behind Blue Eyes: When a stranger kidnaps him from his own back yard, Zach soon finds that the past isn't quite as dead as he might wish. For the time has come at last for Zach and his cousin Cameron to break the wolf curse forever; and his family has no intention of letting that happen.

More Golden Than Day: When his girlfriend Jolie and then Cameron fall into the hands of the wolves, Zach has no choice but to take on his enemies for a second round. Only this time the stakes are horribly high, and if he fails he may end up losing everything he's ever loved.

Truesilver: When a family of wicked ex-wolves is accidentally awakened, Zach soon finds himself locked in a desperate fight for survival that he never anticipated. And even though he's sworn an oath to fight evil to the utmost of his power, there are times when courage is awfully hard to come by.

* * * * * * *

"If you are looking for a story about a boy who learns valuable lessons about family, love, friendship and God this is the book for you. I recommend this book to a pre-teen or adult. I truly enjoyed this book."
-Rae, *My Book Addiction Reviews*

"I found myself captivated with the story and could not stop reading until I reached the final page. Everything about this story is thought-provoking. Readers of all ages will appreciate this wonderfully told story,"
-Jancy, Kansas

The Stones of Song Series
By William Woodall

"There's a thing called magnanimity, or greatness of heart, and to me it's the most beautiful thing that ever there was. It means courage, but it's more than that. It means to cast aside all thought of yourself for the sake of another, like Moses in Gilead or the martyrs who died with a smile on their face. In its own small way it's a reflection of the Lord Jesus at Calvary, and therefore of God, the Light so beautiful that no one who sees it can ever turn away."

So says Cody McGrath, and in many ways that statement is the central theme of this series; the casting away of self for love of another, the scorning of selfishness in all its forms.

These are the stories of the Stone family: Brian, Jenny, Lisa, and Brandon, and some of the people they know and love, most notably Cody. All of them were called for great and glorious things, though sometimes only after great suffering and many mistakes.

Unclouded Day: Brian Stone's life isn't easy. Abandoned by his father, abused by his alcoholic mother, and mocked by his classmates, his only treasures are his beloved little brother and his old guitar. This is the tale of his journey to find the Fountain of Youth, and perhaps to save the world.

Many Waters: Lisa Stone is a small-town waitress with heavy burdens to bear. Cody is a young cowboy with mystical dreams and some very dangerous enemies. But when the two of them must face down an evil witch who tries to destroy their very lives, it seems only a miracle can save them.

Bran the Blessed: Brandon Stone hasn't always made the right choices in life, but he's never found himself in quite such deep trouble as this. But even though his life seems ruined forever, Bran still has a high calling to answer. . . if he can find the courage.

* * * * * *

"I would absolutely, without reservation, encourage you to read this wonderful novel, even if you aren't the fantasy genre type. It was a blessing."
-Sue, *Reflections and Reviews*

"There are so many nuggets of truth in this book. It's about Heaven. It's about bad things happening for a reason. It's about deciding for yourself what truly matters most in life. It's a really good book!"
-Tattie, *Christian Fiction Ebooks*

The Tyke McGrath Series
By *William Woodall*

In the year 2154, the world has become a dangerous place. Extremist groups would like nothing better than to wipe out humanity completely, and even the people sworn to defend civilization against such threats have become deeply corrupt and untrustworthy.

When a virulent plague destroys all warm-blooded life on Earth, a small band of survivors clings to life on the partially-terraformed Moon. But fresh dangers lie in wait for the unwary; nor have they left behind all the wickedness in the hearts of men.

Nightfall: When Micah McGrath suddenly finds himself thrust into a dangerous and ugly future after a lab accident, his only choice is to make the best life for himself that he can. But when the secret police get wind of his research into time travel, he soon finds himself in deep trouble indeed.

Tycho: Tycho McGrath is a high school honor student in Florida when he discovers a terrifying secret: a man-made bacterium is about to wipe out all warm-blooded life on Earth within days. The only hope for survival is to flee at once, a plan which carries its own set of unexpected dangers.

Avenger: After spotting an SOS coming from the abandoned Moon, the survivors must organize a rescue mission. But the expedition quickly becomes far more complicated, leading them to the icy world of Titan in search of a holy mountain that no human eye has ever seen.

Freedom: When a cruel and power-hungry military commander on Venus decides to reconquer Earth, the only thing he needs is the formula for Tyke's Orion vaccine. The survivors soon find themselves locked into a bitter battle over the future of mankind, and who will inherit the Earth after all.

Elysium: What began as a simple mission to recover lost comrades in the Martian desert quickly turns deadly when Tyke and the others find *themselves* stranded on the Red Planet, with only the slimmest of chances to make it home again, or to fulfill the destiny which God has in store for them.

* * * * * * *

"Reminiscent of Freedom's Landing, by Anne McCaffrey, Tycho combines the best of traditional space-exploration sci-fi with modern apocalyptic fiction. For any fans of hard science fiction, it doesn't get much better than this." - **Liz, OH2 Reviews**

Trewick Family Tree

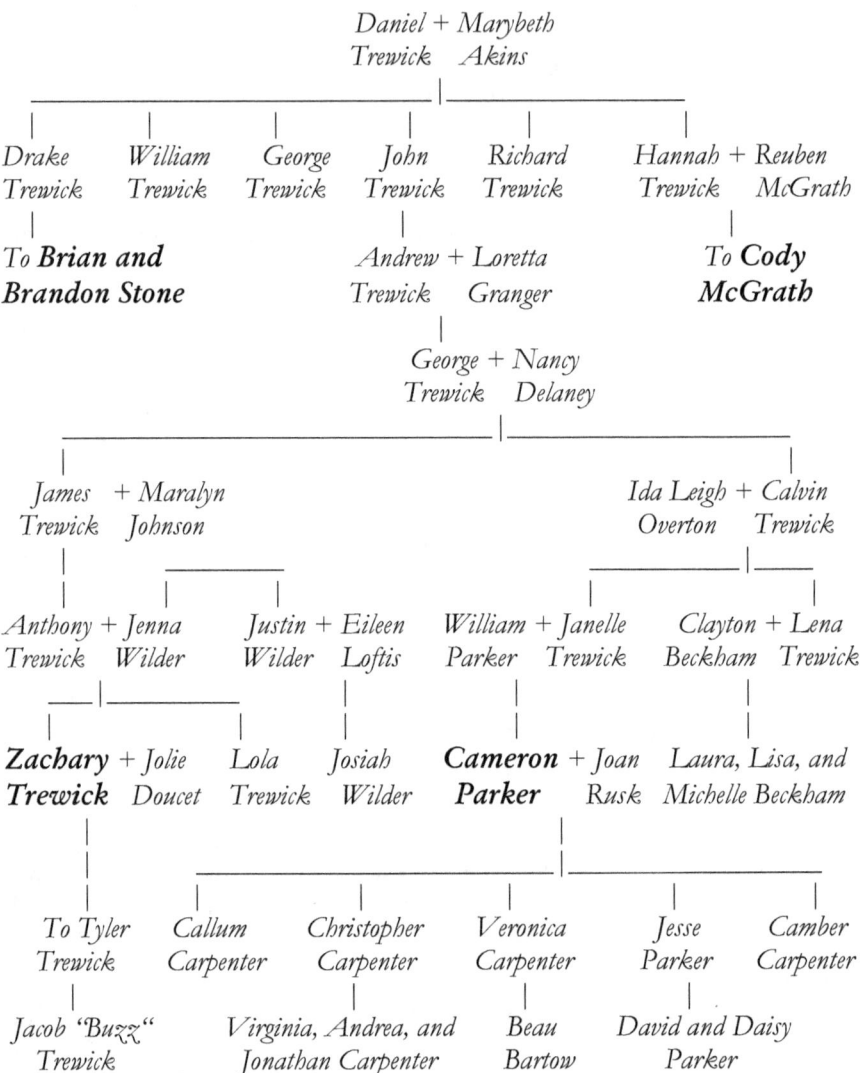

1. **Curse-Breakers are in bold.**
2. **Cameron Parker later changed his name to Philip Carpenter.**
3. **Tyler Trewick is Zach's great-grandson.**
4. **Lisa Beckham's husband is Logan Tygart.**
5. **Laura Beckham's husband is Heath Coates, son of Albert Coates.**

Trewick Family Tree

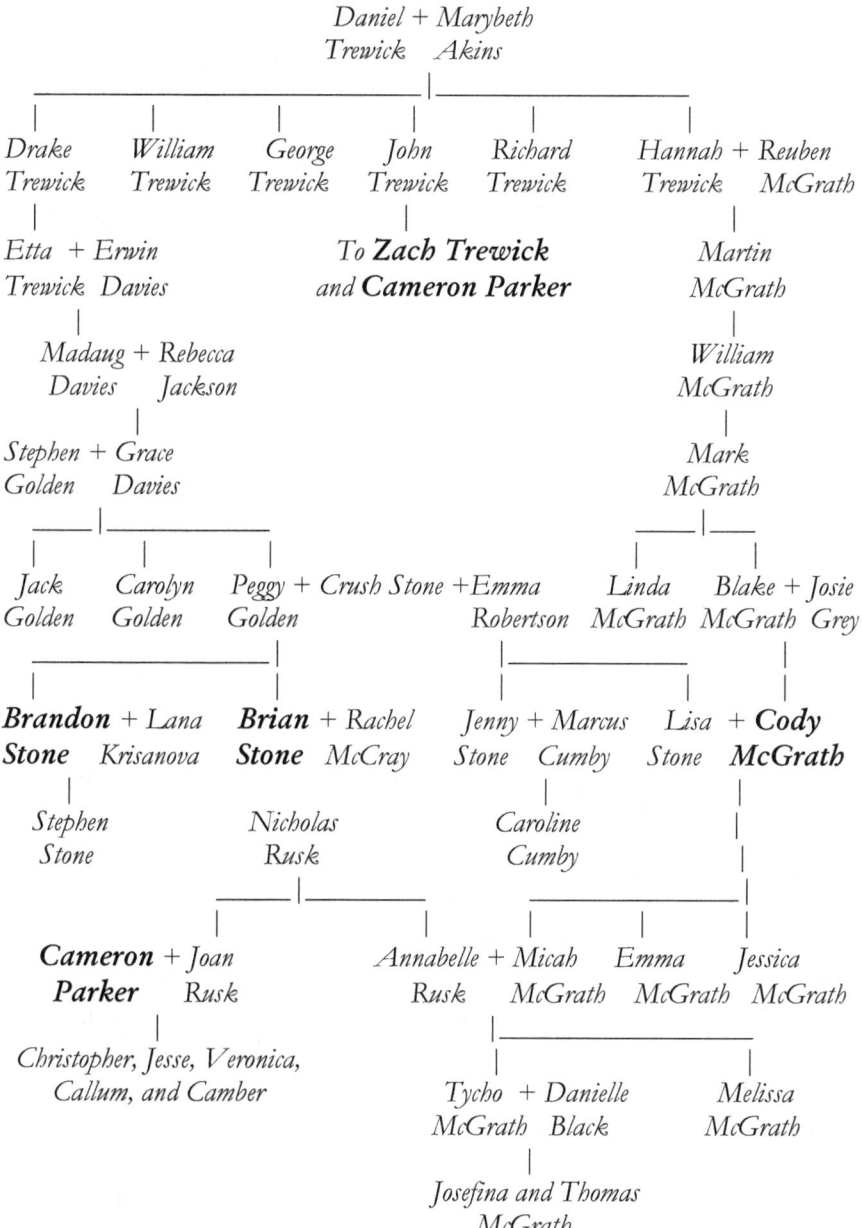

Daniel + Marybeth
Trewick   Akins

Drake Trewick | William Trewick | George Trewick | John Trewick | Richard Trewick | Hannah + Reuben Trewick   McGrath

Etta + Erwin
Trewick Davies

To **Zach Trewick**
and **Cameron Parker**

Martin
McGrath

Madaug + Rebecca
Davies   Jackson

William
McGrath

Stephen + Grace
Golden   Davies

Mark
McGrath

Jack Golden | Carolyn Golden | Peggy + Crush Stone + Emma Robertson | Linda McGrath | Blake + Josie McGrath Grey

Brandon + Lana
Stone   Krisanova

Brian + Rachel
Stone   McCray

Jenny + Marcus
Stone   Cumby

Lisa + **Cody**
Stone   **McGrath**

Stephen
Stone

Nicholas
Rusk

Caroline
Cumby

Cameron + Joan
Parker   Rusk

Annabelle + Micah
Rusk   McGrath

Emma
McGrath

Jessica
McGrath

Christopher, Jesse, Veronica,
Callum, and Camber

Tycho + Danielle
McGrath Black

Melissa
McGrath

Josefina and Thomas
McGrath

Doucet Family Tree

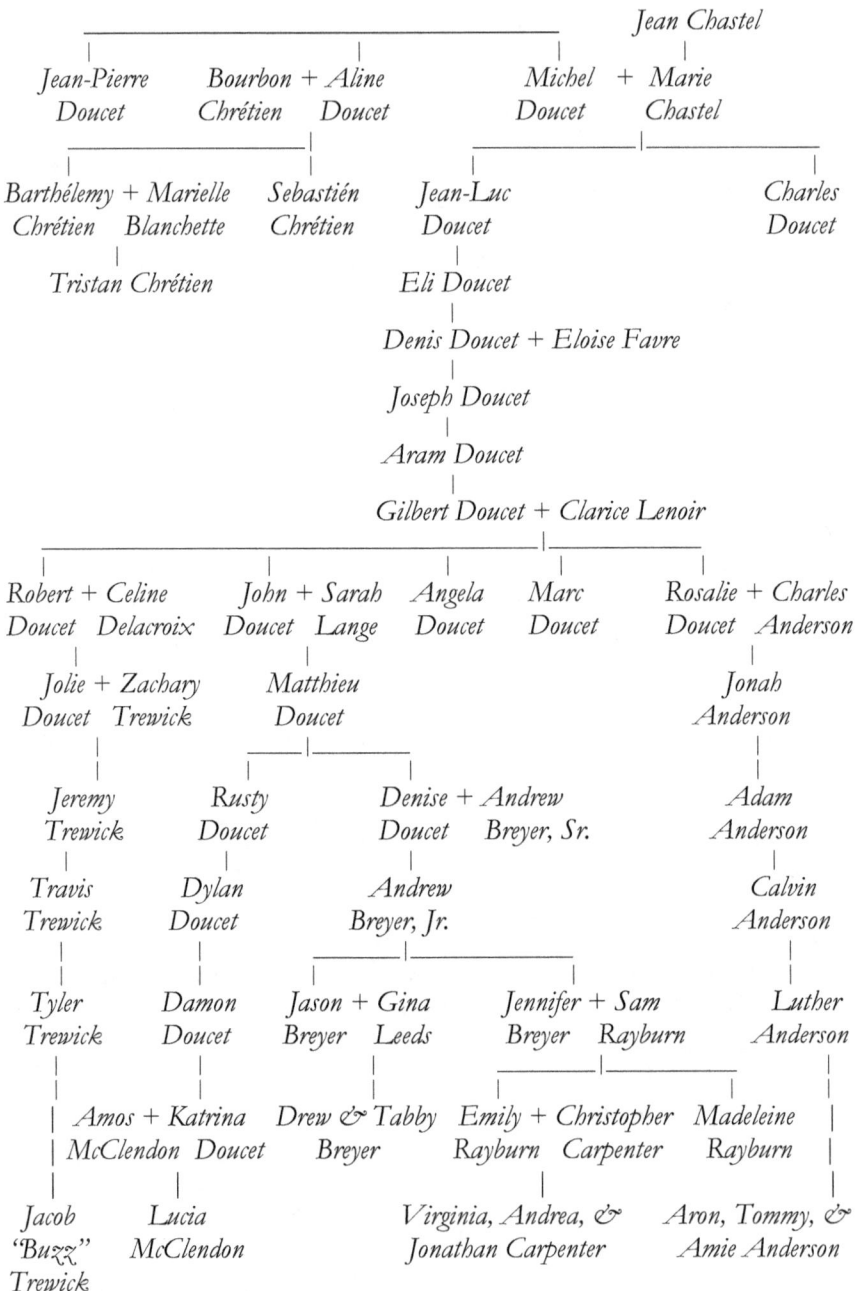

Bartow Family Tree

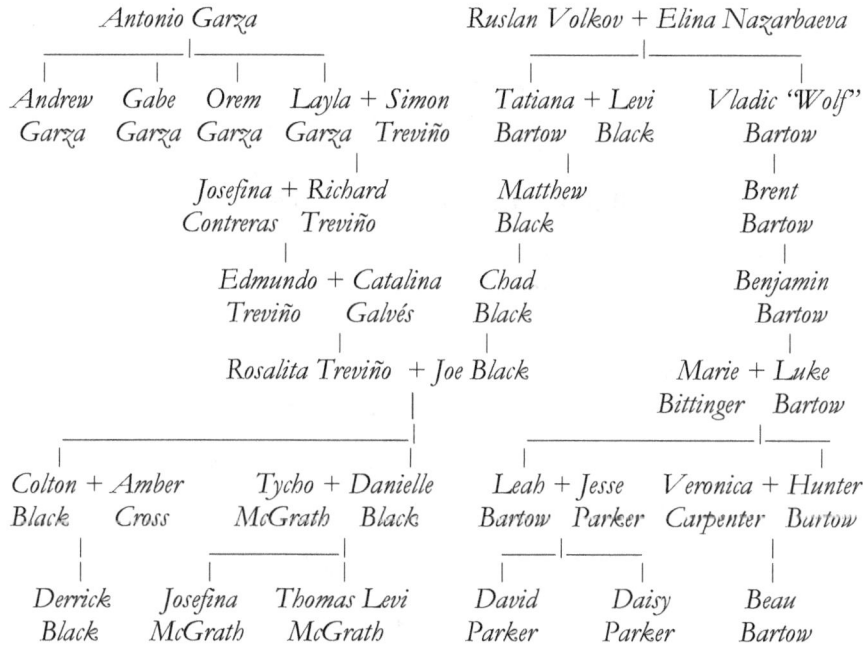

Jones and Golden Family Trees

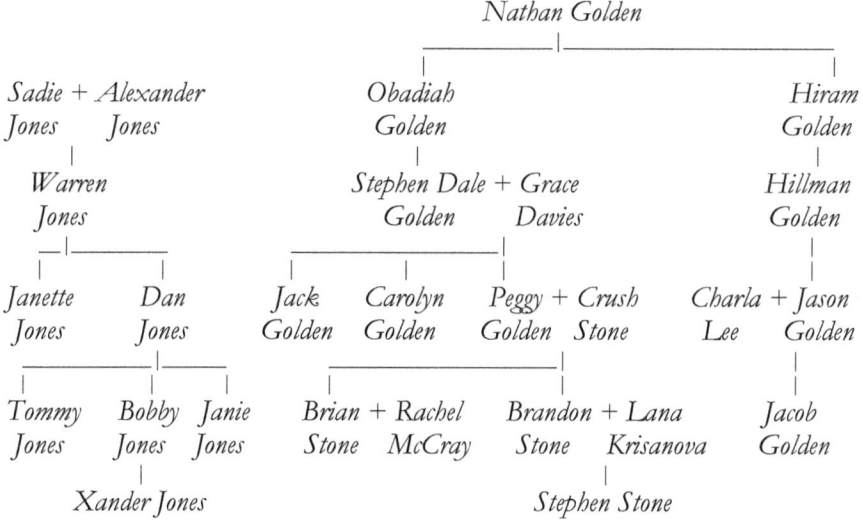

*If you'd like to find out more about
these and other books,
please visit:*

**William Woodall's
Official Author Website**

www.williamwoodall.org

Here you will find:

Free short stories

Discussion questions for teachers and book clubs

Free sample chapters of all my books

Photos of characters and locations for each story

Articles

Interviews

Quotable Quotes

Contact Information

And much, much more!